THE STATION

A LANCE SPECTOR THRILLER
BOOK 9

SAUL HERZOG

1

On Sixteenth Street Northwest, two blocks from the White House and three from the Washington Post building, sits the sumptuous Neo-Renaissance-style Hotel Lafayette. It's a fancy place, with open flame lanterns flickering by the entrance and ushers in long coats and top hats greeting you by name when you walk through the door. Inside, they have everything on file so that even before you've made it across the lobby, the concierge is offering you a dram of your favorite single malt or one of the hand-rolled Cuban cigars you mentioned liking on a previous visit.

Don't worry about smoking laws here. Don't worry about any laws.

The last time a cop had the gall to enter, he lost his job and benefits a month before retirement, and even his own union refused to back him in the appeal. The last time a journalist entered—an uncouth Brit from the *Daily Mirror*—he never came back out. The man simply disappeared. To this day, he remains a missing person, his case pending at DC Metro Police and an official letter of protest lodged by the British Embassy. There is a shrine to him a block from the hotel—a mess of melted candles, withered flowers, and ratty photographs taped to the lamppost like lost cat posters. The hotel would have cleared it up were it not for the fact they liked it being there. "A caution to other prying eyes," they called it. "A warning. Here be monsters."

Welcome to Washington DC, the capital of the richest and most powerful nation ever to plant its flag on the map. In one year, its economy churns through twenty trillion dollars. Its military is capable of projecting absolute dominance over every square inch of the planet's surface. No other nation comes close to rivaling it. At twenty-five miles from the Chinese coastline, a PLA naval vessel cannot sail without US Navy say-so. If a top-of-the-line Chengdu J-20 were ever to cross paths in anger with a Lockheed Martin F-35 Lightning II, even in China's own airspace, the Chinese pilot would have to eject before ever making visual contact. The power gap with Russia, the other supposed superpower, is even greater. The mighty Red Army, the so-called greatest land force on earth, is so diminished by decades of ineptitude and under-investment that it can no longer bring even former Soviet territory to heel. It is a spent force, and everyone from the Ukrainian ambassador to the bellhop in the Lafayette lobby could tell you so.

To say the United States is hegemonic is an understatement. No nation has ever enjoyed such dominance. No geopolitical position has ever been more assured. And no nation's politicians have ever played so fast and loose with its citizens' lives.

They get a bad rap, of course, the politicians. What was it Kissinger said? Ninety percent of them give the other ten a bad name? And it was Khrushchev who said they're the same in every land. And maybe that's true. Maybe the folks in Washington are no worse than their counterparts in Beijing or Moscow or Pyongyang. But then, that would mean they're no better either.

The bar of the Lafayette was at the front of the hotel, overlooking a stretch of K Street that was home to more lobbying firms than any other zip code in the country. Directly behind the bar, dominating the room and looking down sternly on the patrons as they sipped their top-shelf liquors, was an enormous portrait of Abraham Lincoln. *The Great Emancipator,* it was entitled—a previously lost work by the artist George Henry Story that the hotel had purchased at auction for a truly eye-watering sum. The painting depicted *Honest Abe* in the midst of his finest hour, his great address at Gettysburg, preaching to his tattered soldiers that all men are created equal, that the arc of history bends toward justice, and that we, indeed, are not descended from fearful men. Or something to that effect.

It being almost midnight, and a school night at that, the Lafayette bar currently had just a single patron—a fine piece of work by the name of Skadden Arps. Skadden was in his early sixties, slightly overweight, slightly pasty-looking, and he was seated languorously in a leather club chair by the bar's enormous fireplace, as comfortable as if he were in his own bedroom. He'd kicked off his tasseled loafers and was stretching his feet precariously close to the flames as he turned to get the bartender's attention. It was easy to do—the bartender had been watching him like a hawk for the better part of an hour, waiting for him to leave so he could shut up shop for the night. Skadden had no intention of letting him do anything of the sort and raised two fingers in a beckoning motion.

"Sir?" the bartender said when he arrived.

"One more," Skadden said, placing a heavy Baccarat crystal glass in the man's hand. "In fact," he added, "make it a double." And why not, he thought, turning his attention to the window. It was Hennessy Ellipse cognac he was drinking—an ounce of the stuff cost more than a night in the hotel's presidential suite—but then, he wasn't picking up the tab for this, was he? No, tonight's bill would be courtesy of Johnny Q Taxpayer, as would his suite on the top floor and, for that matter, the eighteen-year-old Belarusian hooker named Sveta that he'd just placed a call to. Life was good. It was very good.

Outside, it was one of those wintry DC nights when the air drifts up from the Potomac like a damp plague, the briny stench of the Chesapeake still on it. The street was all but deserted, and directly across it was the brand-new office building that Skadden's firm had just constructed. It was *his* building, constructed by *him*, but if there was one detail he would have changed, it was the height. In his opinion it wasn't nearly tall enough, it could easily have been double, but 130 feet was the limit for office buildings in the city. It was a foolish rule—one might say a superstitious one—introduced in reverence to the Washington Monument and the dome of the Capitol, which, apart from a few radio antennas and church steeples, were the only structures in the District that stretched above it. Skadden could have gotten around the rule, he could get around anything—they didn't call his firm *The God Firm* for nothing—but owning the one building in the city that exceeded the height restriction would have attracted entirely the wrong sort of attention. In any case, seven stories were more than enough for his needs.

"Will there be anything else, sir?" the waiter said, returning with the cognac.

"I'll let you know," Skadden said, not taking his eye from the window. The building was intended as a monument to himself and his achievement. An anonymous monument—everything he did was anonymous—but a monument nonetheless. Naturally, it bore no signage, no clue to its purpose or the identity of its occupant, apart from a small brass plaque by the entrance. Etched into the plaque was a single uppercase 'A' in a Caslon serif font. The 'A' stood for *Arps*, it being his firm, and the font had been chosen to match the one used by Benjamin Franklin in the first typesetting of the Declaration of Independence.

That was a nice touch, he thought, taking a gold cigar case from his breast pocket and holding it up for the bartender to see. People had a lot to say about lobbyists, they had a lot to say about men like Skadden Arps, but he saw himself, ultimately, as a patriot. Sure, he didn't serve his country as directly as some others. He didn't serve in the military, he didn't contribute to the community or give money to worthy causes, but he did, in his opinion, perform a necessary function. And not just any function but one that had been specifically provided for by the Founding Fathers. He opened the case and took out a Cohiba Behike cigar, one of just four thousand ever made, and sniffed the length of it before wetting one end in his mouth.

The bartender had scuttled over with an ashtray, cutter, and light, and Skadden let him stand there holding the flame while he puffed at the end of the cigar to get the thing lit. A thick cloud of gray-blue smoke filled the air, and he said to the bartender, "How about another cognac?"

"Very good, sir."

"And some water."

"Of course, sir."

The bartender bowed, and Skadden was sure he heard him let out an audible sigh. He watched him make his way back to the bar, and his gaze came to rest on the Lincoln portrait, those piercing eyes, that ferocious expression. What would the old man have made of all this, he thought, looking around the room? What would he have thought of the nation he'd helped forge? Eight score years had passed since the battle at Gettysburg. What would the old blowhard have made of the mess that had become of things? The bargaining, the politicking, the compromising, and cattle trading? What would he have thought of the private jets, the offshore bank accounts, the government limousines with their tiny flapping flags and police escorts? And what would he make of the gray men, the quiet men in the shadows, the men like Skadden Arps who skulked the corridors of power in fresh after-shave and thousand-dollar loafers? Was this what the soldiers had died for at Gettysburg?

Government of the people, by the people, for the people, Skadden thought, puffing out so much smoke he had to wave it away with his hand. That's what all the fuss had been about in the end. So much bluster, so much killing, so that men like Lincoln could earn their place in history, and one peculiar form of government would not perish from the face of the earth. And whether they liked it or not, Skadden thought, he was as much a part of that government as anyone. The right to lobby was enshrined in the First Amendment. The right of the common man to petition his rulers. What could be more democratic than that? Skadden Arps was as much a part of the American dream as apple pie or pretty girls in cheerleading outfits.

Now, you might ask, should his work have been performed in complete darkness, with near-zero legal oversight and near-limitless financial resources? And should it have been performed on behalf of foreign powers, on behalf of overseas dictators, or sanctioned organizations, or multinational corporations with budgets larger than nations? Well, that wasn't for Skadden to say. His job was merely to represent the interests of his clients.

And what clients they were. His top ten, in order of monthly retainer, were as follows:

Client List

The Royal Family of Saudi Arabia — $30 million per month

The Government of the Russian Federation — $25 million per month

The Government of the People's Republic of China — $20 million per month

The Kingdom of Saudi Arabia — $18 million per month

Saudi Aramco — $18 million per month

Purdue Pharma LP — $15 million per month

Gazprom PJSC — $8 million per month

British American Tobacco — $6 million per month

Xinjiang Public Security Bureau — $5 million per month

Sberbank PJSC — $4 million per month

If you scanned farther down the client list, you would find the names of eighteen foreign dictators, forty-two foreign governments, and sixty-nine multinational corporations—all of them ambivalent or outright hostile to American global interests and security. Skadden had more open litigation at the Department of Justice than any other individual in the country's history. He represented the leader of the Iranian Morality Police—accused of torturing women for revealing their hair in public. He represented the leader of a private Russian mercenary force that was actively killing US service members in the Middle East and North Africa. He represented the tech company that was illegally monitoring US citizens on behalf of the People's Republic of China.

There was no client Skadden Arps would not accept.

No snake he wouldn't grab hold of.

No check he wouldn't cash.

If you wanted to paint the White House

green, or change the tune of the national anthem to Yankee Doodle, if you wanted the stars and stripes on the flag to be replaced with the logo of Credit Suisse bank, he could find you the congressmen and senators to vote it through.

Certainly, if you needed to get around a congressional export ban on top-of-the-range military equipment—let's say, speaking hypothetically, you wanted to sell twelve F-22 Raptors to the government of Saudi Arabia—he was your man. Or if you wanted certain individuals removed from the Treasury's Sanctions List—let's say Oleg Rusal, the head of the aforementioned Russian mercenary force, or Haj Ahmad Montazeri, the head of Iran's Morality Police—he was your man. And if you wanted to license a semi-synthetic opioid that was chemically identical to heroin, put it in a sugar-coated pill, and make it the most prescribed painkiller in the history of American medicine—selling 250 million scripts a year, almost one for every man, woman, and child in the country—he was your man.

The world is a very big place, filled with some very bad people, and all of them must come to Washington in the end. All must come and pay homage. And when they do, like horseflies to a steaming pile of cowshit, it is to Skadden Arps that they congregate.

Skadden kept a Rolodex—yes, a physical one—and it was stuffed to the gills with hundreds of tattered, alphabetized notecards. The cards represented senators, congressmen, judges, administration officials, journalists, business leaders, op-ed writers, foreign politicians, academics, and anyone else who might conceivably hold sway over the decisions that he and his clients cared about. In short, it contained the names of the most powerful people on the planet. On the cards, written in Skadden's own cryptic hand, were the details of the sordid secrets he had on each of them. These ranged from the merely mundane—extramarital affairs and tax irregularities—to the truly earth-shaking—potentially major political scandals, financial secrets that could bankrupt nations, criminal conduct up to and including mass murder and genocide. He knew who had Nazi treasure in their safe deposit box, who had the most sordid pornographic material on their hard drive, and who had the most blood on their hands. And he knew how to use the information.

He kept the Rolodex in a specially-designed Mosler vault that had originally been built for the US Atomic Energy Commission. He'd purchased it when the Oak Ridge National Laboratory was being renovated—it was one of the few objects in the world that had actually been tested to withstand a nuclear blast—and similar models had been installed at the government's Greenbrier Bunker in White Sulphur Springs, and at the Presidential Emergency Operations Center beneath the East Wing of the White House. Not that Skadden was expecting anyone to launch a nuclear weapon at him. He was just a lobbyist, after all.

The information contained on the cards was his stock-in-trade, his bread and butter, it was the *kompromat* that allowed him to threaten, blackmail, and entrap the most powerful people on the planet. But he only used it when he absolutely had to. Every action created an equal and opposite reaction, and every blackmail created a new and powerful enemy.

What Skadden much preferred to do was sign checks.

That was his real secret power, the thing that truly kept the gears of his giant machine turning. Because the thing Skadden had learned very early on, the thing that gave him a jump on virtually all of his competitors, was that the most common path for a Washington politician was to follow up their stint in public service with a career working for the lobbyists. It was so common they had a name for it—they called it *The Revolving Door*. Politicians from both parties did their time in the public service, they collected their public salary with its 401k and sensible benefits package, they were the model citizen, and then, the moment it was humanly possible, they jumped ship. It was amazing how many former senators and congressmen—men and women would have died before accepting an outright bribe—were only too willing to accept an eighty-thousand-dollar-a-month *consultancy fee*. That was why, of the 154 former US senators who were still alive, fully seventy-seven of them were on Skadden Arps's payroll, all listed as consultants. When it came to former administration officials and congressmen, the numbers were even higher.

Think about that.

It is human nature to look for threats externally, to seek protection from what is on the outside. No one ever wants to admit that their own greatest threat is themself. Certainly, no politician wants to admit that the greatest threat to American security lies inside Washington. Which is why, for eight decades, the one thing they've all agreed on, the one tenet of national policy that has never been challenged by either side of the aisle, is that all threats to American security, to American democracy, and to the very existence of the nation itself, are external. The threat comes from Moscow or Beijing. It comes from Baghdad or Pyongyang. It never comes from within Washington. That's why military spending is so high—higher, in fact, than the next ten nations combined.

Consider the following numbers.

2,996—the casualties from the September 11th terrorist attacks.

6,817—total US military casualties from the wars in Iraq and Afghanistan.

Now consider this one.

500,000—the number of deaths resulting from the FDA's approval of Oxycontin following an intense lobbying campaign by Skadden Arps.

You decide which threat is the greater.

That last one, the Oxycontin application, caused more American deaths than a hundred Iraq wars. The last time a foreign power threatened anything approaching half a million American deaths, twelve million troops were mobilized, and two atom bombs were dropped.

All of this is not to suggest that there are no honest politicians in Washington. It certainly is not to suggest that there aren't thousands of public servants who dedicate their entire lives in service to their country. But only a willful idiot would say there's no rot in the system. And those who know the system best know that at the very top, at the level where wars are declared, and drugs approved, and tax laws implemented, at the level where there's really enough meat on the bone to get a good taste, the system is rotten to the core.

Which brings us back to the 130-foot-tall building that Skadden was so fondly admiring while sipping his cognac and smoking his cigar. Because on the roof of that building, nestled between an air handling unit and an elevator shaft overrun, was a rogue, CIA-trained marksman. It was chilly up there—there was no log fire, no cognac—but there was something far more reassuring. There was a view down the tapered metal barrel of an M40A5 sniper rifle. The marksman breathed deeply, his breath billowing in the cold night air, and adjusted his position slightly. Through his Schmidt & Bender scope he could count the cubes of ice in Skadden's crystal glass. He could make out individual hairs on his chin. He could see that an inch of ash was about to fall from the tip of the cigar onto Skadden's perfectly pressed silk shirt. He inhaled and could almost smell the tobacco smoke.

With the stock of the rifle nestled against his shoulder, he couldn't have been more relaxed. The CIA had spent a lot of time teaching him how to master his nerves, how to breathe steadily, how to slow his pulse.

He was a model student. His pulse was in the forties. A civilian doctor might have worried it was too low.

And he was going to relish the shot.

This was personal.

He adjusted his aim from Skadden's chest to the dead center of his right eyeball.

He touched the trigger.

The bullet left the muzzle at 2,550 feet per second, twice the speed of sound, and a tenth of a second later, the window next to Skadden Arps's head shattered into a thousand pieces. Then, Skadden's head exploded.

The shooter kept his eye pressed to the scope just long enough to confirm the kill, then, in a single movement, was dismantling the gun and packing it into a black canvas carryall.

By the time the bartender in the Lafayette realized what had happened, the shooter was climbing through the rooftop hatch of a service elevator. By the time the hotel's concierge finished dialing 911, the shooter was on the sidewalk of K Street, walking briskly eastward in the direction of Franklin Park.

The man was broad-shouldered, clean-shaven, square-jawed, in his late thirties with an athletic gait and military bearing. He wore a black leather jacket over a green army t-shirt, a black woolen hat, and gloves. As he strode down the street, he removed the hat and gloves and stuffed them into a garbage can. Then he crossed 14th Street and entered a small city park, throwing the canvas carryall into the back of a passing garbage truck. Near the center of the park was a fountain surrounded by manicured shrubs, and he reached behind one of the shrubs to grab a backpack he'd previously stashed there. Inside, it contained a knee-length, camel-colored overcoat, which he put on in place of the jacket. He put the jacket into the backpack and slung it over his shoulder.

Less than two hundred seconds had passed since he'd pressed the trigger of the rifle. He couldn't even hear sirens yet.

He left the park at 15th Street Northwest and continued walking eastward, past the Conrad Hotel, past a Tiffany jewelry store, in the direction of Union Station. He'd just remembered that there was a half-decent twenty-four-hour tobacconist near the train station, and he had a sudden, strong craving for a nice cigar.

2

F*ive days earlier.*

President Molotov brushed past the guards standing sentry outside his new underground office. "Move!" he growled, shoving his way through the door and into a squat, brick room with a low ceiling and reinforced concrete walls. "Go on!" he snapped. "Fuck off!"

He was already past the guards, but they backed away anyway, like lion tamers sensing danger, as he slammed the door.

The security precautions were preposterous now, completely out of control, and getting worse. He couldn't eat, he couldn't sleep, he couldn't even take a shit without some overbearing team of protectors breathing down his neck like hypochondriacal mothers. It was his own fault, of course—Security Edict Number 47 for the Protection and Preservation of the Life of the President of the Federation—but that didn't make it any less suffocating.

Molotov slumped into the seat at his desk and let out a long, drawn-out sigh. This was his life now—reduced to skulking around a bunker deep beneath the Kremlin, hiding from his own shadow, breathing triple-filtered air, and eating triple-tasted food. He looked up at the concrete slab of the ceiling and felt the full weight of it bearing down on him like an oppressive cloud. The whole place had been built by Stalin during the height of his paranoia, and it felt like it. Areas were connected with airlocks. Door fittings were built to submarine specifications. He'd been told that at places, the concrete was thick enough to encase the hull of a twenty-two-foot Kliment Voroshilov tank.

He looked up at the enormous display screen on the wall—just one more of the new security protocols put in place since Osip Shipenko's attempted coup—and grimaced. A little clock in the corner counted down to his meeting—four minutes and forty seconds remaining. This screen was his window on the world now, his only way of communicating with his advisors and ministers. He was more isolated than ever, and while in the past that hadn't bothered him, it did now. It chafed at his nerves, distracted his mind, and colored every thought in the gray, acrid fog of paranoia. But what was he to do? Face-to-face contact, even with his most trusted lieutenants, was just one of the many casualties of Osip's treachery and betrayal. It was a fact. Best to get on with it.

It was all so ironic, he thought. *He*, the man who in the last week alone had summarily arrested and imprisoned over eight thousand people, had become the prisoner. *He,* who owned a country, who owned a hundred palaces, a thousand dachas, a million acres, couldn't leave the confines of a cramped, musty Cold War-era bunker.

He saw no one in person other than his doctors, guards, and domestic servants, and even they couldn't be trusted. They worked only on pain of death—not of their own, but of their children. Molotov had directed that only the parents of young children be allowed to serve in the bunker, and the children themselves had been forcibly taken into state custody. While they were reasonably looked after, and the parents were allowed frequent visits, the children were not free to leave, and everyone understood that they were essentially hostages held at gunpoint. If anything were to happen to the president, if there was even a whisper of sedition or treason within the bunker, every last child would be shot. That was the arrangement.

And there you had it. There was the paradox. The man with the largest ground army in the world, with more self-propelled artillery than America and China combined, was afraid even of his own cook, his own scullery maid, his own doctors and nurses. There'd been a time when he'd been champion of the people, a liberator bringing the country back to greatness after the humiliation of Soviet collapse. There'd been a time when he was a national hero, applauded whenever he appeared in public, the guest of honor at every official event, when he'd stood proudly in Red Square while countless passing soldiers saluted him during Victory Day parades. Those days were gone. Now, he couldn't even enter a room with a window for fear of being sniped by one of his own citizens.

That was the tricky thing about coups. They didn't have to succeed. Just the fact that one had been attempted, just the fact that someone had been mad enough to even try to wrest control, was enough to crack the myth of invincibility. For such myths were fickle things, and Molotov understood that a regime like his, a regime based on fear and coercion, depended more on the appearance of invincibility than it did on power itself. Molotov knew that all politics, all power, stemmed from stories. Wars, contrary to popular belief, were not fought for land, for food, even for oil and gold. Wars were fought for stories—the stories peoples and nations believed about themselves. The fact that someone had had the gall to challenge Molotov's reign was Kryptonite to the story he was telling the world. It was dangerous in a way that all other things—sanctions, economic contraction, the deaths of thousands of soldiers in the

Ukraine—could never be. It infested people's minds. It gave them ideas. It gave them hope. And therefore, it required an answer.

That answer would be as swift as it was merciless. Indeed, the bloodletting had already begun. Anyone involved in the coup, anyone even remotely connected to Osip Shipenko and his cabal of co-conspirators, was already dead. And not just dead but executed using long-outlawed methods that had first been introduced under the reign of Peter the Great. These included the burying alive of a hundred generals inside the grounds of the Peter and Paul Fortress in Saint Petersburg and the drowning of over three hundred members of the Presidential Regiment in the icy waters of the Moskva. These killings were set to continue, with the prosecutors instructed to find or invent the evidence needed for another three thousand executions at a minimum. Sating Molotov's thirst for revenge would take time. And it would take a lot of blood.

And it was happening not just in Russia, but overseas too. There would be killings in London and Berlin, in Paris and Prague, in New York and Washington, and in countless lesser-known places.

If there was one thing Molotov regretted about the whole thing, it was that the international killings would be so quiet. The geopolitical landscape had been deemed too unstable for Moscow to go on a global killing spree in the open. There'd been a time when Molotov's assassins had taken pride in their work. They'd flaunted it, going out of their way to draw attention to what they were doing, regardless of where it took place. They'd used exotic methods, their little *calling cards*, as they called them—Polonium-201, Novichok, the PSS silent pistol with its custom SP-4 ammunition. They'd left these calling cards in every major capital of the world. There'd been a theatricality to Moscow's killings, a flamboyance that spread terror, consolidated Molotov's grip on power, and left no doubt as to the fate of anyone foolish enough to challenge his rule.

But now, according to Ivan Sobyanin, the new head of Political Corrective Action—Molotov's euphemism for the current round of assassinations—the days when Moscow could publicize its global killing campaigns were over. At least for the time being. "The Americans are pulling back on their funding for Ukraine," Sobyanin had said. "They're talking about withdrawing from NATO. The last thing we want now is for them to rethink that."

And so, secrecy was the order of the day.

Molotov opened the laptop on his desk and pulled up the photo of his next victim—a pasty-skinned American in his sixties, dressed in an expensive suit, with slicked-back hair dyed just the right amount to still look natural. The man's name was Skadden Arps, and he'd made a very grave mistake. He'd been a friend once, a reliable ally, a loyal servant, but then he'd gone and done the one thing a Kremlin ally never should. He'd bitten the hand that fed him.

The counter on the digital display reached zero and immediately, Sobyanin's face filled the screen. Molotov adjusted his cufflinks and hit the button to accept the call.

"Mr President, sir," Sobyanin said. "It's all set up. Primed and ready to go."

"The trap is ready?"

"The crime's been committed. Skadden was behind it. All I need to do now is alter the police record, change the name of the victim to Raven Spector, and the American assassin will take care of the rest for us."

"He'll kill Skadden Arps first?"

"He's our useful idiot, sir. He'll do exactly what we're hoping."

"And you're sure you can alter the police record quietly?" Molotov said. "You can change the victim's name without shitting the bed?"

"We can, sir. We have a sleeper agent in the FBI's Seattle office. He'll alter the record for us. None of the bumpkins in the local police will notice a thing."

"You hope," Molotov said. The plan was complicated, but he'd liked it when it had first been presented to him, and he still liked it. Russian agents in Mexico had uncovered information from Spector's past, information that was guaranteed to get his attention. This was the best use of it. "There are a lot of ways we could kill this Skadden Arps character," Molotov said. "It's only Roth that I really care about."

"Understood, sir, but in the view of the Prime Directorate, this is still the best way of killing Levi Roth."

"We have other assets in Washington," Molotov said.

"We do, sir, and we'll activate them, certainly, should an opportunity present itself."

"Good," Molotov said, nodding.

"And I understand, sir, that trying to utilize Spector like this, trying to convince him to kill his own mentor, creates challenges."

"*Challenges* is an understatement."

"Yes, sir, well, as complicated as it may be, the feeling on the top floor is that without Spector, there's simply no guarantee that an attempt on Levi Roth's life will be successful."

"I see."

"And I needn't remind you of the dangers of an unsuccessful attempt."

"You need not."

"I hesitate to say it, but it could open the possibility of the Americans targeting your own person."

"My own *person*?" Molotov said wryly.

"That is to say, sir—"

"I know what you're saying," Molotov said. He wanted Roth dead, but he had to be careful. This plan they were putting before him, as convoluted as it was, had a certain irresistible logic to it. A logic only a GRU-trained officer would appreciate. "As long as Levi Roth is dead at the end of this," he said, "you can go about it however you see fit."

"Thank you, sir."

"Too many people know what he did," Molotov continued. "He crossed the line. He plotted my demise. He went after me personally."

"Of course, sir."

If life was about stories, Molotov needed to make sure that the story this incident told was that targeting him personally was suicide. Anyone who did so died, no matter who they were. "Our shrinks have looked again at this Spector character?"

"Everything he's shown us says he'll follow this bait, sir."

"And when it comes to Roth, his old friend, his mentor, he won't balk?"

"This man doesn't balk, sir. He'll want what we have, and he'll kill to get it. That's what his past actions tell us. What is it they say? When someone shows you who they are, believe them the first time?"

"That is what they say," Molotov conceded, "though the only thing this particular man has ever shown us is a blatant disregard for the proper order of things."

"He's American, sir. They're all like that."

"He's a dog that refuses to be leashed, Sobyanin. I don't like that. Disobedience. Unpredictability. That way lies the path to chaos."

"Trust me, sir. With where we stand right now, if we want a bullet in Levi Roth's skull, this is the best way to do it. This is the way we get the job done. I *promise* you."

"You *promise*?"

"I shouldn't say promise, sir."

"No, you shouldn't."

"It's just that everything this man has done screams ego, sir. It screams classic American cowboy. He thinks he's a superhero. He thinks he can wrestle with us. He thinks he can get into the ring with us and get his hands dirty."

Molotov nodded again.

"He thinks he's Batman, sir. He won't be able to resist what we have."

"Batman?"

"Or Superman, sir. He thinks America can save the world. He thinks the CIA can. I think you know what I'm saying?"

"I know what you're saying," Molotov said, though he wasn't sure everything would go as smoothly as Sobyanin was suggesting. Lance Spector cared about his past, certainly, but pulling a man like that into your plans was like grabbing a tiger by the tail. There was no way of predicting how it would turn out in the end. Molotov was quiet for a moment.

"Sir?" Sobyanin said.

"Fine," Molotov said at last.

"Fine, sir?"

"Do it. Set the trap. Make the American dance

to your tune. But mark my words, Sobyanin, if this backfires, if it looks even for a second like Spector is going to come after us, then pull the plug. Burn everything. I don't need that madman coming after me. Not now. Not ever."

3

Lance Spector let out a long, slow breath, narrowed his eye, and drew a bead on his target. They'd spent a lot of time in the army teaching him to do just this, to steady his hand, slow his pulse, quieten his mind so that nothing remained in the end but his eye, his finger, the trigger, and the face of the enemy. There were three types of shot, they'd taught him—clean, dirty, and miss. "Which is worst," they said, "depends on who you're shooting at, and what manner of death you want him to get." This one, Lance wanted to be clean.

Farther down the valley, he'd seen casings for armor-piercing rounds. He knew what those were for—to cut clear through a body, make it suffer, make it bleed out slow. In the name of sport.

The wolf was five hundred yards distant, white as the driven snow in the moonlight, and if there was any guilt in this country, it wasn't hers. She may have taken down a pair of hikers, she may have tasted the *forbidden fruit*, so to speak—the blood of man—but Lance had no doubt she'd been provoked. Still, here he was, and here she was, playing their roles, one more battle in the eternal war of man against beast. Good against evil. The problem for Lance was that he wasn't sure anymore which side was his.

The wolf's silhouette was clear as crystal against the night sky, her breath billowing in the icy air like smoke from damp wood, and he moved his finger to the trigger of the old thirty-ought-six.

Two days he'd spent tracking the animal—deeper and deeper into the mountains so that now they were so far from civilization they could both pretend to be the last of their kind in the world. For the wolf, it was nearer the truth.

Lance breathed in deeply and held it. He was about to take the shot when the wolf's ears pricked. She looked upward as though about to howl—he wouldn't shoot her while she howled—but she sniffed the air, then turned in Lance's direction. They looked at each other then, neither in any doubt as to the other's purpose, and for the life of him, Lance couldn't touch the trigger. For a moment, at least, he just couldn't do it. There was too much majesty to her. He knew what a sin felt like.

And as he looked at the animal, the face of a woman flashed before his eyes. A beautiful woman. A Russian woman. Her name was Valeria Smirnova, or had been before Lance killed her. He'd taken no pleasure in that kill either. He hadn't wanted to do it. But she'd killed some of Lance's people—Klára, Ritter—and so, Lance had needed to kill her. It was as simple as that. A job that needed to be done. And, if nothing else, Lance was a man who did his job.

He took the shot.

The noise of it rang across the valley like the voice of God himself, and the wolf jerked, yelped, and fell. The soft lead of the bullet did its job instantly. It was a clean kill. At least he'd given her that.

All that was left was for him to collect his proof, hike back to his truck, and get his pay.

4

It was a six-hour trek across treacherous mountainside, through dense forest, criss-crossing a fast-flowing stream of ice-cold water that made him curse his shoddy, foreign-made boots, before he was back at his truck. By that time, the sun was just beginning to inch above the treeline to his east, spilling over everything a crystalline light that shimmered as if the air itself was frozen. He was cold, and he climbed into the cab and fired up the engine to get the heat going before loading the back. There was always a moment's tension in the old truck when he first turned the key after an absence like this. The ignition was cold as a witch's tit, but it sputtered and caught fire on the first try. He put his foot down and really gave it to her until the vent was blowing warm air like a hairdryer, then he went to the back of the truck and loaded up. He had some dry socks and a fresh t-shirt in a bag, and he put them on before getting back into the cab. All that was left to do was a quick check of the radio, but it hissed nothing but static, so he switched it off and rode in silence.

The road was a muddy, frozen four-wheeler track that a power company had cut into the sharp, craggy rock of the mountainside to allow service access to a remote transformer. Driving on it was a treacherous affair—the rocks seemingly carved specifically to cut up a tire—and it took Lance two more hours to go twenty-five miles. After that, he was on a stretch of road owned by the Elk Mountain Logging Company that was no walk in the park either, but better, before emerging finally onto a paved government road near the town of Flathead. On the paved road, he tried his radio again and managed to get something going—country music. It could have been worse.

He entered the town—if town was the right word for the settlement of two dozen wood cabins that looked like a set from a Sam Peckinpah film—and pulled into its sole business, a gas station. Gas station was also probably a generous term for the overground diesel tank that was connected by hose to a hand pump. Logging company vehicles used it to fill up. A cabin next to the fuel tank served as a store, and Lance grabbed the empty thermos from the seat next to him and climbed out of the cab, leaving the engine running. Before he even reached the door, it swung open to reveal an older man with prickly white stubble on his chin, dressed in a red flannel one-piece and a pair of camouflaged hunting boots.

"Don't you look a treat," Lance said, eyeing the sizable bulge at the front of the man's crotch.

"You're the one come knocking on my door," the man said, giving the crotch a defiant scratch.

"I'm looking for coffee, not company," Lance said.

The man retreated into the cabin, leaving the door open, and Lance followed. "I'll take one of these, too," Lance said, picking up a cinnamon pastry in a plastic wrapper that had been flown in from someplace distant. It was one of those foods that would survive a nuclear war, its sell-by date four years in the future.

"Did you get your kill?" the old man said, taking Lance's thermos and rinsing it for him before filling it from the pot.

"I did," Lance said. "Took a while."

"What price did they put on it?"

"Five," Lance said.

The man raised an eyebrow. Lance nodded, though he didn't do it for the money. He did it to keep his mind busy.

"Well, drive careful," the man said. "The road's soft with the thaw."

Lance paid and left, got back into his truck, and drove on toward the sun as it inched higher in its arc. An hour and a half later, he was rolling down the main street of Deweyville, passing the Farmers and Merchants bank and the bar called The

Eureka, which he sometimes went to. At the edge of town, he pulled through a drive-thru and got some fresh coffee and two breakfast sandwiches—there was nothing in the fridge at home. The house was a few miles farther out of town, perched high on an outcrop overlooking the valley, and he ate one of the sandwiches on the way.

When he reached the house he parked, yanked the brake, gathered his things, and carried it all up the steps to the front door, spilling coffee all over his leg as he did so. Once inside, the first thing he noticed was the flashing light on the phone answering machine—a red, digital nine, as high as the machine's counter went.

Not good, he thought.

5

Lance unpacked, showered, got the fire and a fresh pot of coffee going, and only then directed his attention to the landline telephone in the entryway. He walked over to it like a man approaching a coiled snake, holding his breakfast sandwich absently in one hand, and eyed the digital nine on the display screen. On that phone, he received one, perhaps two calls maximum *per year*. He couldn't remember the last time he'd been left a message. He unwrapped his sandwich and took a bite, chewing deliberately as he pushed the play button. Whatever the message was, it would be nothing good, he knew that much.

There was a beep, a timestamp from two days prior, and then a woman's voice.

Hello. My name is Lola Quinn with the police here in Black Swan, Washington.

> This message is for Lance Spector. If you could give me a call back at this number I'd be most grateful.

There was a click when she hung up, another beep as the machine proceeded to the next message, another timestamp from a few hours after the first call, then the same voice.

> This is Lola Quinn again with Black Swan Police. If Lance Spector could please give me a call back, I'd very much appreciate it.

When the third message began with the same voice, he stopped it and hit the return call button. Black Swan, Washington, he thought. Who did he know there? Had he even heard of the place? He didn't think so.

The voice of an older woman came on the line and said, "Black Swan Police."

"Yes," Lance said, wondering how some out-of-the-way police station in god-only-knew-where had managed to get his number in the first place. It wasn't like he was in the book. He cleared his throat. "My name is Lance Spector. I got a call from you folks."

"Mr *Spector*, yes," the receptionist said—from

the sound of it she'd been expecting his call. "It was Quinn who's been trying to get hold of you."

"Quinn," Lance said as if testing the name aloud. "That's right."

"She's at her desk. Let me transfer you over."

Lance waited, eyeing the sandwich in his hand, wondering if he had time to swallow another bite before Quinn picked up. He waited fifteen, twenty seconds, then threw caution to the wind and took the bite. The instant he did, Lola Quinn's voice came on. "Is this Lance Spector?"

"Yes," he said through a mouthful of biscuit.

"Thank you for calling back," she said, sounding more irritated than grateful. "You're a difficult man to get a hold of."

"Yes."

"I must have left a dozen messages. Your machine...."

"I was out of town."

"Of course, well, as I said before, I'm calling from Black Swan, Washington."

"I gathered that."

"And I've got a case here," she said, clearing her throat, "if it will just open on my screen."

"A case?" Lance said.

"Yes," Quinn said. She made a tutting sound while waiting for her computer to load, then said, "Okay, here we go, file open, concerning one... Raven Spector."

Some biscuit went down the wrong pipe, and

Lance fell into a fit of coughing. *This,* he should have seen coming—he had enough feelers out—but for some reason, it still felt like a bolt of lightning.

"Mr Spector? Are you all right?"

"I'm fine," he said, gasping for breath, and despite himself, there was a trace of emotion in his voice. It was just a crack—a hairline fracture, you might say—but it was there, nonetheless.

"May I ask what agency you're with?" Quinn said. "I've scoured this flag, but it doesn't seem to have a marker."

She was right. There was no marker. Lance had used his CIA clearance to place the flag years ago, but this was business purely his own. It had nothing to do with Langley or any other government agency.

"Mr Spector?"

"I'm here."

"The agency?"

"Special Operations Group," he said, unable to think of a lie.

"Special Operations Group?"

"That's right."

"That's not on my list here. Is that—"

"It's federal."

"No, I have federal."

"It's sensitive," he said, hoping that would be enough for her. "I can get you a civilian reference number if you want."

"No, no," she said. "The flag's valid. That's all I need. I just thought...."

"It's *sensitive*," he said again, his tone suggesting they move on.

She went quiet then, and he waited, his mind racing through a million things at once. When she spoke again, her voice jarred him from his thoughts. "I couldn't help but notice..." she said haltingly.

He knew what she was going to say and beat her to it, "That's nothing."

"It's just, the name here, and your name—"

"They match. I know."

"Right."

"Coincidence," he said. "I noticed the same thing. Just plain old..."

"*Coincidence?*" she said, sounding distinctly unconvinced. "In that case, I won't tell you to take a seat or anything."

"A seat?"

"Before I break it to you."

Lance didn't doubt he was about to get some bad news, but after so many years, so much water under the bridge, he didn't think there was much she could say now that would faze him. "I think I'll manage," he said.

"Well, I'm working this file."

"Like you said," he said curtly. He didn't mean to be rude, but his sister had been missing for more than thirty years. His sister and his mother. If this cop had found some old bones and closed the case, he really just wanted to know.

"As I'm sure you know, the first twenty-four hours in a case like this—"

"Twenty-four hours?" he gasped.

"Obviously we've blown past that now—"

"Twenty-four hours?" he said again, his mind failing to process the information.

Lola let out a sigh and began explaining. "In a missing persons case, the first twenty-four hours are known as—"

Lance let out a quiet laugh.

"I'm sorry," she said. "Did I say something funny?"

"Funny?" he said. "I wouldn't say funny."

"Have I.... Is this a bad time, Mr Spector?"

"A bad time? No, it's just, you're talking about hours. The Raven Spector I was looking for disappeared more than three decades ago."

"Really?" she said, beginning to let her irritation show. "Well, if I'm wasting your time—"

"Ms Quinn, let's not—"

"Because frankly, Mr Spector, I've got better things to be doing than leaving messages across the country for people who don't even pick up the phone."

"If I could have returned your call—"

"Well you didn't," she said, cutting him off, "and I've got a case on my desk, a *serious* case, clock ticking."

"I think there's been some sort of mistake."

"You can say that again. A woman's life is on the line, and every time I try to access my system, your name flashes across my screen in big red letters like some sort of computer error."

"The flag *was* triggered in error."

Lola kept going, talking over him. "So before we start quibbling about wasted time, Mr Spector, let's make one thing very clear. You're the one wasting *mine*."

He said nothing for a moment—it seemed safer given that his famous charm wasn't having the desired effect—and thought about what she was saying. It made sense enough, as far as it went. Lance had put the big red warning there himself—not only on the federal database, but on the Texas files from back in the day, on all state databases, and on both his sister's and mother's names, just in case any new matches were ever created. It was a long shot, he knew, but he'd wanted to know if the bodies ever showed up. He'd wanted to give them a proper burial. Now, here was this cop telling him someone named Raven Spector had gone missing from a town in Washington State just days ago. Anyone under that name, living there, would have triggered his flag long ago. He'd have looked into it and disregarded her as a false match. Raven Spector wasn't a common name, but there had been more than a few that he'd had to sift through over the years. This was another Raven. Had to be. Simple as that.

"So?" Lola said. "Do you have something to say for yourself, or is this flag just here to make my job more difficult?"

"I'll have it removed. Sorry to have wasted your time. I hope you find your missing person."

"Removed?"

"That's what you want, isn't it?"

"I would have thought there was a reason for its existence in the first place."

"There is," Lance said, "but it's overly wide. The name's a match, but it's not my vic."

"How do you know that? I haven't even told you about my case yet."

"You said it was a missing persons file. Twenty-four hours. The Raven Spector I'm looking for disappeared three decades ago."

"Birthdate of January 26th, 1981?"

Lance felt his blood run cold. That was his sister's birthdate. And his own. That information wasn't part of the flag.

"Mr Spector? Are you there?"

"You've got a missing persons file open on a Raven Spector, born January 26th, 1981?"

"You catch on fast."

"I'm sorry, it's just...."

"I gave you the chance to take a seat."

That was true. He reached out for the wall now and leaned against it. Had his sister been alive this whole time? Living in Washington? And had Lance —for all his bluster and top-level security clearance —missed it?

"Why don't you tell me what's really going on, Mr *Spector*?" Quinn said, this time emphasizing his name.

Lance made to speak, but no words came out. He looked at the receiver in his hand as if it were the source of the silence, then brought it back to his ear.

"Mr Spector?"

"I'm here."

"Are you connected to this case, sir? I mean, connected personally?"

"Personally?" he echoed. So many years had passed that the memories almost felt like they belonged to another person. His mother and sister had disappeared from a roadside Texas motel when he was eight years old, and the details of that night—the plastic feel of the motel bedsheets, the smell in the room of stale cigarette smoke, the enormous sign on the roof of a neon cowboy swinging his leg and waving his hand at the passing highway traffic—could have come from any of a thousand case files. God knew he'd pored over enough of them, tens of thousands of pages from old cases—state, federal, CIA. He'd stared at so many old photographs that the images that came to him now in his dreams—women with their throats slit, their wrists tied, plastic bags over their heads, lying in filthy bathtubs or the trunks of abandoned cars—could have come from anywhere. There'd been such a tidal wave of sex trafficking and child pornography along the border in those years that it was hard to know where one case ended and the next began. "Personal is a strange word, don't you think?"

"In what sense, Mr Spector?" Quinn said, her tone growing less patient by the second.

"If the same thing happens to a thousand women, to ten thousand, is it still...." His words trailed off.

Quinn cleared her throat. "Look, Mr Spector, I'm getting the sense—"

"I'll tell you what's personal," he said, cutting her off. "The feeling in my chest when I think about them. My own mother and sister. There's a tightness right here," he touched his neck even though she couldn't see it, "below my Adam's apple, like someone just jabbed me in the throat."

A silence grew between them. Lance had given up on finding his family alive a very long time ago. Short of a miracle, even finding the bodies was a stretch. Which meant his mother and sister's file in the Texas criminal database would remain open, unaccounted for, for as long as it was conceivable the two victims were still alive. According to his calculation, their file wouldn't be closed until sometime around the turn of the next century. That stuck in his craw.

Lola broke the silence. "I think it's best if I—"

"Don't hang up."

"I don't know how you managed to flag your own—

"I know it's irregular."

"It's not just irregular, it's illegal, as far as I'm aware."

Raven had been eight years old too when it

happened, them being twins. His mother, for her sins, had been scarcely twenty-three. It was hard to believe now, but in her day, in her neck of the woods, getting knocked up at fourteen or fifteen wasn't that unheard of. And, indeed, if that had been the worst thing ever to happen to her, the rest of the story might not have been so bad. It wouldn't have been a fairy tale by any stretch—his mother's impeccable taste in men would have assured that much—but they might all have at least kept their names out of the crime databases.

Sandor Grey was where it all went south. Sandor Grey. Lance sometimes said the two words to himself like a mantra. Sandor Grey. Sandor Grey. Sandor Grey. The first name was actually Sándor—a Hungarian name—though the man Lance's mother married was born in Cheboygan, Michigan. Punchy son of a bitch, he was. As in, he liked to throw punches. And not just at other men, but at women too, and little girls and boys.

He beat Lance all the way to the emergency room one time—he'd almost died, the police got involved, Child Protection Services—but Sandor talked his way out of it. The thing Lance remembered about him most was the mustache. It made him look like Burt Reynolds' character in *Smokey and the Bandit.*

"You said you have an active file?" Lance said. "Raven Spector. Missing."

"That's correct."

"*Still* missing?"

"Correct."

"Not deceased?"

"Cases like this—"

"When did she go missing?"

There was a pause, he heard a keyboard clacking, then she said, "Forty-eight hours ago."

"Two days?"

"If that's what your math tells you."

"Sorry, I'm just caught off guard here. The Raven Spector I'm looking for went missing in 1989. She was eight years old at the time."

"I see," Quinn said. "That's not in the note on my screen."

"The original case would have been opened in El Paso, Texas."

"Texas? That's why I don't see it."

"You can't get hold of it?"

"I can fire off an email. Wait for a clerk in Austin or somewhere to check their inbox and get back to me. It'll take a few days."

"What else does your file say?" he said. "A struggle? A suspect? A husband?"

"None of the above."

"Then what happened?"

"Raven was out walking. She was staying at a trailer park on the outskirts of town, and there's a convenience store less than a mile away. According to a neighbor, that's where she was headed when she was last seen."

"She never made it?"

"No, she did not."

"And this happened forty-eight hours ago?"

"Correct."

"Any witnesses? Anyone see anything?"

"No."

"A suspicious van? Anything like that?"

"Nothing."

"Then why jump on it so quickly? The woman's an adult. How do you know she didn't just take off on her own?"

"She left the park on foot."

"She could have had a ride waiting. She could have hitchhiked somewhere. She could have hopped on a bus. If the Queen of England disappeared, you wouldn't raise the alarm this quick without some sign of foul play."

"The Queen of England?"

"Or the king."

"Mr Spector, around these parts, when a woman disappears on that stretch of road—"

"What's wrong with that stretch of road?"

"You haven't heard?"

"Heard what?"

"Black Swan, Washington?"

"I don't know what you're talking about."

"The disappearances?"

"What disappearances?"

"We've been in the news. It went national. The *New York Times* did a big profile a few years back—"

"I let my subscription lapse."

"This town has a problem, Mr Spector. It has a history."

"Of disappearances?"

"Women. Girls."

"I see."

"So when this came in, I wasn't of a mind to just let it sit in my in-tray without doing anything."

"How do these cases usually end up?"

"You mean—"

"I mean, I'm not imagining from your tone that many of these women make it home again in one piece."

"No, they don't. If we're lucky, we recover the bodies."

Lance had his back to the wall and he put his weight against it, then slid down until he reached the ground. "I see," he said.

6

Lola Quinn inched the cruiser forward and shook her head. Despite all her promises to the contrary—packing a lunch, making her own hummus, bringing carrot sticks to snack on, food that wouldn't actually kill her—here she was again, back in line at the drive-thru. This, combined with the desk she parked her ass at for eight-to-ten hours a day, was starting to show.

She was twenty-six years old, unattached—unless a tabby cat she'd adopted from the local shelter two months ago counted—and categorically could not afford to let herself go. Not yet, at least. That's what her mother told her every time Lola mustered the courage to answer one of her calls.

"A little bit longer, sweetie," her mother would say, imploring her with the desperation of a woman who'd already decided she had nothing left to live for other than grandchildren. "A guy with his own teeth and a half-decent job. It's not beyond you to snag one of those, is it?"

"We'll have to wait and see, won't we?" Lola said back.

"Once the ring's on your finger, you can eat whatever you like. Look at your cousin." Her mother's voice would take on a conspiratorial tone then, as if she were about to impart womankind's greatest secret yet in the eternal battle against man. "She's put on thirty pounds since the wedding."

Lola's cousin Kerry, born two months before her, two towns over, was the daughter her mother had always wanted. That was what it felt like, at least. There wasn't a single category in which Lola felt she'd won out. Kerry's father had stuck around—Lola's hadn't. Kerry placed in their childhood beauty pageants—Lola never did. Kerry made the varsity cheerleading squad—Lola didn't. And now, Kerry was ensconced in a suburban Tacoma townhouse with a kid, two dogs, a Lexus sedan in the driveway, and a three-karat ring on her finger that Lola secretly hoped was cubic zirconia.

No one ever mentioned the fact that the prince charming who'd made it all happen—a man in his fifties with two ex-wives, six children Kerry's age, and a packet of wooden toothpicks in his breast pocket that he pulled out after every meal—was having an affair with the nineteen-year-old receptionist at his law practice. Nor did they mention that Lola was the youngest ever police detective in Black Swan's history. And the first female.

"Order, please?" the drive-thru speaker said.

Lola hesitated—they sold salads here—then surrendered to the inevitable. "Cheeseburger, please."

"Fries?"

"Why not?"

"Soda?"

"No, coffee."

"Cream, sugar?"

"Two of each."

"That's it?"

"That's it."

"Drive on up."

It had been a tough morning. The call with the man from Montana had been trying. She assumed he was the brother, though he hadn't said so explicitly, and speaking to him only hammered home the fact that there were real people, real lives, on the line. Not that she was in any danger of forgetting—she'd been working round-the-clock since the case came in. It had been midnight when she'd collapsed into bed the night before and scarcely seven when she was back at her desk this morning, going over the details with a fine-tooth comb. She told herself that that was the reason she hadn't packed the hummus. No time. She'd eat healthy when the case was solved.

She picked up her food and pointed the cruiser back in the direction of the station. She would have liked to swing by the crime scene for another look, but she'd been there half a dozen times already, and there were other things that needed doing. The clock was ticking, and every second that passed lessened the chances of finding Raven Spector alive. She felt like a death row inmate on her final day. She had no leads, no witnesses, no suspects, and the last time someone disappeared from that stretch of road—a sex worker from the Yakama Reservation named Gloria Cavalier—her body was found on day three.

Today was day three for Raven Spector.

She pulled up to the station and parked in a visitor spot because it was nearer the door. Then she grabbed her lunch and hurried up the steps. Marlene, the receptionist, looked up from her computer screen as she passed and said, "Chief brought pastries."

Lola looked at the white *Dutch Bakery* box on the counter and said, "That's the last thing my ass needs."

"Oh, shut it," Marlene said, taking a bite from a cruller. "Your ass is fine."

Fine wasn't exactly what Lola was aiming for, not Marlene's idea of *fine* in any case, but she didn't say as much. Instead, she passed the box without even looking inside, planting her fine ass back in the seat at her desk. "Any calls?" she said, unpacking her food.

"You were gone all of twenty minutes," Marlene said.

"Will you call Jo for me?"

"You've already left her two messages."

"Those were from my cell. You call her."

"My calling's not going to make a difference."

"It might," Lola said. "And I can't run this investigation on the say-so of a semi-retired trailer park supervisor. If she doesn't pick up soon, I'm going to drive back over there. Tell her that in the message."

Marlene sighed, then called Jolene's number at the trailer park and transferred the call to Lola without waiting for an answer. Lola had to hustle to pick it up and was surprised when Jolene answered on the first ring.

"What is it now, Marlene?"

"It's not Marlene. It's Lola."

"Oh."

"You've been avoiding my calls."

"Only because I already told you everything I know."

"A woman and child are missing, Jo. I have to keep digging. Sorry if it's a bother."

"I told you I'd call if I remembered anything else."

"You said the woman smoked."

"Yeah, she smoked. They all smoke."

"You're sure?"

"I can picture her now, sitting on the stoop of her trailer the other night, worrying about her bills and sucking down Pall Malls like they were going out of style."

"They are going out of style."

"Not around here."

"And you're certain they were Pall Mall?"

"I think—" Jolene said, then stopped and said, "I could check. She stubbed them out in a paint can by the stoop."

"Please," Lola said. "I'll wait."

Jo put down the phone and left. When she came back a minute later, she said, "Like I said, Pall Mall."

"One hundred percent?"

"Same brand as me, Lo."

"Okay," Lola said, "and what makes you say she was worried about bills? I thought she'd only been there a week."

"Bills, men, her sagging tits. I don't know what she was worried about. I just assume it's the same shit I worry about."

"You don't have saggy tits, Jo."

"Oh, you're too kind."

Lola popped a fry in her mouth. "She get close to anyone while she was there? She have any visitors? Anyone come looking for her?"

"No, no, and no. I already told you this. Besides, how would I know if she had friends? I wasn't exactly watching her like a hawk."

Lola sighed. "All right," she said. "If anyone comes looking for her—"

"I know, I know. I'll call you right away."

The line went dead, and Lola ate a few more fries.

There was a banker's box on her desk, it contained the entirety of the evidence recovered in the case so far, and she took off the lid. Inside were two clear plastic bags. One contained the key to the 1988 Winnebago LeSharo that Raven Spector had rolled into town in ten days ago. It was on a gray and blue Seahawks keychain, along with another key that had yet to be identified. The second contained a single cigarette butt. They'd been found by the side of the road, about midway between the trailer park and the convenience store, and the butt hadn't had time to get wet in the rain.

Lola took the bag containing the butt out of the box and held it up to the light, squinting to read the brand. Marlboro.

"Marlene?"

"Yes?"

"The evidence list for the Cavalier case? There was a cigarette butt that time too, wasn't there?"

Marlene tapped some keys on her keyboard and scanned the screen. "Yes, there was."

"Brand?"

Marlene shook her head. "Not specified," she said.

"Do we still have the box?"

Marlene hit more keys on her computer. "Should be in the shed. Row H. Top shelf. I'll get the key."

The shed was a climate-controlled shipping container at the back of the station. They kept evidence in it before having it transferred to a more secure facility once a case was closed. Gloria Cavalier's case was technically still open.

"I'll get it," Lola said, marching toward the chief's office, where it was usually to be found in a pencil organizer on his desk.

"Lola," Marlene said after her.

"Yes?"

"You done with those fries?"

7

Lance drove directly to Glacier Park Airport, six miles outside of Kalispell, and parked in the long-term lot. He had no idea how long he'd be gone. He'd called ahead for a ticket on the first flight to Port Angeles, Washington, and checked in with no luggage. There was no lineup to get through security, and he was in the departure lounge considerably earlier than he needed to be. He looked at his watch, he had hours to pass before boarding, and the terminal didn't offer much by way of distraction. He sat and stared out the window at the runway for as long as he could bear it, then went to the little Italian-themed café close to his gate and ordered coffee and a sandwich. There was a stack of newspapers by the counter, and he picked up a copy of the *Post*.

Raven Spector, January 26th, 1981, he thought. What were the chances that was another person? He'd run the combination through every government database in existence and never found anyone. As far as he knew, there was no one with that name and birthdate other than his sister. But how could she pop up now, after thirty years, while having remained completely off the grid the whole intervening time? Had she returned from overseas? He had a flag on the passport database as well as border control. This didn't add up. Was it a mistake? Possibly.

There was another possibility, of course. There was always another possibility when you were in his line of work. It was the possibility someone was fucking with him. But who? Who had that information?

He took a table where he could see the gate and sipped his coffee. It was good and strong. He picked up the newspaper then, glanced at the front page, and froze with his coffee raised halfway to his mouth. He literally felt the blood drain from his face. There it was in boldface type.

Ex-CIA Director Levi Roth Feared Dead in Car Crash

He stared at the headline for he didn't know how long. When he finally had the wherewithal to take another sip of his coffee, it had gone completely cold.

"You all right, hon?" the lady behind the counter asked when he looked up at her.

"What's that?"

"You look like you just saw a ghost."

"Oh," Lance said, thinking she was more correct than she knew, "it's just... I let my coffee go cold."

She brought him a fresh cup and took away the old one. He hadn't taken so much as a bite from the sandwich.

The article in *The Post* was brief.

Former Director of Central Intelligence Levi Roth feared dead, along with his driver and security guard, when his Cadillac Escalade went off the Taft Bridge in Washington DC in the early hours of the morning. The vehicle fell a hundred-thirty feet into Rock Creek, where it exploded on impact. Both Roth and the driver were last seen entering the vehicle just before it left the grounds of the Eisenhower Executive Office Building in the White House compound. As of writing, the wreckage was still being searched for the bodies, and CIA spokesperson William J Leahy confirmed that the agency would be taking over the site.

Speculation is rampant that some sort of foul play is involved, though neither the CIA nor the White House has commented

> on this angle. The President, who just days earlier announced that Levi Roth would be stepping down from his role as Director, has yet to comment.
>
> Levi Roth's relationship with the White House, as well as with congressional oversight committees, had grown increasingly fractious, with rumors abounding that he played a key role in the recent failed coup-attempt in Moscow against President Molotov.
>
> "How could this not be Moscow?" said one congressional aide when asked for comment. "Molotov's not going to stand back idly after a thing like that. If Roth's really dead, and I'll only believe it when I see a body, my guess is the Kremlin did it."

The article went on, but Lance pushed the paper aside and took out his cell. He had a personal number for Laurel and he tried it. It rang a few times before connecting.

"You've got some nerve calling now," she said when she picked up, her voice frail, as if she'd been crying.

"Is it true?" Lance said. "Is he dead?"

"You should have been here, Lance."

"What happened?"

"What do you mean, what happened? His car

went off a cliff, Lance. He's dead. That's what happened."

"Have they recovered a body?"

"They're still digging through the wreckage. The whole thing will take days. Anything they find will be burnt to a cinder. Even the steel of the chassis melted."

"I see."

"I know what you're thinking."

"What's that?"

"You're thinking, without a body, who's to say he's really dead?"

"Well?"

"You're unbelievable, you know that?"

"What did I say?"

Laurel was quiet for a second, then sighed. "Whatever," she said. "Is there a reason for this call, or are you just looking for an update?"

"Is anyone looking at the Russian angle?"

"He was the head of the CIA, Lance. He just tried to have Molotov overthrown. Of course they're looking at the Russian angle. But you know what everyone's saying behind the scenes?"

"Who's everyone?"

"Cutler, Schultz, Schlesinger. Even the president."

"What are they saying?"

"They're saying that he asked for it. That he went courting this. That he poked the bear. That if you live by the sword, you've got to expect to die by it."

"Well, if that's true, it applies to whoever killed him too."

"Lance! Give it up. It's over."

"Not for me."

Laurel was quiet again. Lance didn't know if it was grief or anger that was keeping her from speaking, and if it was the latter, whether it was directed at him or the killers, whoever they turned out to be. He cleared his throat. "Listen—"

"Why did you call, really, Lance?"

"To check on you."

"Are you coming back?"

"I'm not sure if I can."

"I see."

"Laurel, I would, it's just, right now—"

"It's fine, Lance. Forget it. Forget everything."

It was Lance's turn to be quiet.

Laurel cleared her throat. "You're really going to miss the old man's funeral?"

"I'm sorry, Laurel. Something else has come up."

"What something?"

"Something from my past. Something to do with my sister. Possibly."

"Your sister?"

"Possibly."

"You should have been here," she said again.

"I know."

"We all knew they'd come for him."

"I know, Laurel. I do."

"But you keep dropping off the radar. You disappear. Every time we really need you."

"I'm sorry."

Lance looked across the lounge at his gate. They'd announced the flight, and people were beginning to get in line to board. "You don't know everything about me and Roth," he said.

"I know enough."

"Not everything."

"You're talking about Clarice," she said.

"And other things."

She sighed, and a silence filled the line again. Lance shut his eyes and tried to blank his mind.

Laurel said, "You know, you're going to have to move on eventually, Lance. You can't keep stewing in the past like this, like a ghost in an old house that can't move on. Clarice, your mother and sister, all of it's in the past."

"The past is all we have, Laurel. It's all we are. If something's not right there, it's not right here."

He thought she was going to say something else, there was another pause, but then the line went dead. She'd hung up. He tried calling her back but she didn't pick up. They were making the final boarding call for his flight. He rose to his feet, put some money on the table, and went to the gate.

8

Lola returned from the storage shed thirty minutes later and let the door slam loudly behind her.

Marlene looked up, startled. "What's happened?" she said, rising from her desk.

"Who says something's happened?"

"Don't get fresh with me, Lola. Whatever it is—"

"Is the chief back?"

"Lola," Marlene said, her tone leaving no room for argument. "Tell me what's going on?"

Lola glanced toward Chief Glanton's office, then back at Marlene. "The evidence," she said, "the box for the Cavalier case. There's nothing in it."

Marlene's eyes widened. "What do you mean, nothing in it?"

"Is he back, or isn't he?" Lola said, marching toward the office. "I can see from here the light's on."

"Hang on," Marlene said, hitting some keys on

her keyboard. "Come over here." Lola hesitated, then went around the counter to see what was on the screen. Marlene had pulled up the evidence log for the Cavalier case. "According to this," she said, "there are thirteen items logged for that case. None have been signed out, so…."

"The box is there," Lola said, "dated and labeled perfectly, everything in order, but there's nothing in it."

"It's completely empty?"

"Yes!"

"How is that possible?" Marlene said.

Lola shook her head. "Unless…" she said but didn't finish the thought. The number of people with access to the evidence shed wasn't long. It included members of the police force, so long as they got the key from the chief's desk first, as well as a few authorized people in the county courthouse and prosecutor's office. It also included the feds, of course, if and when they decided to roll in and grace the town with their presence. Lola's eyes darted around the station, at the vacant desks of her colleagues, looking at them suddenly as if for the first time.

"Unless someone took it," Marlene said, finishing her sentence.

Lola nodded. Her chest felt tight. She went to her desk and sat down, breathing deeply to catch her breath.

"Honey, are you all right?"

"I'm just tired," Lola said, looking at the older

woman. They both knew they understood each other. They both knew something very wrong was going on in their town, and had been for a very long time. "I'm very tired," Lola said.

"You're too young to be tired," Marlene said.

Lola smiled. If only that were true. "When's enough going to be enough?" she said quietly. "When is this going to end?"

Marlene looked at her but said nothing.

"It's been going on our entire lives," Lola said. "Mine and yours. We've been...."

"I know," Marlene said, her eyes begging Lola not to go on.

"It sullies everything."

And that was true—it touched everything and everyone—Marlene more than most. And not just murders—though they were the most visible symptom of a disease that ran deep in the veins of Black Swan and the surrounding country—but abuse too, prostitution, drugs, violence, alcoholism, all the things that poverty and oppression and a malevolent world could impose.

"Keep the faith," Marlene said. "Things change. Things get better."

"What things?"

"Trust me," Marlene said, her gravelly rasp giving her words an added weight, "things could be a lot worse. I've seen them a lot worse. There was a time in this town when even investigating a disappearance was asking for trouble."

"It's still like that," Lola said, "and it just keeps

happening. Even here, in the police station, evidence is disappearing and we're still no nearer to solving the crimes than we ever were."

"We'll find the missing evidence."

"No we won't," Lola said. "It's gone." She threw her hands up. "It's just... *gone*."

Marlene nodded sadly. "You're right," she said. "It's gone."

Lola went to her desk and opened the drawer. She pulled out a bottle of aspirin, then went to the sink and poured herself some water. "This isn't the first time, is it?" she said, throwing her head back as she swallowed two pills.

"Lola, there are a lot of things—"

"You've seen this before."

Marlene looked at her, there was sympathy in her eyes, but she didn't speak.

Lola said, "If I'm going to work this case, if I'm going to get up in the morning and keep coming to this station, then you're going to have to trust me."

"I trust you, Lola, but I worry for you."

"Don't."

"There have been...."

"What? What have there been?"

"Deaths."

"I know that."

"Not like this. I mean cover-ups. Dead police, Lola. Dead prosecutors. Dead investigators."

Lola breathed out, long and slow. She'd known, of course, about the deep-rooted problem the town was facing. It was impossible not to know. But being faced with it so blatantly now, finding an evidence box empty in a case she was responsible for was a slap in the face. It rocked her. But it wasn't new. She told herself that now, in a vain attempt to regain her composure. This wasn't new. She'd known all along. You didn't get this many disappearances, this many killings, in one place without something very bad going on beneath the surface. The whole town knew it.

She looked at the glass of water in her hand. It was shaking and she had to put it down before she dropped it. Then she went back over to Marlene's desk.

"The chief's not...."

"The chief?" Marlene gasped.

"He's not involved, is he?"

"Heavens, no. He's one of the good ones, child. Don't ever let anyone tell you otherwise."

Lola felt a wave of emotion rush over her. "I don't think I could take it if you'd said anything else."

"He's been here longer than anyone, Lola, and believe me when I say he'd give his life for this town. For the town and each and every one of its people."

"Well, he's got his work cut out for him."

"Yes, he does."

"And something's not working."

"If you're suggesting he could be doing more—"

"I'm just saying," Lola said, shaking her head, "I mean, I'm not blaming him."

"I know," Marlene said. "I know what you're saying."

"It's just, how many women have gone missing even in the last five years?"

"Too many."

"And the five years before that? And before that?"

Marlene nodded.

"Something's got to give, Marlene."

"I know," Marlene said. "You're right, but...."

"But what?"

"There are still things you don't know. Things you haven't seen. There are factors at play."

"What factors?"

"Dark ones," Marlene said. "Dark and powerful." She became quiet then, as if thinking about what she'd just said. As if regretting it.

Lola glanced over at the chief's door. She could still see the light on behind the frosted glass.

"Don't," Marlene said when she saw Lola looking at it.

"Don't what?"

Marlene's face was very sad. Sadder than Lola had ever seen it.

"Don't what?" Lola repeated. "There's a woman missing. The clock's ticking. And this keeps happening. They keep disappearing, they keep showing up dead, and nothing ever changes. We don't solve anything. We don't catch anyone. The state police and the feds ride in like the cavalry, guns blazing, but they don't catch anyone either. The politicians helicopter in but stay just long enough to get their faces in the newspaper. No one's actually doing anything, Marlene. And whoever's responsible for these heinous, monstrous crimes—"

Lola suddenly went silent as the chief's door swung open. Out walked the man himself, Bill Glanton, oblivious to everything but the coffee machine he was headed toward. In one hand was his 'World's Best Grandpa' mug, which he filled from the pot as he looked over at Lola and Marlene. "What are you two plotting?"

Marlene put a hand on Lola's arm to stop her from speaking and said, "Who says we have to be plotting something?"

"I know that look," the chief said, stirring cream into his coffee. He looked at them a moment longer, but he'd learned long ago not to press the two of them when they were like this. Instead, he had the good sense to turn around and go right back into his office.

Lola looked at Marlene then and said, "We need to tell him about the missing evidence. There's only a handful of people who have access to that shed—"

"I think you'll find there's very little that goes on around here that the chief doesn't already know."

"You think he knows about this box?"

"I think he's been around this a lot longer than you or I, Lola. And however bad things are, they'd be a whole lot worse without him. I promise you that."

Lola wasn't sure what to make of that. She was about to ask Marlene what exactly she meant when, as if on cue, the Deputy Chief, Jim Belcher, came barging in through the main entrance. He was on the phone, talking overly loudly to his wife, Cathy. "Not the rib eye," he was saying. "It's too good for them. We can grill burgers."

Lola felt an involuntary shiver run down her spine. Belcher was not her favorite person on the Black Swan Police Force, not by a long shot. The girl he'd married had been in the Academy with Lola, they'd both come back to Black Swan and started on the force together. They were both also a good fifteen years younger than Belcher. For the life of her, Lola still couldn't fathom what had persuaded a seemingly smart girl like Cathy Martin to hitch her cart to a deadbeat like Jim Belcher's.

He'd been married to someone else when they'd arrived, not that he was the type to let that stop him from making a move. He'd started out hitting on them both, and they'd hated it. Lola had even reported it to the chief, and the chief—or so Lola thought—had more or less put a stop to it. But something must have continued with Cathy—Belcher had somehow overcome her resistance—because one day, about a year after they'd started, Cathy simply announced that she was leaving the force. It made no sense to Lola—she knew how hard Cathy had worked to get there—but when she pressed her about it, Cathy simply broke into tears. Lola knew something wasn't right. She tried to find out what it was, too, but Cathy eventually told her to back off.

"We're getting married, and that's that," she'd said. "So stop prying."

"Getting married doesn't mean you can't keep your job," Lola had said.

"Lola," Cathy said then, "it's my life. My decision."

"I hope so."

"It *is*," Cathy said, and Lola could tell she was close to tears.

She was lying, but Lola didn't know why. "He's already got a wife," she said.

"They're splitting up," Cathy said. "Now, do me a favor and back the fuck off."

The whole thing had certainly left Lola with a bad feeling, and she'd tried to bring it up a few more times before Cathy broke off contact altogether. It had been months now since they'd spoken, though she'd seen photos online of the shotgun wedding Belcher had thrown in his backyard in the summer.

"Best tits this office has ever seen," Lola heard him brag to McEnearney and some of the other guys after the wedding. "A real pair of milkers." As he said the words, he'd looked up at Lola and gave her a wide, toothy sneer. "And she knows how to stay in her place, if you know what I mean," he added.

Lola watched him now as he breezed through the office without acknowledging her or Marlene, slowing down only to take a pastry from the box on his way past.

"Prick," Lola muttered under her breath.

"Don't," Marlene said.

Belcher went into his office, only to reemerge a moment later, still on the phone. He left the same way he'd come in.

"He's clocking off already, isn't he?" Lola said.

Marlene shrugged and said, "What's a woman's life when there are hamburgers to be had?"

9

It was pushing eight thirty when Lola finally shut down her computer for the night. She was going cross-eyed from staring at the screen, and the police station's eerie quiet was beginning to give her the heebie-jeebies. Every sound, every rustle, gave her a fright. What she needed was to go home and get some rest. Tomorrow would be a new day.

She'd spent hours out in the shed, rooting through old evidence boxes, and hours more poring over digitized evidence on her computer, looking for something, anything, that might connect the Spector case to previous disappearances. She needed something concrete, something new, that hadn't already been exhausted. What she'd come away with was no less than six references to Marlboro cigarette butts from various cases going back eight years. She was certain she'd find more if she kept digging.

On its own, it didn't seem like much. Smoking Marlboros didn't narrow the field a whole lot, and it certainly didn't paint a path to the killer's doorstep, but it was a start. She would send the cigarette butts she had to the state lab in the morning and see what they could come up with. If they got a DNA match from multiple cigarettes, it would tie the disappearances to a single individual. That was something all prior investigators had failed to do.

Which meant it was progress.

But it was depressing work. The one thought that never left her mind as she sifted through all that old evidence was that not one of the cases had been solved. She'd gone back almost a decade, twenty-four cases, twenty-four women, and still no one knew what had happened to any of the victims.

It was haunting. The killer could be right there among them, living in town. The talk was that outsiders were responsible, and Lola herself tended to believe that, but it was an assumption. The police never proved it as fact.

She wondered how many women had truly been taken. And she wondered how far back it went. Her own database access only went to 1989—which was when the county started going digital—but even that put the caseload at well over a hundred and fifty.

How many more weren't in the database? It wasn't hard to imagine a woman drifting into town—so many of them had been transient—and disappearing without anyone ever raising the alarm.

Almost all of them had been Native American, and many had prior run-ins with the law—addiction issues, mental illness, homelessness, prostitution. People like that could disappear without a case ever being opened, they could slip through the cracks.

The whole thing was enough to make her lose sleep at night.

There was a sound from the direction of the offices and she turned around startled, ready to draw her gun if she needed. No one was there.

Right, she thought. She was hearing things now. Definitely time to go.

She brought her coffee mug to the sink and washed it, then peeked inside the pastry box as she walked by. It was empty now, though she hadn't noticed it being pilfered earlier. She was wondering what she'd do about dinner—it was too late to cook and eat healthily—when a car pulled up outside. She watched it through the window—a taxi from Port Angeles, the biggest town within a half-hour's radius, and the only airport. A man stepped out and waited for the cab to drive off before turning his attention to the station. Lola found herself pinching apart two slats in the blind to get a better look. When he glanced up at her, she looked away hurriedly as if caught doing something she shouldn't.

He was well-built, wearing an open jacket over an army t-shirt. The shirt was pulled taut across a muscular chest. It was difficult to tell his age. He was older than she was, certainly, but by a year or fifteen, she wasn't sure.

When he pushed open the door, cold air rushed into the office with him. He glanced at Marlene's vacant seat before zeroing in on Lola. She felt his gaze on her like a physical grip, and her voice caught when she tried to speak.

"Help you?" she croaked, clearing her throat. "That is, can I?"

"Can you?"

"Help you?"

He nodded. "I'm looking for Lola Quinn," he said.

"You're the—" she said, clearing her throat again before trying a second time. "You're Spector."

He took her in like some sort of tracking system assessing a target, and she subconsciously took a half-step back from him. He wasn't Native American. When she'd spoken to him earlier, she'd imagined that he was. Raven was. This man was white. It didn't mean they couldn't be siblings, but it did make her wonder.

"I am," he said.

He looked tired—ragged, perhaps was the word she'd have used—and there was a rough, frayed quality to his voice. Lola had seen it enough times to recognize it. As a cop, she was used to entering people's lives when they were at their absolute lowest, when all their deepest, darkest fears were being realized. There was a certain look to times like that, a certain feeling. She said, "You must have come as soon as we hung up."

He nodded. "Took a few hours to get a flight but here I am. Is there any update?"

She shook her head. Nothing he needed to be made aware of, in any case. The standard procedure when dealing with family members was to keep them as far out of the way as possible for as long as possible. You went to them when they had something you needed, but apart from that, you told them nothing. The information flow was one-way. For one thing, involving them could get them hurt. It could certainly jeopardize an investigation if they went crashing around, scaring off suspects. And then there was the fact that they were often suspects themselves.

Something about this man told her this time would be different. She couldn't picture him leaving town until he had whatever it was he'd come for. She said, "You look like the type of man who knows his way around an investigation."

He said nothing, and she continued, "In which case, you'll know what the rules are."

"I know all the rules," he said as if they had absolutely nothing to do with how things were going to play out, one way or another.

She looked at him again. She couldn't remember if he'd been told Raven was an Indian. Anyone familiar with the town's history would probably have assumed as much, but he hadn't heard of the town. Something told her she'd better clear that up sooner rather than later. "Have you received a description of the missing person?" she said.

"A description?

"A physical description? Have you seen the drawing we distributed?"

"I don't know that it would make much of a difference," he said. "I haven't set eyes on my sister since she was eight years old."

"Even still," Lola said hesitantly, "just so there aren't any misunderstandings."

He contemplated her a moment, then nodded. Lola went around to Marlene's desk and shook the mouse. The screen lit up, and she entered Marlene's password—the name of her cat followed by a dollar sign and four zeroes. She was about to navigate to the composite drawing the sketch artist had created—they still had no photos—but at that very instant, as if on cue, the door swung open and Jim Belcher stormed in.

"What's all this?" he said, eyeing Lance suspiciously.

Lola was surprised to see him. It wasn't like him to come back to work after he'd already clocked out. For some reason, her mind jumped to the thought that he'd been watching the place, though she couldn't think why that would be the case. "It's nothing," she said.

Belcher walked past the two of them, all the

way to his office, and stopped at his door. "Lo, can I see you a minute?"

Lola looked back at the computer screen.

"Lo," he said again, an insistent, whining quality to his voice.

She hated when he called her that. She'd told him as much, though that had only made it worse.

She looked apologetically at Spector—he was still standing in front of the reception desk, as if he hadn't made up his mind yet whether this was the right place for him—and she said, "Would you give me one second, Mr Spector?"

He nodded, and she logged out of the computer and hurried over to Belcher's office. She entered, and he looked at the open door. "Shut that, would you?"

She glanced across the office—Spector was out of earshot, he hadn't moved from where she'd left him—and shut the door.

"What do you want?" she said irritably. "I have someone—"

"That's him, isn't it? That's Mr Montana?"

"Mr Spector," she said. "And what do you know about it?"

"I know you need to get rid of him."

"He's trying to find out—"

"This is an open investigation. He can find out when everyone else does."

"He just walked in the door. He hasn't done anything wrong."

"I said get rid of him," Belcher said, trying to put an air of finality to his voice that he lacked the authority for. She was about to argue with him, but she knew there was no point. There were better ways. Belcher wasn't exactly the most intelligent man ever to put on a Black Swan Police uniform. Lola had learned early that it was generally easier to go around him than through him. "Is that all?" she said tersely.

He nodded dismissively and she left, shutting the door behind her a little harder than was necessary. Across the office, she saw that Spector was behind the counter, leaning over Marlene's computer, his hands on the keyboard.

"Excuse me?" she cried. "What do you think you're doing?"

He ignored her, typing on the keyboard as she stormed toward him. He wouldn't be able to access anything without the password, but that was hardly the point.

She was halfway to him when Belcher's voice thundered from behind her. "What the hell's going on here?"

"It's all right, Belcher," Lola said, trying to diffuse things before they got started, but there was no way of explaining why Lance was behind the counter.

For his part, Lance hadn't even looked up at them from the screen. He was still hitting keys on the keyboard, and he said, "If you've got a file open on my sister, I need to see it." From the way he said it, Lola had the distinct impression that if they didn't give him what he wanted, he would take it anyway.

Belcher must have gotten the same impression and—master de-escalator that he was—drew his firearm and pointed it at Lance. "Step away from the computer right now."

Spector looked up then, first at Lola, then at Belcher. "Are you going to use that thing?" he said.

"If you don't do as I say, I will."

Lola caught Spector's eye, wordlessly pleading with him not to push the situation. She empathized with him—if someone in her family had been snatched from the side of the highway, she'd want to know what the police had on it too—but the way he was going about it was going to get him killed. Spector looked at her, and she flitted her eyes toward the door. Directly across the street was a diner. Spector followed her eye toward it, then looked back. "Fine," he said, stepping away from the computer. "Have it your way."

He began making for the door, and Belcher said, "Wait here just one goddamn minute."

But Spector ignored him.

Lola turned to Belcher and said, "For the love of God, let him go."

"He just broke the—"

"Do you want a fight on your hands or not?" she said.

Belcher sighed as Lance disappeared through

the door. Lola watched him cross the street toward the diner, then turned back to Belcher. “The chief would have given him something,” she said.

Belcher let a sneer cross his face then. “Chief ain’t here, sweet cheeks. I am.”

10

It was fifteen minutes later when Lola pushed open the door of the diner and stepped in from the cold. She'd had to wait for Belcher to screw off home for the night and was relieved that Spector was still there, sitting at the counter with his back to the door. He didn't seem like the type that liked to wait.

She glanced around the diner, taking in the scattered handful of customers in the booths. The place wasn't busy at this hour, but there were still more than a few faces she recognized. She walked up to the counter and sat down, leaving one empty stool between herself and Spector.

"Thanks for coming," he said under his breath, not taking his eyes from the newspaper in front of him. It was the local rag, *The Enquirer*, and Raven Spector's composite drawing was on the front page, which meant he'd seen it. That was one less thing to worry about.

He had a cup of black coffee, and she could see from the cutlery he'd been given that he'd ordered something to eat.

The waitress, a woman Lola's age named Carla, came out from the kitchen and delivered some food to a table. Lola caught her eye, and she came over.

"Just a coffee, Car."

Carla nodded officiously, then glanced from Lola to Spector and back again. She gave Lola a knowing look. "Nothing to eat?"

"No thanks," Lola said.

Carla nodded toward Spector and arched an eyebrow. He'd taken off his jacket to reveal two well-muscled arms and a t-shirt that looked in danger of being torn in half if he moved too suddenly. Carla and Lola had spoken too often of the town's dearth of eligible men for this one to slip by without comment, and Carla said conspiratorially, "The meatloaf's *real* good."

"Is it?" Lola said, shooting daggers at her.

"And we're almost out, so if you don't have it, I think *I* will."

"Will you?" Lola said tersely.

Spector looked up from his newspaper. "Ladies, I'm sure there's plenty to go around."

Lola felt her face flush. Carla, for her part, spun around and hurried back to the kitchen as if she'd just been urgently summoned.

"Friend of yours?" Spector said.

Lola was so embarrassed she'd covered her face with her hands. "Sorry," she said through the gaps in her fingers. "Carla was dropped on her head as a child. She's never been the same since."

Spector smiled, then turned back to the newspaper. Lola said, "Mind slipping me your flier section?"

He looked at her blankly for a second, then realized what she wanted and slid the advertisements from the paper over to her. In her purse, she had a full printout of Raven Spector's case file. It wasn't a lot to go on, four pages of single-spaced type that covered the basics of the case and transcripts of the witness statements. It included pictures but the station's black and white inkjet printer had done such a poor job that they were next to useless. She took it from her purse and slipped it between the pages of the newspaper section, then slid it back across the counter to Spector.

Carla came over with Lola's coffee and some cutlery.

"What's that for?" Lola said as Carla set the cutlery on a napkin.

"I put in an order of meatloaf for you," Carla said. "You'll thank me later."

She hurried off then before Lola could say anything, though, truth be told, Lola was ravenous. She glanced at Spector, who was studying the pages of the report, reading intently.

"This is everything?" he said when he came to the end.

Lola nodded. "It's not a lot, I know."

"No ID was found?" Lance said.

"No," Lola said. "No wallet. No license. No bank cards. Nothing."

"None of the witness statements gave a name," he said. "It says here she signed in to the trailer park with just a first name. Ray."

"Right," Lola said, leaning on the counter to see the file. "Where did the name come from?" she said to herself. "Must have been the DMV. We have her RV."

"I see that," Spector said, looking at a blotchy black-and-white picture of the vehicle.

"Not a lot to go on, I know," she said apologetically.

"It's a start," he said.

Carla came over with Spector's order, a BLT with fries, and asked if he wanted a top-up on his coffee.

"Sure," he said.

When she left, he placed the printout back inside the pages of the flier section and slid it to Lola. She put it in her purse.

Carla arrived with the coffee pot and topped up both their cups. "That's going to get cold," she said when she saw Spector hadn't touched his food.

Spector picked up the shaker and sprinkled salt over the plate without tasting it first.

Carla turned to Lola. "Yours will be right up."

When she left, Spector said, "Why don't you tell me about the history?"

"The history?"

"The town history."

Lola sighed. "Well," she said, "it's as bad as they say. A string of disappearances going back years and years. None of them has ever been solved. I don't think there's ever even been an arrest made."

"How many cases have there been?"

"A lot."

"A lot?"

"You won't believe me if I say it."

"Try me."

Lola hesitated. It was difficult for her to say the number aloud. She was ashamed of it. She was a cop in that town. A detective, no less. This had started long before her arrival, but it was happening now on her watch. That made it her fault, as far as she was concerned. "Over a hundred," she said.

"A hundred?"

"More," she said, depending on how far back you want to go. She braced herself for what was going to come next. She'd forgive him for saying something disparaging.

But all he said was, "Hmm," shaking his head slightly.

"Definitely a lot more if you keep digging," she said, feeling guilty now for downplaying the number. "For all I know, they go back to the town's founding."

Spector said nothing. She looked at his plate. He really was letting the fries go cold.

"I didn't realize," she said, feeling a need to fill

the silence, "how many there were until I started digging today. The way people talk around here, you'd almost think it was normal."

"How do they talk about it?"

"Just..." she said, shaking her head. "I don't know. Like it's...."

"What?"

"Like I said, *normal*."

Spector nodded. "You'd be surprised at the things people can get used to."

He said it like someone familiar with the subject matter, like he'd seen more than his share of it. She wondered what he did for the government? What federal agency he worked for? If any. "You'd think," she said hesitantly, " that when the story went national...."

Spector just shook his head. "Words on paper," he said. "Words on the airwaves."

"You're not a big believer in the power of the press?"

"To do what?"

She shrugged. "Shed light?"

"What light?" he said with a sigh.

She didn't know what to say to that. She felt like she was speaking to the most jaded man she'd ever met. The way he was acting, it was like a hundred missing women was just another day at the office. Maybe it was for him.

"One thing's for certain," he said. "You don't get this many missing women over this many years without some sort of organization."

"Organization?"

"This isn't a case of a lone man gone bad," he said.

She nodded.

"In the wild," he continued, "you'll get an animal that goes bad, gets a taste for blood, and starts killing for no reason. But it's only with people that you'll get a whole pack that turns at once. A whole town. A whole country."

"There are good people in this town."

"I'm not saying otherwise."

"You're making it sound like our whole town—"

"Every town's the same," he said. "None's any better or worse than the next. But you've got a problem here in this one. Something's gone sour, something's gone rotten, and someone's going to have to do something about that."

"What agency did you say you were—"

"Someone needs to root out whatever's rotten and burn it all to hell."

Lola's eyes widened. She looked at Spector, startled by his words, and said, "Tell me you're not thinking of taking the law into your own hands."

"Look, Ms Quinn, this is a job that needs doing, same as any other job. That's all I'm saying."

"I'm an officer of the law," she said. "I can't be complicit in some vigilante—"

"You said yourself the police can't be relied on."

"I don't think I said that."

"A hundred missing women. No arrests."

She was going to answer, but there was nothing

she could say. She didn't even disagree with him. He was right. Something needed to change. What they were doing now wasn't working.

"What if it was someone in your family?" he said. "What if it was your sister that disappeared? If you had to choose between the law and—"

"And what?" she said. "Some stranger riding into town and killing the first person he thought did it?" She shook her head again. "Who even are you?"

"I'm the man who's going to find out who did this," he said. "I'm going to find them, and I'm going to kill them. Every last one of them."

"Revenge, then? That's your plan?"

He shrugged. "Revenge. Justice. If you can tell me the difference—"

She looked at him in amazement. "Are you for real?"

He looked at his food, then let out a long sigh. "Look," he said, "I'm telling you this because you've helped me."

"And if I get in your way?"

He shook his head. "You won't."

"How do you know that?"

"Because you know as well as I do that this isn't about revenge. This isn't even about justice."

"Then what is it about?"

"Like I said, this is just a job that needs doing. Nothing more."

She let out a laugh. "A job?"

He shrugged again.

"Like filling a pothole?" she said.

"If you like."

She didn't know what to say. Who was this guy? What had she done in showing him the file? She'd assumed he was some sort of government agent, but the way he was talking now, he sounded more like a crazy vigilante intent on getting himself killed. If not by the murderers, then by the cops.

But there was another side to it. The way he was speaking, there was something in it. It was like he'd said the words a thousand times before, like he was speaking from experience, like he knew exactly what was going on and exactly what needed to be done about it.

"Sometimes," she said, finding herself speaking in spite of herself, "I feel like there's a malignant cloud hanging over this town."

Spector nodded.

"Some sort of thick black smoke," she continued, "that strangles everything."

"A monster," he said.

She nodded. "It's like, everything's normal, people go to work, they walk their dogs, the kids go to school, it's the perfect, happy community. But beneath the surface, there's this hidden…" her words trailed off.

"Darkness," he said, finishing the sentence for her.

Carla arrived with the meatloaf and put it on the counter with a little jug of gravy on the side, the way Lola always ordered it.

"Thanks, Car."

"Everything all right over here?" she said. "Sounded for a minute like things were getting a little heated."

"We're fine," Lola said.

"If you want me to...." Carla nodded at the police station across the street.

"It's fine," Lola said again. "Really."

Carla shrugged. "All right." She turned to Spector then. "Something wrong with that food?"

"Oh," he said, looking again at it as if he'd forgotten it was there. He pulled the plate in front of him, and Carla watched as he picked up the sandwich in one hand and took a bite.

"All right, then?" she asked. "All to your satisfaction."

"Fine," Spector said, taking another bite.

"We like to satisfy our customers here," she continued.

"That'll do, Carla," Lola said, watching her until she turned and left.

It wasn't a small sandwich, but the way Spector ate it made it seem small. He took another bite, then turned to Lola and said, "Someone knows something."

Lola poured the gravy over her meatloaf. She'd intended to only pour half, but somehow, the jug was empty when she was done.

"Someone close," he continued. "Someone you likely know."

She found herself thinking of the empty

evidence box in the shed. And she thought of the chief, of Belcher, of the local politicians and steady stream of state officials and federal agents who poured into town every time the media turned its attention to the missing women.

Spector's sandwich was gone. She hadn't even taken her first bite, and his plate was empty but for the fries, which he didn't seem interested in. He took some cash from his wallet and placed it on the counter beneath his coffee mug.

"Promise me you're not going to do anything stupid," she said, watching as he rose to his feet.

He looked down at her, a mischievous glint in his eye, and she could tell he was about to say something witty—something charming and witty, maybe even ask her what she was up to—when a police cruiser, lights flashing, siren wailing, sped into the lot across the street at top speed. It skidded to a halt outside the police station and two cops—it looked like Wheelan and McEnearney—jumped out.

Lola looked at Spector. He looked back, then he turned and made straight for the door.

"Spector!" she called after him, but he marched on as if he hadn't heard a thing.

Lola looked down ruefully at her untouched meatloaf. "Damn it," she said aloud, then put a twenty under her plate and hurried after him.

11

Lance strode toward the police station, narrowly avoiding a second cruiser that was speeding in after the first. It swerved around him wildly and screeched to a halt, horn blaring. A cop in his twenties emerged from the driver's side and yelled, "Hey asshole, you trying to get yourself killed?"

Lance stared at him for a second, then turned away and continued toward the police station.

"Nut job," the cop called after him, but when Lance turned back, the cop didn't say anything else.

Lance pushed his way through the police station entrance and saw the two cops from the first car speaking animatedly to Belcher. "What's going on?" he said.

All three turned toward him in unison, but it was Belcher who spoke. "You again."

"That's right," Lance said.

"I'm not going to warn you a second time, *pal*. You get the hell out of my station, or I'll have you arrested for—"

Lance cut him off midsentence, addressing the other two. "What did you find?"

The cops looked from him to Belcher.

"Don't look at him," Lance said, "look at me. Tell me what you found?"

That made Belcher so angry that it looked like his eyes were going to pop out of his head. "Who the hell do you think you are?" he spat. He began coming toward Lance, and as he moved, his one hand undid the clasp on his baton.

"Don't go doing anything you'll regret," Lance said as Belcher got closer, his short legs making him waddle like a duck with every step.

"Oh, I'm not going to regret this one bit," Belcher snarled, pulling out the baton. "In fact, I believe I'm going to enjoy it."

He took another step, just enough to bring himself within range, and Lance shot out a quick jab at his flabby neck. It wasn't so hard, just enough to shut him up, but Belcher doubled over like a collapsing step ladder, grabbing his throat in pain.

That was the moment that Lola Quinn chose to enter the scene, bursting through the doors with a look on her face that gave even Lance pause. She took one look at Belcher on the floor and yelled at Lance, "Are you *trying* to get yourself killed?"

Lance looked around to see that the two

younger cops had both drawn their pistols, pointing them squarely at him.

"Come on," Lance said, eyeing Belcher, who was writhing and flailing on the ground in agony. "I've seen dying men make less of a fuss."

"What the hell do you think you're doing?" Lola said.

Lance only shook his head.

"I'm going to get you for this," Belcher croaked, holding his throat like a man who'd been shot through the neck and was trying to stem the flow of blood.

"Mister," one of the younger cops said, "you better raise your hands right now."

Lance looked him over. His name tag said McEnearney, and he was quite young. It wouldn't have taken much to make him jump. Lance raised his hands slowly, maintaining eye contact with him.

"Let's everyone calm down," Lola said. "There's no need for anyone else to get hurt."

"To hell with that," Belcher croaked, still coughing and spitting phlegm. "Shoot the son of a bitch. You saw what he did."

"Come on," Lola said, motioning to McEnearney and his partner to lower the guns. "It's all right. I'll take it from here."

The two of them looked at Belcher, but they had the good sense to follow Lola's lead and holstered their weapons.

This made Belcher positively apoplectic. "What

the hell are you doing?" he yelled at his officers. "Arrest that man. Cuff him. Right now."

McEnearney brought out his cuffs. "Tell him not to try anything," he said to Lola.

"I won't try anything," Lance said.

Lola looked at Belcher, struggling now to get to his feet, and shook her head. She turned to Lance and said, "For the love of God, please don't."

Lance let the two cops take his arms behind his back and put him in cuffs, and while they did so, he said, "These boys were about to say what they'd found, weren't you boys?"

"Not to you, they weren't," Belcher said, his voice hoarse and throaty. He was on his feet now, leaning on the reception desk, still touching his neck as if he couldn't quite believe everything was intact.

"Come on, Jim," Lola said, helping him over to one of the chairs in the reception area. "Let's get a look at that neck."

"You should be calling me an ambulance," Belcher said.

She looked at the two younger cops and said, "Go on, then. Tell us what you've got."

"You sure?" McEnearney said, eyeing Belcher.

"Yes," Lola said.

Belcher looked of a mind to raise an objection, but Lola had her hand on his throat and she gave him a look that shut him up before he could get the words out.

"We found the body," McEnearney blurted.

Lance took a deep breath.

"Where?" Lola said.

"Forest out by Dickey."

Lance looked at Lola, gauging her reaction, then took another breath.

"You all right?" Lola said to him.

He was all right. He already knew that this woman, whoever she was, wasn't his sister, but he also knew that he wasn't about to get shut out of the case. Something ugly was going on, and he needed to find out what. Not just so that it could be stopped, but because it seemed like someone, he still didn't know who, had gone out of their way to drag him into it.

He shut his eyes as if in grief and let his body sag.

"I'm sorry," Lola said.

"Give me a fucking break," Belcher said, getting back to his feet. He looked a little sturdier now, and he paced over to Lance. "Hold him up straight," he said to the two cops.

"What the hell are you doing?" Lola cried as Belcher pulled out his gun, raised it up, then smacked Lance clear across the face with the butt of it.

It was a hard blow, and Lance's ears rung from the force of it.

"Belcher!" Lola cried.

But Belcher only sneered, his beady eyes bulging with rage. "That's right, you little shit. Not so tough now, are you."

"Come on," McEnearney said. "He's cuffed."

Belcher looked at McEnearney then like he was going to hit him next. "What did you say?"

"Nothing. Sorry, boss."

Turning back to Lance, Belcher said, "Assault an officer? See how far that gets you."

Belcher began walking toward his office then. Over his shoulder he spat, "I want that man in jail."

McEnearney and the other guy, Wheelan, began leading Lance toward the holding cell at the back of the station. Lance looked over his shoulder at Lola.

"Don't look at me," she said. "There's nothing I can do."

"Should have thought," Wheelan said, "before you hit Belcher in the throat."

"He had it coming," Lance said.

"Yeah," McEnearney said, "and now you've got a night in the lockup coming."

"Where did you find the bodies?" Lance said as they led him into a square, brick room with a bench along three walls. It was empty, and it had that same institutional smell as a Greyhound bus station—bleach and filth in equal measure. "You said something about a forest."

Belcher's shrill voice came out of his office. "Don't tell that son of a bitch a single thing, McEnearney."

McEnearney gave Lance a look, as if in apology, then he and Wheelan slammed shut the door of the cell and locked it.

As they were leaving, McEnearney stopped and turned back. “Is that your sister’s body we just found?”

Lance sat down on the bench and let out a long sigh. “Who knows?”

12

Chief Bill Glanton straightened the collar on his uniform and gave himself a final once-over in the mirror. All things considered, not bad for sixty-five, he thought. He straightened his badge and wiped some lint from his shoulder.

"Coffee's ready," his wife called from the kitchen.

He joined her at the table and poured some cream into the mug that was waiting for him. His wife, Annessa, was stirring hers, and when she was done, he took the spoon from her.

"Lola called," she said, "while you were in the shower."

The chief had already been apprised of the situation by Lola the night before and said, "This fellow from Montana can't wait?"

"She told me the whole story, and I think you

need to hurry down there and sign him out pronto."

"He spent the night in there," the chief said, "I don't see how my getting a proper breakfast is going to make much of a difference."

He could smell the bacon on the stove but the look Annessa gave him said that he wouldn't be getting any of it, or any of anything, until he did what she wanted. "How much, exactly, did she tell you?" he said.

"Enough."

He sighed. He knew the two women talked, and he knew Lola would have brought Annessa up to speed on just about everything to do with the case, whether it was proper to do so or not. Annessa cared a great deal about the subject and people tended to treat her as an authority figure. They looked up to her, especially where the disappearances were concerned. Not only was she native herself, Suquamish to be precise, but she was also chairwoman of the town's *Women in Crisis* center. She'd spent the better part of her life trying to help these women, and each time another one went missing, she took it personally. It could just as easily have been their daughter, she'd reminded the chief a thousand times, and he knew she was right.

"Can I at least finish my coffee?" he said.

"You can take it with you," she said. "And you can take your breakfast too."

Glanton poured his coffee into a thermos while

Annessa put his bacon between two slices of bread and wrapped it in foil.

"Thank you," he said, giving her a kiss on the forehead.

"And you look out for that girl," Annessa said, referring to Lola. "She doesn't know what she's getting herself into."

Glanton nodded, pulling his parka on before he let himself out.

It was seven fifteen when he left the house, and by seven twenty-five, he was in the parking lot of the police station. Lola's car was already there. He entered the building and she stood up from her desk the moment she saw him, positively racing to intercept him.

"He's awake," she said.

"By *he,* I take it you mean our prisoner."

"He's not a prisoner. He's just trying to find out what's going on."

"And assaulting police officers is how he hopes to achieve that?"

"Not *all* police officers," Lola said, suppressing a grin.

The chief nodded, and he knew that Jim Belcher had more than asked for whatever he'd gotten. In fact, the thought of him getting a punch to the throat made the chief inclined to like this man from Montana before he'd even met him, not that he was going to say as much. He went over to the coffee machine to refill his thermos and saw that there was a *Dutch Bakery* box on the table next to it.

He peeked inside and said, "Who brought these?"

Lola's expression remained blank. "Consider it a bribe," she said.

The chief sighed. "Let's get one thing clear," he said. "I can't have some vigilante running around town, taking the law into his own hands, mucking up our crime scenes."

"Wouldn't want to confuse our crack CSI squad," Lola said defiantly, not even attempting to hide her sarcasm.

The chief eyed her as he sipped his coffee. Nothing but trouble, she'd been, since she arrived—trouble, and the best new cop the town had seen in a generation. She'd also grown up with his granddaughter, the two had been inseparable since kindergarten, which only served to make him even more protective of her. "What did you say this guy's name was?" he said.

"Spector. Lance Spector."

"Why does that sound familiar?"

"It's the missing person's name. Raven Spector. At least, according to the *file*."

"What's that supposed to mean?"

Lola shook her head.

"What is it?" the chief said, watching her carefully.

"It's just...."

"Just what?"

"Something Spector said last night."

"What did he say?"

"He asked how we got the name."

"The name?"

"Raven Spector's name. It wasn't in any of the transcripts."

"And how would *he* know what was and wasn't in our interview transcripts?"

Lola looked away, avoiding his gaze, and the chief shook his head. Where *had* they gotten the name from, though, he thought? If it wasn't in the transcripts, then where on earth had it come from? "I thought the trailer park gave it to us," he said.

Lola shook her head. "No, Jo said the vic signed in only as Ray." She handed the chief a printout of her first interview with Jolene.

"Ray?" the chief said, reading the transcript. "Just a first name?"

Lola nodded.

"Ray could be short for Raven," the chief said.

"It could be," Lola said. "But where did that come from in the first place? Raven Spector? What put us onto it?"

"Must have been the DMV," the chief said.

Lola shook her head again. "That's what I thought too, but then I looked up the record. The RV isn't registered to a Raven Spector. It's registered to a Ray Strickland of King County, Washington. Male. DOB May 13th, 1987."

"And you contacted him?"

"Yes. He said he sold the RV to a woman matching our vic's description four months ago."

The chief had taken a pastry from the box. He was about to bite into it but stopped himself with it midway to his mouth. He looked at Lola.

"I know," she said.

He put down the pastry. "So you're telling me that we've been calling this victim Raven Spector, and we don't know why?"

"Oh, I know why now. I checked the log."

"And?"

"The name was entered remotely."

"Remotely?"

"FBI field office in Seattle. Someone logged in on their end and updated our file."

"Who?"

"The metadata was erased, but whoever did it, did it almost as soon as we'd opened the file. Almost as if they were watching us. Waiting for us to report the case."

"That doesn't make any sense."

"It gets worse when you look at the timeline," Lola said. "I cross-referenced everything. Jo at the trailer park raised the alarm. I remember because I took the call. I drove out there and walked the route from the trailer park to the grocery store."

"And found her key on the side of the road."

"Right," Lola said. "And that's when I called it in. Because of the key."

The chief nodded. He knew all this. He'd

agreed to it. Ordinarily, in an ordinary town, in ordinary times, a grown woman going off for a walk and losing her car keys wouldn't be enough to raise too much concern. But this wasn't an ordinary town. "Okay," he said.

"Well, if you look at the log, within minutes of my elevating the case, the file was updated in Seattle with the name, Raven Spector."

"So they were adding details to *our* case then, from Seattle, before we had any idea of who'd gone missing or why. How in the world could they possibly know anything about our case at that point?"

"They couldn't," Lola said, "unless...."

"Unless?"

"Unless someone on their end was somehow involved."

"Now that's a leap," the chief said. "That's a very big leap."

"Is it? You give me another explanation that makes sense."

He couldn't think of another explanation. Not one that held water. He let out a long, tired sigh.

"Well?" Lola said.

The chief said nothing. He didn't know what to say. This wasn't the first time he'd seen things like this, things that didn't make sense, signs of interference from some unseen, powerful source. But how to tell her that?

He could see she was shaken, and he understood why. She was still young. She was still naive enough to have faith in the system. She hadn't seen yet just how deep the rot went.

But she was learning. Fast.

"There's something else," she said.

He nodded slowly. Of course there was.

"Another thing I'm not sure how to explain," she said, and he could see that she was hesitant to say what it was.

"Well?" he said. "Don't hold back now, Lola."

"There's evidence missing." She blurted the words, then let them hang there in the air between them.

The chief let them hang too, then said, "From where?"

"From the shed. The boxes."

Lola was smart, smarter than those who'd preceded her. He'd known it would eventually come to this. It had been only a matter of time. And he'd known that when this time came, it would be very difficult to protect her. From herself. "Lola," he said, "there's more to this case than you realize."

"You knew?" she said, and the thing that broke his heart most, apart from the danger, was the suspicion he could hear in her voice. That hadn't been there before.

"Lola," he said, lowering his voice even though they were the only people there. "There are things you don't know about this case. About this town."

"Like what?"

"Dangerous things."

She regarded him silently for a few seconds,

and he knew she understood him. You couldn't grow up in Black Swan and not develop a sense for it. Something lurked in the darkness there, like a wolf prowling the forests beyond the town, and she knew it as well as anyone.

The time had come to give her more. Not everything, but something. He said, "You remember the incident out on 101?"

She nodded. Of course she did. Everyone did. It had been almost twenty years ago now, well before her time, well before Glanton was chief. Six officers shot dead on a remote stretch of road while responding to a report that a woman had been taken from a local shelter. It had been the talk of the entire state, a huge inquiry was conducted, but no finding was ever made. And no one had ever been caught for it.

"What are you saying?" Lola said.

"I'm just saying we need to be careful. People get hurt when they start asking too many questions about this thing."

"You're saying that incident was connected to this?"

Glanton nodded. "Everything in Black Swan is connected. That's what makes it so dangerous."

"Those officers were killed because they were getting too close to the truth?"

"I don't know it for a fact."

"That's the reason you've never cracked this?"

"Trust me, Lola," he said, and he could see the disappointment in her eyes. He knew why. She thought he was a coward for not digging deeper, for not ruffling whatever feathers were behind these disappearances. But the truth was, he'd tried. And then the death threats had come in. Not against himself—that he could have handled—but against his wife and daughter. That had been his limit, and not even Annessa knew about it. "Everything I've done in my role as chief here has been to protect the people of this community. *Everything*."

She looked at him for what felt like a very long time, then said, "Okay."

"Okay?"

She nodded.

"Sometimes," he said, "our job is to slay the beast." She didn't say anything, and he continued. "And sometimes, it's simply to recognize that the beast is too big to slay, and just do our best to keep the people we care about out of its reach."

"I get it," she said, holding his gaze. "I do, chief."

He truly hoped she did, for her own sake, because if she ended up dead because of this, he'd never forgive himself.

But he was scared. Scared that she wouldn't know when to back down. Scared she'd go too far. And so many things were beyond his control. That was one thing being a father had taught him. And he knew that if he pestered her about this, if he tried to warn her off the case, tried to order her to stay away, that he'd drive her toward the very thing he feared.

She glanced back toward the holding cell, and

he followed her gaze, glad of a chance to shift the topic. "How's our guest holding up?"

"He's all right."

"Not going to need any stitches?"

"He says no, and I suppose he'd know."

"You looked into his file?"

"I pulled everything I could."

"And?"

"You'll see," she said, giving him a coy smile.

"I'll see?"

"Or rather," she said, "I guess it's more a case of what you won't see. I made some calls to Olympia last night to fill in some blanks, and the woman at the VA basically told me I shouldn't even bother. She said she'd never seen so many redactions on a single file."

"He must have been involved in something sensitive," the chief said.

Lola nodded.

"The type of thing you don't put on your résumé."

"That's the impression I'm getting," she said.

"All right," the chief said. "Well, let me set eyes on the man himself before we go too far down any rabbit holes."

Lola led the way back to the holding cell, moving, it seemed to the chief, with a bit more pep in her step than was warranted.

"All right," the chief said, approaching the cell, "so what's all this fuss about that I have to miss breakfast?" He found a man in an army t-shirt sitting on the bench, looking back at him, a paper coffee cup in hand. Across his forehead was a long gash where Belcher's pistol had caught him, and it looked like some pretty nasty bruising was coming in around the eyes too. Nothing life-threatening, the chief agreed, and not completely without its advantages either, truth be told. That injury was the reason Belcher wouldn't be able to make a stink when he found out the man had been released. "You look like you had yourself an accident," the chief said.

"Accident!" Lola scoffed. "If you call walking into someone else's fist an accident."

There was a lot of sarcasm in her voice, and, not for the first time, the chief thought she was acting awfully protective of a guy whose only achievement since arriving in town had been to get himself locked in a jail cell. The man's looks, no doubt, were a factor, and he gave Lola a quick sideways glance.

Her eyes were glued on Spector.

On a napkin next to him was one of the donuts from the box Lola had brought, and the chief said, "I trust you're not finding the conditions here too harsh?"

"I've definitely experienced worse," Spector said.

The chief smiled. "Yes, I have no doubt you have. And I take it you've had a chance to cool off, too?"

The man looked up and said, "Yes, sir, I have."

The chief nodded again. He appreciated

people being agreeable. Too often in his line of work, people chose to be argumentative just for the sake of it, as if it fit some role they'd been assigned. He could appreciate, too, why this man might have been on edge the night before. He was worried about a family member. The chief would have felt the same way if he were in his shoes. He said, "So I can take it that if I let you out of there, you're not going to go punching any more of my officers?"

Spector took a sip of his coffee and let out an almost imperceptible sigh. "I'm not one for making promises I can't keep," he said.

"Well, can you tell me, at least, what you intend to do while you're here in Black Swan?"

"Certainly," Spector said, looking from the chief to Lola, "I intend to find out if the body you recovered last night belongs to my sister."

"And if it does?"

The look on Spector's face left little doubt as to what he intended, but he gave an answer all the same. "I'm just the same as anyone else, chief."

"How so?" the chief said.

"I cross my bridges as I come to them."

"I should warn you, the State of Washington doesn't take too kindly to people taking the law into their own hands."

"I'll bear that in mind."

The chief looked at him for a minute, trying to get a read on the man, then said, "I hope that you do, son."

"He will," Lola said, and the chief gave her a long, steady look.

"I hope he appreciates you going out on a limb for him, Lola."

Lola did something then that the chief didn't think he'd ever seen her do before. She blushed, red as a beet.

"Come on," the chief said to her, as much to spare her from further embarrassment as anything, and led her back to her desk. "Open up his file for me," he said when they got there.

"Spector's?"

"Yes, Spector's. Who else's?"

"All right," she said. "Just asking."

"Sorry," the chief said, "it's just, I hope you're not losing your head over this guy."

"Losing my head?"

"He's...."

"He's *what*?"

"Well, he looks like he just stepped off a movie set."

"*No* he doesn't!"

"He looks like Paul Newman."

Lola said nothing then, just scoffed, and the chief could tell he was annoying her. She chewed her lip for a minute, then said, "Would you talk to the other guys like this?"

"Like what?"

"Warning them off a woman?"

"I'm not warning you off anything. I'm just looking out for you."

"Well don't," she said, bringing her attention back to the computer screen. A moment later, Spector's file came up, and she stepped aside to let the chief have a look.

Ordinarily, there wasn't much to these things. Unless, that was, the person in question had been in trouble with the law. In this case, however, there was row after row of redacted type. It wasn't law enforcement related, but military—he could see the military codes in the redaction notes. What was left was a name, a birthdate, and nothing else. Not an address, not a social security number, not any vehicle registrations, nothing.

The chief had seen a lot of files over the years. Never had he seen anything like this. "What have we gotten ourselves into?" he muttered.

Lola shrugged.

He looked at her again. "I can't help but get the feeling you're tickled pink by this," he said.

"You have to admit," she said, "we could use a little shake-up."

"A shake-up?"

"I think he's going to do something, Chief. I think he's going to find out who's been doing this shit in our town, and he's going to hurt them."

"*Do* you," the chief said. "And need I remind you that anyone willing to do all that would be breaking about fifty separate laws in the process."

"Not if he's one of us."

"One of us?"

"Law enforcement."

"He's not law enforcement."

"Government then. Military."

"Hmm," the chief said, thinking how best to handle the situation. She was right that they could use the help, but he wasn't so sure he had the same confidence she seemed to have that this Spector was the man to deliver it. In any case, his primary goal in the matter wasn't to slay the beast, as he'd put it earlier. It was to keep her and everyone else in the town safe. "Will you promise me one thing?" he said to her.

"What's that?"

He caught her eye and held it. "Will you give this guy enough space that if the shit really does hit the fan, you're far back away so as not to get covered in it?"

She smiled then as if he'd just given her the green light she'd been waiting for. "Does that mean you're going to let him help?"

13

The three of them, Lola, Spector, and the chief, rode out to the county morgue in the chief's car. As they were pulling out of the station, Belcher passed them coming the other way. His eyes widened when he saw Spector in the backseat, and Lola, unable to help herself, gave him a little wave.

"He didn't look happy," Spector said.

The chief chuckled. "No, he didn't, did he?"

"Well," Lola said, "if he'd stopped to think before hitting you with the butt of his pistol, he might have been able to keep you behind bars for more than a few hours." She looked over her shoulder at Spector. "We should get those bruises photographed. I'd like something to hold over him. Another day or two and you're going to look like a raccoon."

The morgue was a five-minute drive, and it was still before eight when they arrived.

"Is this place even open?" Lola said, glancing at her watch as they got out of the car.

"It better be," the chief said, leading the way.

The door was locked when they reached it, and the chief rapped his knuckles on the window. They waited a minute, and he knocked a second time. Eventually, the duty officer showed up, his hair disheveled like he'd just been sleeping and the top few buttons of his shirt undone. "Chief!" he said. "I didn't know you were coming."

"It's almost eight, Scotty," the chief said. "You might want to button up that fly before the day shift arrives."

Scotty turned his back to fix his fly, then led them to the morgue's reception area. Lola had been there many times, but the smell of formaldehyde never failed to turn her stomach.

"I take it you're here to ID the body," Scotty said, eyeing Spector. "I'll warn you now," he added, "it doesn't make for easy viewing."

The chief looked at Lola as if to give her an opportunity to excuse herself, but there was no way she wasn't going in with them.

Scotty nodded toward the enormous leather register at the reception, and the chief signed in for the three of them. Then they followed him down a tiled corridor, past a few offices and an administrative section, and through to a set of stainless steel double doors wide enough to wheel a gurney through.

"Now, before we go in," Scotty said, taking a

moment before opening the door to the cold room, “I really do have to reiterate that what you’re about to see is pretty disturbing.”

They stood there for a second until Spector said, “All right, let’s get it over with.”

The chief nodded, and with a hint of reluctance, Scotty swung open the door. The icy air immediately enveloped them, and Lola found herself holding her breath. They filed into the room, a large, clinical space dominated by cooling units and extremely bright fluorescent lights that hung from the ceiling on long chains. Directly beneath one of the lights was a single gurney, and on the gurney was a body draped beneath a thin white sheet.

Spector looked to Scotty and the chief, then stepped forward and pulled the sheet back from the face of the corpse. Lola’s eyes weren’t on the corpse but on Spector’s face, watching for any sign of recognition.

There was nothing. His face was completely unmoved, a study in impassivity.

She glanced at the corpse then, her eyes focusing on the face, and only then did she see why Scotty had been so adamant in warning them. Lola had seen her share of bodies, but nothing that even remotely prepared her for this. The face was almost unrecognizable as a person at all. Both eyes had been gouged out, and the eye sockets had been burned with some sort of poker so that all that remained was two black holes, staring upward toward the fluorescent light as if in some sort of act of oblation. The mouth was open like it had been caught mid-scream, and the teeth were gone. They hadn't been pulled out but rather chiseled, and imprecisely at that—as if the person doing the chiseling had purposely made a mess of it, or the woman had been alive and struggling at the time. The lips were gone, torn to shreds, revealing a snarl of bloody gums and shattered, broken teeth. Inside the mouth, there was no tongue.

Without even realizing it was happening, Lola was doubled over on the floor, retching. The chief put his hand on her back, but she shrugged it off. "I'm okay," she said, her voice a dry rasp as she spat on the floor in front of her. "Sorry."

"It's all right," the chief said. "Scotty will clean that up."

Scotty rushed off for a mop, and Lola tried to regain her composure. She looked up at Spector and said, "Is it her? Is it your... sister?"

Spector looked for a second like he was going to answer but then pulled the sheet off the rest of the body. Lola saw it, then turned away and began retching all over again. The body was as mutilated as the face. The breasts were gone, hacked off by something blunt, and, as if to add insult to injury, black crow feathers had been stuck into the raw flesh where the breasts had been and around the genitals. On the stomach, an intricate network of cuts had been hacked into the skin, and the pattern looked to Lola like some variation of a pentagram.

She'd seen similar markings in some of the other files she'd examined, but nothing as gruesome as this.

"What the hell?" she said. "Who would do something like this?"

The chief's face was pale, he looked like he wasn't far from throwing up himself, and he cleared his throat before saying, "This isn't like the others."

"It's been getting worse for some time," Scotty said, wheeling a bucket and mop toward them. "Almost as if whoever's doing it is getting desensitized to the effect."

"They're getting bored," Spector said.

Scotty nodded. "In a manner of speaking."

Lola said, "I wonder if she was dead when they did this."

"The autopsy will tell us," Scotty said.

The chief nodded. "If it's the same as the last few," he said, "it will confirm that the torture started while she was still alive."

The four of them stood in silence then, looking over the body like a strange medical delegation pondering a patient, then the chief pulled the sheet up over it and said, "I think we've seen what we came for."

"Agreed," Lola said, making room for Scotty to mop the floor before her.

"Scotty," the chief said, "would you mind giving us a minute alone in here?"

Scotty seemed only too willing to oblige. "Not

one bit," he said, finishing up with the mop. "I'll be right outside if you need me."

When he was gone, the chief let out a long sigh. It was clear he had something he wanted to say, but he seemed hesitant to bring it up. When he spoke, his voice sounded different from his usual self. Lola was used to thinking of him as a kindly old man, a sort of fatherly or even grandfatherly presence. Now, he suddenly sounded like something different, a man from a world that was too cruel and harsh for kindly old men. "This goes deep," he said at last.

"It goes deep?" Lance said. "What do you mean by that?"

"I mean, there are powerful people involved."

"You know who's involved?" Lola said.

The chief shook his head. "Not exactly."

"Why don't you tell us what's going on?" Lance said.

"I don't know what's going on," the chief said. "But the point I want to make to you now, the both of you, is that I don't think you do either."

"What are you talking about?" Lola said.

"People who go digging into this tend to end up dead."

"You didn't," Lance said.

"I slipped through the net," the chief said. "And I learned early to keep my nose clean."

"So you want us to walk away from this?" Lola said.

"Whatever this is," the chief said, glancing

toward the gurney, "it's not something I can rightly make sense of. I told you earlier about the Highway 101 incident."

"What incident?" Lance said.

It was Lola who answered. "It was something that happened twenty years ago," she said. "Six police officers were shot dead. The chief told me this morning that they'd been investigating a missing woman at the time."

"No one was ever caught for it," the chief said. "And that's just the surface. This problem runs deeper than anyone knows. There were so many more cases back then that never got reported."

Lance nodded.

The chief continued. "There was a time when an Indian woman around here could disappear, and the police would just shrug it off without even opening a file."

"Chief," Lola said. "Do you know who's behind this?" The chief said nothing for a moment, and she added, "Tell us what you're holding back?"

He sighed. "Well," he said hesitantly, "here's something. Back when I first joined the force, before the incident on 101, before I knew how deep of a problem this was, there were reports of a private plane flying in and out of a small airfield out by the old lumber mill."

"There's no airfield out that way," Lola said.

"This was a long time ago," the chief continued. "Back then, you couldn't just google the registration of a plane. There was no Google."

"What happened?" Spector said.

"I started scoping out the airfield. I must have spent two months sitting out there, on my own time, in my own car, waiting for a plane to come in."

"And one did?" Lola said.

"Yes, and I had a buddy at the aviation authority in Seattle look up the tail number for me."

"Who was it registered to?" Spector said.

"Dead end," the chief said. "Some offshore company somewhere. No one could tell me who it led back to. I even got the AG's office in Port Angeles to look into it."

"AG?" Spector said.

"Attorney General," the chief said. "Anyway, they couldn't crack it. It was all shell companies and blind trusts and such."

"So what happened?" Lola said.

"A few weeks passed, then I got this phone call. I still remember where I was when it came in. I was in bed with Annessa. The call woke us up."

"Who was it?" Spector prodded.

"It was the girl at the AG's office. She was crying. She told me that the guys they had looking into the plane ownership for me were all dead."

"Why?" Lola said.

"I think they found something," the chief said. "Though I never found out what it was."

"How did they die?" Lance said.

"Different things," the chief said. "Someone fell asleep in his garage with the engine running.

Another guy drowned in his own bathtub. The lead investigator supposedly killed himself one night for no apparent reason by jumping off the Tacoma Narrows Bridge."

"That's a lot of bad luck for one team of investigators," Spector said.

The chief nodded. "I went to one of the funerals. I didn't know the guy but he was young, in his twenties. There was a wife there. She was holding a little baby. I didn't ask any more questions after that."

"But who could have done all that?" Lola said. "Orchestrating deaths all over the state? Killing cops? Killing women as if it was some sort of sport?"

"I lay awake at night thinking about that," the chief said. "There have been so many deaths."

"Other investigators?" Spector said.

"Investigators, cops, lawyers, prosecutors, even politicians. This thing is toxic. It's the kiss of death. It kills whoever gets near to it."

Spector looked from the chief to Lola, then said, "And you're afraid that's going to happen to us now?"

The chief nodded. He turned to Lola and said, "Look, Lola, I don't mean to sound patronizing—"

"Then don't," she said back, cutting him off.

"I can't let you walk into a firestorm and not say something."

Lola didn't know what to say. She wasn't looking to get herself killed, but she also hadn't signed up to be a cop so that she could shut her eyes to something like this.

"And you," the chief said, turning to Spector, "I don't know who you are, but it looks to me like you've got your head screwed on straight." Spector said nothing, so the chief continued. "You came here because you thought you might have found your sister."

"That's right," Spector said.

"And?" the chief said.

"And what?"

"Have you? Is this woman lying before us your kin? Is she your sister?"

"She's not," Spector said.

Lola said, "If you think we're going to just shut our eyes to this—"

"I'm not saying shut your eyes," the chief said. "I'm just saying, there's solving the case, there's standing up for justice, and then there's getting yourself killed for no reason at all."

Spector said, "I appreciate you telling us all this—"

"Look," the chief said. "I'm not saying I'm proud of what's happened, but this isn't a question of my pride. It isn't a question of getting myself killed just so that I can get a hero's funeral. I had a family to protect. I still do. I can't afford to go out in a blaze of glory."

"But you always knew something would change," Spector said.

"Excuse me?"

"You knew," Spector said, "that one day something would happen. Someone would step in. This wouldn't go on forever."

"Nothing goes on forever," the chief said.

"Right," Spector said. "Eventually, this ends."

The chief regarded him for a moment, then let out a brief laugh. "You're saying you're the man to end it?"

Spector shrugged. "Someone's got to be."

"But she's not your sister," Lola said.

"No, but she could have been."

"What does that mean?" Lola said, though she knew well enough what he meant. And she knew he was right.

"If you want to go after this," the chief said, "I won't stop you."

"Good to know," Spector said.

"But once you start, you'd better be prepared to take it all the way."

"I've had some experience in taking things all the way," Spector said.

"I don't doubt that you have," the chief said, looking at him intently. "But I do have one condition."

"A condition?"

"A request, if you will."

"All right," Lance said.

"I can give you some information, I can get you started on the right path, but you have to promise me you won't take Lola with you."

"Excuse me!" Lola gasped.

"I'm not giving you information that might get her killed," the chief said.

"Done," Spector said.

"Are you kidding me?" Lola said. "What gives the two of you the right—"

The chief put something in Spector's hand then —Lola didn't see what it was—and Spector put it in his pocket without looking at it.

14

Lance sat alone at the diner counter and ordered coffee. He was in the same seat he'd occupied the night before, and Lola would have been with him had the chief not threatened her with a stint in a cell if she dared go against his orders. She'd been furious when they dropped him off, but there was nothing she could do about it.

The same waitress—Carla, if he wasn't mistaken—came over, eyeing him as if he'd run out on his last bill. "You!" she announced.

"Yes, ma'am," Lance said.

"I heard you spent the night in jail."

"It was worth it."

She rolled her eyes, unimpressed by his wit, and handed him a menu. He ordered the same sandwich he'd had the night before.

"You actually going to eat it this time?"

"I ate it last time."

"Eventually," she said, then left to get his coffee.

Lance watched her go, she moved with a nice sway of the hips, then reached into his pocket and pulled out the business card the chief had given him. There was a phone number on it and a little pixelated graphic of a pole dancer in silhouette. On the back was a handwritten address.

He put the card back in his pocket, and Carla came over with the coffee pot. As she was pouring, the door opened, and a gust of cold air rushed in. Lance turned to see his three friends from the police station, Belcher, Wheelan, and McEnearney, crowding in. They spotted him immediately and took the booth directly behind him.

"Gentlemen," Carla said as they sat down. "I'll be right with you."

"Oh, we're just here to make sure our out-of-town visitor is having a nice time," Belcher said. Lance felt something light hit him on the back. He turned to see a paper sugar packet on the floor. He picked it up and put it on the counter in front of him.

Carla gave him a meaningful look, then went over to the three men with three coffee mugs and the pot. She poured them coffee at the table and said, "You sure you're not eating?"

"Depends what's on the menu," Belcher said, then gave her a light tap on the ass.

Lance watched, eyeing Carla for a sign the

attention was welcome. He could see from her face it wasn't—surprise, surprise—though she didn't say anything, just hurried off to serve another table.

Lance turned his back on the three men, then felt another sugar packet hit him. It was followed by another. He could hear Belcher, too, laughing like a schoolboy.

"Hey, Montana," Belcher said, another sugar packet hitting Lance on the back, "I heard you wasted a trip."

Lance replied without turning. "Trip's not over yet, Belcher."

Another sugar packet, this time missing and flying by his head. Lance removed his jacket and placed it neatly on the stool next to him. Carla came over with his sandwich, and he said, "I'm really sorry about the mess."

"What mess?" she said.

He swiveled in his stool to face the three cops. "And you guys should probably call an ambulance."

"What are you talking about?" Belcher said.

"You and you," Lance said to Wheelan and McEnearney. "How much pain would you say you're willing to feel on behalf of your friend here?"

Belcher scoffed. "Is that supposed to sound intimidating?"

"Why don't you go across the street," Lance said to McEnearney, "and tell the chief that Belcher won't be making it back to work for the rest of the day."

Belcher laughed again, but the two younger cops seemed a lot less skeptical of Lance's words. When they looked like they were considering going across the street, Belcher said, "Come on! What is this?"

"Last chance," Lance said.

They didn't move.

Belcher flicked another sugar packet, missing again, and Lance turned away, following its trajectory, and grabbed his plate from the counter. Sending the sandwich and fries flying, he flung the plate like a frisbee at Belcher's face. It hit him square in the jaw, and before its shattered pieces even hit the floor, Lance was off his seat and had his hand on the back of Belcher's head. He smashed Belcher's face down on the table, feeling the soft crunch of his nose, and when he pulled him back up, blood spattered everywhere. Lance looked at him, judging the injury, then smashed him down a second time. With the face held firmly down, he undid the clip holding Belcher's gun. Then he pulled out the gun and slammed it on the table in front of Wheelan and McEnearney. "Take that," he said to them, and when they did, he said, "Go on, now. Tell the chief what I said. A day at least before he gets back to work."

He felt Belcher pushing against him and let him up. Belcher seemed ready for a fight, but one look at Lance made him reconsider. He just sat there then, holding his broken nose, while McEnearney and Wheelan began climbing out of the booth. Lance watched all three of them leave, then went back to the counter and picked up his jacket. “Sorry again for the mess,” he said to Carla, counting out some money and placing it on the counter.

“What’s that for?”

“The damage.”

She shook her head. “Don’t worry about it,” she said.

Lance left the money where it was and looked out at the street. He hadn’t hurt Belcher that badly, a bloody nose, maybe broken, and he didn’t think he’d be back looking for more trouble any time soon.

“You might want to make yourself scarce,” Carla said as she swept up the shattered plate and cleaned up Belcher’s blood. “Before the chief comes over to arrest you.”

Lance shook his head. “The chief isn’t going to come over.”

Carla nodded knowingly and said, “Then why don’t you take a seat? I’ll get you a fresh sandwich.”

“That’s okay.”

“No,” she said. “I insist.”

Lance glanced out the window and shrugged. “All right,” he said, sitting back down at the counter. Carla had already cleaned up the mess and came right over with the coffee pot and fresh place setting. While she was pouring, she leaned in toward him and lowered her voice. "Very bad business, if you ask me."

"You mean the disappearances?" Lance said.

She nodded. "I've been here my whole life," she said, "and there hasn't been a time when this wasn't hanging over us like a miasma."

"A miasma?"

"A stench," she said, then went to serve some other customers.

A minute later she brought over his sandwich and put it in front of him, then hesitated, hovering over him.

"Is there something else?" Lance said, looking up at her. "I got something on my face?"

"No, no," she said. "Just want to make sure it meets your standards."

Lance nodded, looked at the sandwich, then took a big bite out of it.

Carla leaned in close again and said, "Someone close to you?"

"What's that?" he said through a mouthful of food.

"This latest disappearance?"

"Oh," Lance said, taking another bite. He shook his head.

Carla nodded, then said, "Well, that's something."

"Something?"

"Good news?" she said uncertainly. "For you, I mean."

Lance said nothing. She hadn't seen the body.

She remained hovering over him and he tried to think of something else to say. When nothing came to mind, he put the rump of the sandwich in his mouth all in one go.

"They don't like to chew in Montana?" she said.

15

From the diner, Lance walked back toward the center of Black Swan, past vacant lots with grass growing through cracks in the concrete and abandoned commercial plazas where even the pawnshops and payday loan places were boarded up. He crossed a rusted metal bridge over a muddy river bank and reached the Main Street. Lance had seen his share of war zones, and Black Swan's Main Street—the tarmac so cracked and broken it looked like it had been shelled by artillery—could have competed with any of them.

The hunting supply he was looking for was at about the midpoint between the bridge he'd just crossed and the railway line. He went inside and nodded to the storekeeper.

"Fishing's that side," the storekeeper said. "Up there's camping."

"And hunting?"

"Hunting's behind the counter, for the most part. What are you looking for?"

Lance looked at the guns and pointed to a used Remington 700. He asked if he could look at it. There was no shortage of 700 variants on the market, some better than others, and this one was familiar to him. He judged it to be about thirty-five years old, in decent condition, parkerized to protect against rust. He looked at the bolt lugs and action screws, then checked the crowns and the cleanliness of the bore. The rifle had been used, the wear and tear was plain to see, but he didn't see any sign of abuse or damage. "Is she a straight shooter?"

"I haven't tested her," the clerk said.

"Mind if I do?"

The man gave him a shrug. "You ready to part with some money?"

"Let's take her outside and find out."

They went out to the lot behind the store and the clerk let Lance fire off a few shots on a makeshift range. The gun shot true. He'd be able to trust it, even at long range, if it came to it.

Back at the counter, he picked up two boxes of .308 Winchester cartridges.

"We've got cheaper ammo if you want," the dealer said.

"That's all right," Lance said. "I'll take a knife, though, and a scope if you've got one."

The dealer had numerous hunting knives. Lance chose a clip point skinner with a six-inch fixed blade and a guard. For scopes, there was only one option, which Lance also took, along with a flashlight and nylon carrying case to hold it all.

"How about a map?" Lance said when he had everything slung over his shoulder and paid for. The store owner gave him a 1:20,000 scale topographical map of the county, free of charge.

Lance left the store and located the brothel on the map with his finger. It was on the main road south out of town, a windy two-lane that wound through steeply forested mountain slopes. He walked south along the main street and continued walking when he reached the edge of town, stretching out his hand for a ride whenever he heard a vehicle behind him. He made an unusual sight with his rifle bag slung over his shoulder, and he'd walked over a mile before a truck finally stopped for him. He heard the driver downshifting and turned to watch. It was a logging truck, and it came to a halt right next to him.

Lance climbed up to the window and looked in. Straight away, he knew why the driver, a three-hundred-pound Seahawks fan with a beer gut and stubble, had stopped. He was looking for a good time. For a free ride, Lance didn't mind disappointing him. "You staying on this road a while?" he said.

"Long enough."

"I'm going as far as this intersection," Lance said, showing on his map the point where the highway crossed a logging road. It was about a mile farther along the highway than the strip club.

The driver, sensing this wasn't the type of passenger he'd hoped for, looked at the map disinterestedly. "All right," he said with a sigh. "You might as well hop in."

Lance watched the road in silence. When they passed the strip club, he leaned forward to get as good a view of the place as he could. It made a sorry sight in the light rain, the gray clouds almost touching the tops of the trees above it. A sign bearing the same pole dancing silhouette as the business card made it clear what the place was for. Next to the bar was a motel of sorts, a series of rooms, each with their own door opening to the empty parking lot. A neon sign in the window read, "Massage, Aromatherapy, Hourly Rates."

"Thinking of paying a visit?" the driver said.

"Oh," Lance said, leaning back in his seat. "Never been much for the aromatherapy."

The driver laughed. "Aromatherapy," he scoffed. "Right." He began slowing down as they approached the crossroad and said to Lance, "You sure you want to get out here?"

"Yes," Lance said.

The driver shrugged. "Happy hunting then."

"Thanks," Lance said as he climbed out of the cab.

He watched the truck head off southward, then doubled back toward the brothel, walking in the forest a few yards off from the road. Any time a vehicle passed, he stopped and crouched so as not to be seen. It had started to rain again, and his breath made a cloud in front of him. It was chilly. They'd gained altitude since leaving the town.

When he reached the brothel, he cut a wide three-hundred-yard perimeter around the building, making sure there were no surprises in the woods. The area behind the brothel was fenced, though the fence was old and rusted with big gaps and gashes in it. He looked for any sign that they kept dogs and saw none, then made his way back toward the front. He watched the road for a few minutes before crossing. The terrain rose steeply on the other side, and he found himself a good vantage point from which to watch the club, the motel, and both sides of the parking lot in front. He lay down then on the wet moss and waited, watching everything through the rifle scope.

It was an ugly place—paint peeling, roof leaking, termite and vermin-infested. It looked like it might have been a roadside restaurant once, as well as a motel. There was plenty of space for parking, and it looked like someone had tried using part of the lot for scrapping vehicles. There was a stack of four tires on one end, and an old refrigerator and an engine block on the other. A lean-to against the side of the bar was piled with firewood. The sign bearing the pole dancer was electrified—fluorescent tubes inside a cracked plastic lightbox. One of the tubes flickered constantly. There were some vehicles parked outside the bar—a fancy BMW sedan with custom rims, an Escalade with blacked-out windows, and a yellow pickup with the logo of a local logging company on the door.

A line of smoke rose from the chimney.

Periodically, a car arrived or left. The drivers were all men. Lance got as good a view of their faces as he could through the scope. He memorized the license plates. The men entered the bar, and every now and then, one of them would come out of the bar and go into one of the motel rooms, accompanied by a female.

As it got later and the light began to fade, the traffic increased.

At about seven, a big guy, he looked like the bouncer of a nightclub—which is what he probably was—came out of the bar smoking a cigarette. He climbed down the steps, crossed the muddy lot, climbed into the Escalade, and drove off. About thirty minutes later, he returned with three women. The women climbed out of the back of the vehicle dressed like off-duty hookers—velour tracksuits with logos across the ass, sequined sneakers, oversized faux fur coats. Two wore ball caps, and the third wore sunglasses despite the dim light. One was Indian, one black, one white.

Lance watched them file toward the door of the bar, then noticed something strange—something he hadn't seen coming, something that caused his breath to catch in his throat. The big guy was holding a pistol, as if afraid the women might make a run for it.

16

Lance kept watch of the brothel as evening gave way to night, keeping careful track of whoever came and went, trying to build a picture in his head of how many people might be inside the building at any given time. It got cold but nothing that would kill him. Traffic to the club peaked at about ten, and by midnight was beginning to trail off.

The yellow pickup had left a few hours earlier, and its driver—a man in a plaid shirt and Timberlands—Lance pegged as a customer. The Escalade left and came back one more time, leaving with two women and returning with four. The BMW that was there when he'd arrived, a new 7-series with aftermarket upgrades, was the only car he hadn't seen arrive. He figured whoever owned it was running the show and had likely arrived with some heavies or perhaps a woman or two.

In addition to it and the Escalade, there were

two other BMWs—a sedan and an SUV—both black with blacked-out windows, that had arrived mid-evening and still hadn't left. They'd contained a thug apiece, dressed in styles that wouldn't have been out of place in the Moscow underworld. One wore tight-fitting jeans and a leather jacket, the other a flamboyant Versace tracksuit.

There were also four vehicles Lance assumed belonged to customers.

A man stumbled out the door and climbed into the cab of a late-nineties Ford Ranger, leaving three customer vehicles. Lance decided he'd waited long enough. He got to his feet slowly, stiff after hours of lying still, and stretched his frozen limbs. He took the hunting knife from the bag, it hadn't come with a sheath, and slid it into his belt at his back. He also took the two boxes of ammo and double-checked that the rifle was loaded and ready to go.

All in all, he figured the building contained at least four, and possibly seven or eight heavies—that included the Escalade driver and whoever had arrived in the 7-series. It also contained at least five hookers and probably a few more, as well as seven customers. There may have been a few more people inside—someone must have been tending the bar, and there must have been women inside when he'd arrived—but he doubted there were many. He'd circled the building and confirmed there were no additional vehicles at the back.

He'd certainly faced worse odds, he thought. The goons would have been drinking. They also had no idea he was coming. That was to his favor. Against was the fact he didn't have a handgun or any kind of silencer.

With the knife in his belt and rifle in hand, he began climbing down the slope from his perch. He was about halfway to the road when the door of the bar opened. Blue light spilled into the parking lot, accompanied by the steady drone of European techno.

Lance crouched in the brush and watched. First one, and then a second of the beefy Russians came out the door. Both were holding cigarettes, and one of them had a beer bottle in his hand. The first man began taking a leak right from the top of the porch onto the steps below, and the second man was pulling someone with him—a woman. She seemed to be resisting, and he went back inside and then pushed her out in front of him. He followed, giving her a hard shove. She slipped and fell head-first down the steps into the mud below. The man laughed uproariously, then flicked his cigarette after her.

She wasn't moving, she might have been seriously hurt, but that didn't stop the other man from adjusting his aim so that the stream of his piss landed right on her. He laughed then, and when he finished, the other man walked down the steps and grabbed her by the hair.

"You disgusting bitch," he snarled in Russian. "I should make you wash out the car."

The woman said nothing, struggling to get to

her feet. She was shoved again and stumbled across the lot toward the SUV. When she reached it, she climbed into the back and the two men got in front. Then the engine fired up, the lights came on, and the vehicle pulled out into the road. Lance watched until its taillights disappeared from view.

Two less to deal with, he thought. The rifle held four rounds. When he was near the road, he found a place with a clear view of the parking lot, put the two ammo boxes on the ground, and raised the rifle. He had a line of sight on the bar door, as well as most of the doors leading to the motel rooms. He listened for the sound of approaching vehicles. There was none. He then drew a bead on the flashing red light inside the front windshield of the 7-series and pulled the trigger.

A sharp crack filled the air, followed by the shattering of the windshield. Before the cold night air filled with the sound of the car alarm, Lance had shifted his sights to the front door of the bar.

A man appeared almost instantly—the big guy wearing the Versace. Lance waited until a second man showed up behind him, then—Pop, Pop.

Blood misted from their skulls as their bodies slumped down the steps. A third man appeared at the door, saw his two fallen friends, and then mindlessly, like an imbecile, ran out into the middle of the parking lot, looking for whoever had caused it.

Same pop. Same mist of blood. Same slump to the knees as he fell face forward to eat the dirt.

Lance dropped the rifle and was on his feet, running parallel to the road through the low brush. When he was opposite the Escalade he crossed, keeping low, using the vehicle for cover. He scanned the lot, empty but for the three bodies, and dashed to the side of the building. One way led to the front entrance of the bar, the other to the motel rooms. Between the bar and the long, squat structure that housed the motel rooms was a narrow gap. He went to the corner and looked down the gap. There was a side door into the bar.

He darted to the door and checked it. It was unlocked, and he shoved it open. It led to a long, dark corridor. From the far end, he could hear the muffled sound of the techno music. He stepped in and hurried along it, the music growing louder as he went. He passed a door to his left, a sign on it read 'Office', and stopped when he heard noise from inside. He pushed open the door to see a man and a woman going at it. With the music as loud as it was, the sound of three gunshots and a car alarm hadn't been enough to disturb them.

From the ceiling hung a bare bulb, which was switched off. The only light in the room came through a small window with a slatted blind. On the wall was a calendar featuring farm machinery, and beneath it was a desk.

Facing the desk, his back to the door, was a man —an average Joe, about fifty years old judging from the love handles. His buttocks, the palest part of his body, caught the moonlight with each backward thrust of his groin.

In front of him, blocked from Lance's view by the man's torso, was the lucky recipient of these thrusts. Her splayed legs were the only part of her Lance could see, her feet pointed upward at the ceiling, a red stiletto on each. She moaned as the man pulled out of her. He hadn't climaxed, and he bent down to put his face between her legs. As he did so, she opened her eyes to see Lance standing in the doorway, watching them with a six-inch hunting knife in his hand and a bemused smile on his face.

"Oh my God," she cried, and the man, whose mouth had only just made contact, took it as a sign of encouragement.

Lance raised a single eyebrow at the woman, put a finger in front of his lips, then took two strides forward and struck the man on the back of the head with the handle of his knife. The man slumped forward, and the woman pushed him off her instantly.

"Who are you?" she gasped, her eyes wide with fear.

There was a chair that had been pushed away from the desk, and on its back was a wool blanket. Lance handed it to her. "Stay in here," he said.

She looked at the knife, then the blanket, and nodded.

Lance went to the window and pulled open a gap between two slats in the blind. The SUV was just coming back into the lot. He hadn't expected it to return so soon. The man who'd pissed from the porch hopped out and made for the door of the bar. When he saw the bodies on the ground, he froze. He couldn't be certain what they were in the darkness, but he crouched next to one for a closer look. Instantly, he rose up and drew a gun.

Lance went back out to the corridor and almost collided with another man coming the other way. He was a customer, and Lance gave him a single punch to the face, the knife in his hand giving it extra weight. The man fell to the ground and didn't move. He'd come from a room across the hall, and Lance pushed the door open with his foot and peered inside. He saw two naked girls sitting on a bed, their backs to the wall, holding their knees. A photographer's studio light lit them up, and in front of them was a camera on a tripod. They sat, eyes wide with terror, staring at Lance.

No way in hell they were eighteen.

"Don't leave this room," Lance said. "There's going to be gunfire."

He was about to step back into the corridor when he heard footsteps. Tight against the wall, just inside the door, he waited. The door nudged open slowly. He couldn't see who was on the other side of it, but he could see the girls' faces. They looked at whoever it was blankly, not giving anything away. Then, a man stepped into the room and growled, "Where is he?"

Lance raised his foot and brought it down hard

against the door, sending it slamming into the man's face. Then he rounded the door and grabbed the man by the shirt. It was the pisser. Lance pulled him into the room, spun him around, and then slid the blade of the hunting knife across his sinewy throat.

Blood spurted everywhere, landing on the bed inches from the girls' feet. They drew back in horror.

Lance pushed him away and turned just in time to avoid being struck by a bullet. It hit the door frame and was followed by another and another, sending splinters flying. Someone was emptying a perfectly good magazine.

Lance waited. When he heard the click of an empty gun, he leaped into the corridor and collided instantly with an absolute bear of a man—two-hundred-fifty pounds of pierogis, cabbage soup, and pure muscle. The man wrapped his arms around Lance like a wrestler, and Lance pulled back and rammed his forehead right into his chin. The man let go, and Lance ducked as an arm swung for him. Then he rose up and thrust the knife deep into the man's sternum. It felt like driving an axe into solid wood. The man stared at his chest, a look of surprise on his face, then grabbed the knife by the hilt and tried to pull it out. Lance put a hand on each side of the man's head and twisted his neck as hard as he could. It snapped, and the man crumpled like a puppet whose strings had been cut.

Without stopping, Lance continued through the

door at the end of the corridor into the bar proper. The music was louder, and a few customers were still there, one at the bar, one in front of the stage, and a third who'd realized something was up and was hurriedly putting on his coat.

Behind the bar was a topless woman looking at Lance with wide eyes. On the stage, a dancer held onto the pole, standing still with a look on her face like she wasn't sure if she should finish her performance or run for cover. She stared at Lance and then perceptibly nodded toward the exit.

Lance wiped the knife on his pants and strode toward the door, kicking it open but immediately ducking back. Bullets flew from the parking lot, shattering glass and wood. Lance crouched and shielded his eyes. The door swung wildly on its hinge and slammed shut. Lance waited until he heard the steps creak, then got up and kicked the door hard. It hit someone, and a gun went off. Lance stepped forward, kicked the door a second time, and then stepped out to find a man falling backward down the steps. In a single motion, he leaped into the air, landed on the man, and gutted him like a pig.

Another man appeared in the doorway behind him, firing bullets as Lance pulled the man he'd just killed on top of himself as a shield. He threw the knife, and as it spun toward the man's face, Lance got out from under the dead man and rose to his feet. The man on the steps swatted blindly and got lucky, blocking the knife and taking only a gash on the arm in return, but Lance was just behind it.

He rushed up the steps and lunged, grabbing the man around the waist and forcing them both backward into the bar. The man landed hard on his back, his head hit the floor, and his pistol fell from his hand. Lance grabbed the gun instantly, and bang! A bullet to the brain.

Outside, across the parking lot, an engine fired up. Without seeing it, Lance knew it was the 7-series. The alarm, which had been sounding the whole time, stopped. Lance got up and ran, leaping down the steps of the porch and sprinting across the lot.

The man in the car couldn't see through the shattered windshield, but that didn't stop him from flooring the pedal. The car lurched forward with a spray of mud as Lance jumped, stretched out his arms, and landed hard on the hood. He held on with one hand as the car accelerated, and punched the shattered windshield with the other. The car swerved, and he was almost thrown off. He held on with both hands, and when it straightened out, he punched the windshield again, trying to break through. It wasn't easy, and his fist bounced painfully off the shatterproof glass.

The car skidded and careened out of the parking lot and onto the highway, almost throwing Lance off again. He managed to hold on, but the car continued to gain speed. It veered into the shoulder, spraying water and gravel as it did, then swerved back into the road, crossing its lane and veering into the oncoming lane. Lance jammed the knife into the bullet hole in the windshield as the car crashed into the other shoulder. He looked back over his shoulder and saw that the car was headed right for the trees. He braced for impact, but at the last second, it swerved again back onto the road.

Desperately, he pounded the handle of the knife. It passed through the glass, leaving a hole large enough for his arm to fit through. He released his grip on the hood and thrust his hand through the hole in the windshield. The driver jammed on the brakes, and Lance was thrown forward. He was flung from the car into the road, the entire windshield coming with him in a single shattered sheet. Lance landed on it and slid about twenty yards before coming to a halt.

Without the glass in front of him, the driver could see now, and Lance could see him. And both knew what the other was thinking. Without a moment's hesitation, the driver revved the powerful engine of the 7-series once, then jammed his foot on the gas. The car leaped forward like a sprinter out of the starting block, and in the same instant, Lance jumped into the air.

He grazed the hood of the car, then smashed into the driver, feet first, his boot right in the driver's face, knocking him out cold. Lance was sprawled across the driver, and as the driver's foot let off the gas, the car slowed to a gradual halt, its momentum taking it another hundred yards down the road. Lance climbed out of the car, and the driver slumped forward, the weight of his chest sounding the horn in a monotonous wail. Lance stood in the middle of the road and caught his breath. Back toward the bar, he could see two women running in his direction. Behind them, two cars—the bar's remaining customers—pulled out of the lot and sped off in the other direction.

17

The man in the car was a wiry son of a bitch—dressed in a ridiculous linen suit as if he was holidaying on the Riviera rather than overseeing a seedy strip club. He wore a pencil mustache and had a black mole next to one of his eyes. In his breast pocket was a packet of Marlboro cigarettes.

"Seems like he was *trying* to look like a pimp," Lance said when the two women who'd been running toward him arrived. They were breathless and severely underdressed for the cold. Both were in heels that decidedly did not look like they'd been designed for running. "I'll take him back to the bar," Lance said. "You two see if you can get that car started."

Lance retrieved his knife, then checked that the son of a bitch hadn't died on him. He pulled him out of the car and slung him over his shoulder. As he walked back to the bar, he heard the women behind struggle to get the car started. Eventually, they succeeded and drove back behind him, the lights illuminating his path.

Lance was breathless when he flung the pimp on the ground in front of the bar. Five other women had gathered there, looking down from the porch. The pimp was beginning to come to, and Lance gave him a solid kick in the gut to help him along.

"Who are you?" the pimp stammered when his eyes opened. "What is this? You killed—"

Lance put his foot on the man's hand and pressed down.

The man let out a wail of pain and grabbed Lance's ankle with his free hand. Lance ignored him, grinding the hand into the ground. The man cried out again, and Lance said, "I think we're all smart enough to know how this is going to go? I'm going to get the information I want. The only question is what I have to do to you to get it."

"I don't know anything," the man wailed as Lance increased the pressure.

Lance felt bones in the man's hand break. He said, "Who took the woman who disappeared?"

The man might have known, he might not, but he was the only lead, and Lance didn't mind cracking a few eggs to make this particular omelet.

"I don't know what you're talking about," the man cried as Lance mashed the hand into the gravel like he was putting out a cigarette butt.

"Well, you better think of something to tell me,"

Lance said, "or I'll start siphoning gasoline out of that car and light you up like a bonfire."

The man looked up at Lance and knew he was in trouble.

Lance didn't have much time. The next car to come down the highway would see the carnage and call the police. It was only a matter of time.

Lance raised his foot from the man's mangled hand, and the man immediately cradled it in his other hand. It looked like it had been in a pit bull's mouth. Lance then placed his boot on the side of the man's head.

"What are you doing?" the man stammered.

"Listen," Lance said, leaning on his knee, putting just enough weight on his foot that the man would feel the very real danger that he was in. "You see that road?"

The man said nothing, and Lance repeated the question louder.

"I see it," the man cried.

"When I see two headlights coming our way, I'm going to crush your skull, you understand me?"

"What?"

"That's how much time you've got to tell me what I want to know. Next car, and you're dead."

"But I don't—"

Lance pressed down with his boot.

"Okay, okay," the man cried out. "What do you want to know?" He spoke rapidly, in a blind panic.

Lance said, "What did you do with her?"

"Me?" the man gasped in horror. "I didn't take

her. I didn't have anything to do with it." Lance pressed harder and the man flailed and squirmed wildly, grasping at Lance's leg, clawing at the boot on his face, trying in vain to release himself from its weight. "I whore them," he cried. "I make them dance. I make them work. That's all I do."

"Is that all he does?" Lance said, looking up at the women on the porch.

"Uh uh," one of the girls from the room with the video recorder said. "He does a lot more than that."

Lance pressed harder, and the man said, "I don't do the weird shit. I swear to God, I don't."

"What weird shit?"

"You know. The rituals. The torture. All that fetish stuff."

The words made Lance's blood boil, and he found himself pressing down harder than intended. "Who told you about that ritual shit? If you don't do it, how do you know about it?"

"Everyone knows about it," the man gasped. "This has been going on for years around here. Everyone knows."

"Looks to me," Lance said, "that if I wanted a woman to torture, all I'd have to do is come to you."

The man was crying, and Lance began to grind with his foot, tearing the man's cheek and ear against the sharp gravel beneath his face. "It's not like that," the man cried. "I swear. These girls come to me. I don't take them. I don't have to."

“That true?” Lance said, turning again to the women.

None of them spoke.

“You all here by choice?” Lance said.

“Sort of,” one of the other women said, “but he’s not telling you everything. He knows more than he’s letting on.”

“What could I possibly know?” the man cried. “I’m a pimp. I’m a businessman.”

“Any of you ever seen anything related to these disappearances?” Lance said, speaking to the women.

The women looked at each other, but none of them gave an answer.

“You see?” the man gasped, squirming under the boot.

Lance let out a long sigh, then reached behind his back and pulled the knife from his belt. He leaned down, grabbed the man’s ear, and cut it clean off his head in a single motion.

A blood-curdling scream filled the air. Lance turned to the two girls who’d been in front of the video camera. “How old are you?” he said to them.

One made to speak but stopped when the other touched her arm, shaking her head.

“They’re sixteen,” one of the others said, answering for them. She was the woman from the first room, still wrapped in the blanket Lance had given her.

“Do any of you know anything that could help

me figure out what's going on with these disappearances?" Lance said to the women.

He knew they had more to say, but they were still hesitant.

He turned back to the man on the ground, still crying and holding his ear, blood gushing from it like a hose. "Listen up," Lance said. "You've got a real peach of an operation here. I saw these girls arrive with a gun pointed at them. I'll tell you right now, I could slit your throat and sleep like a baby tonight. You hear me?"

The woman in the blanket spoke up then. She said, "He's got a computer inside with names on it. I don't know what they all mean, but he's up to something."

"And there's the basement," another woman said.

Lance looked down at the man and felt an animal rage rush through his veins. It was a feeling he was used to, though he still hadn't given up trying to resist it. Every atom in his body wanted to kill this man, to make him feel the pain he'd inflicted on the world, to make him pay for his crimes. Lance grabbed the man by the hair and yanked up his head.

"All right," the man gasped. "All right. I sell them on. Some of them. Some of the women."

"Who do you sell them to?"

The man gasped for breath but didn't answer.

Lance held the knife to his other ear.

"I don't know. I swear to God, I don't know. He

messages anonymously. He pays anonymously. I don't know who he is. I don't want to know."

Lance gritted his teeth. He knew that was probably true, but there were other ways to know who the customer might be. "How do you deliver the women? Does the buyer come here?"

"Never," the man said. "He tells me where to drop them off. It's always at night, always in the woods. These woods are riddled with logging tracks. He tells me to tie up and gag the women and then leave them somewhere specific."

"Somewhere specific?"

"He sends coordinates. Different places always. Middle of nowhere."

"And you leave women there, naked and gagged, in the dark?"

The man said nothing.

Lance looked at the women. "Any of you seen that?"

They shook their heads, but one of them, the one who'd been bartending topless earlier and had now pulled on a jacket, said, "He's telling the truth. That's how he does it."

"You've seen it?"

"Sort of."

Lance nodded. That was enough. That and the computer. "You know how to access the computer?" he said to the bartender.

"I do," she said.

Lance yanked the man's head back by the hair, revealing his taut, throbbing carotid artery. Putting the blade of the knife against it, Lance said, "This should have been done a long time ago." He ran the blade across the man's throat, and it slit the flesh like it was cutting through butter. Then he pushed the body forward, face down in the mud.

The women wasted no love on the man but they gasped in horror all the same. The man gurgled and spasmed on the ground like a dying chicken, blood pulsing from his neck in weakening spurts. They all watched as the movement gradually subsided, to be replaced with a permanent stillness.

"Sorry about that," Lance said to the women.

"He deserved it," one of them said.

Lance nodded. "It was a job that needed doing. Nothing more. Don't none of you lose sleep over it."

"If we lose any sleep," one of the sixteen-year-olds said, "it won't be for that piece of shit."

"It's a shock," Lance said. "Seeing a thing like that."

"We're big girls," she said.

The bartender stepped forward. "Who are you, anyway?" she said.

Lance thought for a minute, then said, "I'm just trying to find out what happened with the latest disappearance."

The woman nodded and said, "Whatever happened to her, that's what happened to all the other women who went missing."

"What was she to you?" the sixteen-year-old said.

“The woman who disappeared?” Lance said.

The girl nodded.

“She was nothing to me.”

“Really?” the girl said skeptically, nodding at the dead body on the ground in front of him.

“I thought she was,” Lance added, “or, at least, there was a chance she might be. But she wasn’t.”

“What do you mean, there was a chance?”

“My sister disappeared a long time ago. There was a chance this was her.”

“Was your sister Indian?”

“No,” Lance said. “Let’s go inside. We’re running out of time.”

“Why are you doing all this?” the girl insisted. “If it wasn’t your sister, why keep going? You could get in a lot of trouble going around like this.”

Lance smiled. *Trouble*, he thought. If only.

18

Inside the bar, Lance said to the women, "Is this everyone that's on the premises? Are there any more goons? Any more men? Anyone out in the motel?"

They shook their heads. The woman who'd been bartending said, "You got them all. You took out the whole crew."

"So no one else is coming?"

"Not unless someone called the police."

Lance nodded. "Did any of you call the police?"

"No," the bartender said, "but one of the customers might have."

Lance nodded. He looked at the seven women. The bartender looked the oldest, probably in her mid-thirties, and the rest descended in age. The two girls who'd been in the room with the video camera were the youngest. "You'd better get dressed," he said to them.

They went in different directions, some to the

corridor Lance had entered through, the rest to a room behind the stage where they had lockers. Lance went back outside to the lot and dragged the bodies out of sight of any passing highway traffic. He piled them behind the Escalade and then found an old canvas tarp to pull over them.

When he returned, the women had congregated around the bar. Lance said to them, "Who can show me this basement?"

The bartender was the first to move. She went behind the bar and got a ring of keys from a hook next to the phone. Then she led Lance into a storage area behind the bar filled with old kegs, stacks of soda cans, and cleaning supplies. There was a large corkboard on one wall, and she took it down and moved some mops and a fridge. Behind was a steel door. Using two separate keys, she unlocked two deadbolts and pulled the door open. Just beyond the door was a light switch, and she reached in from where she was and turned on the lights.

From where he stood, Lance could see a set of wooden steps leading downward.

"If I go down there," Lance said, "what am I going to find?"

"Nothing now," the woman said. "At least, I don't think anyone's down there. You'll see what they do, though."

Lance nodded. "This door's not going to lock behind me?"

She smiled, then handed him the ring of keys. "I'll come with you if it makes you feel better."

"All right," Lance said, glancing back into the bar where the other women had started pouring a few drinks. He led the way, checking that the steel door could be unlocked from the inside before descending the steps. The bartender followed, and each step creaked under their weight. When the steel door swung shut behind them, slamming loudly, they both jumped.

"Sorry," the woman said. "I forgot to warn you."

Lance looked up at it—it made him uneasy that it was the only way back out—then looked forward. The basement seemed to have been cut raw out of the ground, the walls lined with limestone like the walls of an old foundation. The building above them must have been built on a much older site, he thought. At the bottom of the steps was a small hallway with a single steel door at the end. The floor was compacted dirt. There were no windows or means of ventilation. The air was heavy with a fetid, animal stench.

"What's behind the door?" Lance said.

The woman just shook her head. She'd pulled part of her shirt up over her face to block out the stench.

"You've never been down here?"

"Once," she said. "Briefly."

"What about the keys? They were right by the bar."

"I never touched them. None of us did. I don't

think I'd have touched them now if he was still alive."

Lance nodded. "But you knew what was going on down here?"

Her eyes filled with tears. "Something dark. I knew that much. I could hear when there were women down here. Sometimes. I should have done something."

"You never wanted to call the police?"

"Of course I did."

"But you didn't do it?"

"Around these parts, calling the police is the type of thing that gets you killed."

"Do the cops know about this?"

"I don't know what they know," she said. "All I know is we don't call them. That, and, well, you asked what's behind that door? The one time I came down here was ten years ago. It was right after I arrived. I saw as soon as I arrived that I'd made a mistake, that I'd gotten into a bad situation, but the boss—"

"The man whose throat I just slit?"

She nodded. "What you did was too good for him. You should have stripped him naked and fed him to wolves. You should have doused him in gasoline like you said."

"What did he say to you?"

"When I first got here?"

Lance nodded.

"He brought me down here and showed me what was behind the door. It was empty, but I knew what I was looking at. He said if I ever tried to run, if I ever helped anyone escape, if I ever spoke to the cops or to anyone about what was going on, this is where I'd end up?"

"And you believed him?"

She nodded. "I saw it happen. There'd be a girl causing trouble, then she'd disappear. I knew, we all did, that she'd been brought down here."

"And you never went to the police?"

"Not about this."

"Did anyone else?"

"I don't know."

"Did you go to them about anything?"

She looked at him for a minute, then said, "There's a guy who comes by here."

"A cop?"

She nodded. "His name's Belcher."

Lance said nothing.

"He saw me once getting slapped around by a guy I was mixed up with."

"What guy?"

"It doesn't matter. He's gone now. He was a mistake."

"And the cop? Belcher?"

"It happened back in the bar there. Belcher had one of the girls on his lap. He was having a good time."

"Was he in uniform?"

The woman nodded. "But he wasn't working. He didn't lift a finger to help me."

"Did you ask?"

"I got slapped right in front of his face, and the look in his eyes, it wasn't good."

"You didn't get the impression he'd help?"

"When you're in this line of work, you learn how to read people pretty quick. What I read from this guy, let's just say, if I called the police station, I wouldn't want it being him who picked up."

"All right," Lance said. "You ever see him around here doing other stuff."

"What other stuff?"

"Picking up money. Getting involved."

She shook her head. "No, he's just a regular Joe Schmo creep, as far as I ever saw."

"All right," Lance said. He went up to the door and tried the keys, one after the other, until one of them worked. He heard a heavy bolt unlock and then pushed the door open. It took all his weight to move it. "You wait here," he said to the woman.

She nodded, and Lance stepped into the darkness. The stench almost overwhelmed him, and he gagged as he felt on the wall for a light switch. He found one and flicked it. Another incandescent bulb came on to reveal the squalid space that filled the rest of the basement. It was a room of about a thousand square feet, windowless, though there must have been air getting in from somewhere. The air was chill, though not as cold as outside. The floor was the same compacted dirt and the walls the same raw stone he'd seen in the corridor. The ceiling was just about high enough for Lance to stand at a slight hunch. In the center of the room, directly beneath the lightbulb, were a number of dog cages, about six by six feet in size. They were solidly built, not bought off the shelf, but welded together with strong steel by someone who knew how to work with it. In the corner of each cage was a bucket for human waste. On the floor inside one of the cages was a filthy dinner plate.

Lance's eyes darted around, making sure he'd missed nothing, then he doubled over and retched.

19

Lance backed away from the room and shut the door.

"Seen enough?" the woman said. He could see on her face she was eager to get back upstairs.

"Yeah," he said.

They climbed the stairs but stopped at the door. She turned around. "You know the Cavalier woman?" she said.

"No," Lance said.

"Gloria Cavalier?" she said. "She went missing a year ago. They found her body in the woods, just like this current case."

"Okay," Lance said.

"I saw her."

"What do you mean?"

"I mean, I saw her picture in the newspaper, back when her disappearance was in the news. I recognized her."

"Because you saw her down here?"

"Not down here but in the parking lot. They were taking her out of a car. She looked drugged."

"And they brought her down here?"

The woman nodded. Lance could tell that what she was saying was difficult for her. She said, "And a few weeks later, I read in the newspaper that her body had been found. Mutilated."

Lance nodded. They looked at each other for a minute, and the woman said, "I should have done something."

"You're doing something now."

The woman shook her head. "It's too late now, though. I should have done something then."

Lance swallowed. He thought of his sister. He wondered if he'd ever find out what had happened to her and his mother. He wondered if there was more he could have done to find their killer. He said, "We all have our regrets. The best we can do now is keep moving forward."

She looked at him for a moment, unconvinced, and then they both went back out to the bar where the other women seemed to be settling in, pouring a second round of drinks. Lance wondered what was to become of them now. Whatever place they'd found in the world—bad though it was—he'd just shattered. They were homeless now. Jobless. They'd be back on whatever streets they'd been on when this life found them, and there was nothing to say they'd be better off.

That, too, was a guilt he was used to. The work

he did for the government, if *work* was the word for it, the value of it, the good it did the world, was ambiguous, to say the least. He'd done things that, even now, years after they'd happened, woke him in a cold sweat in the middle of the night. And who was to say if they'd helped anyone?

He realized the women were looking at him. "Mister, you want a drink?" the bartender said.

He looked at each of them, then said, "Where do you live?"

"There's a house a few miles down the highway. They keep us there."

"What's going to happen now that I killed these guys?"

One of them shrugged. "I don't intend to be around long enough to find out."

Lance looked at her. She was probably in her early twenties, very skinny, with long black hair that went well past her shoulders. "Where will you go?"

"Why?" she said. "You looking for a roommate?"

The others laughed.

Lance shook his head. "The woman that got murdered this week," he said. "Did she pass through this place?"

"I never saw her," the long-haired woman said.

"He got paid, though," the bartender said. "He had money. That came from somewhere."

"The boss got paid?" Lance said.

She nodded.

"Paid by who?"

"I don't know," she said, "but he had money to throw around."

"And more blow than I've seen in a while," the long-haired woman said.

Another added, "Plus, they all went to the casino."

"They've definitely been living large these last few days," the bartender said. "They'd come into cash."

"And you think that was related to the disappearance?"

"Why don't I show you the computer?" the bartender said. "Since you're not having a drink."

She led him down the corridor and into the room where the video camera was. The room was brighter than the others, with its studio-style lights pointed at the bed. There was a small desk behind the door, Lance hadn't paid much attention to it before, and he saw now that there was a computer on it.

The woman opened the email application and began scrolling through the junk. She did a few searches, searched the deleted folder, and after a minute, found what she was looking for. "Look here," she said. "I've seen messages like this before. This one is from last week."

"He let you read his email?"

"No, but I did other stuff on the computer. Placed orders for the bar. Scheduled the girls. He was too much of an idiot to know everything on his phone synced up here."

Lance sat down in front of the computer and began reading the first message.

Got one for you. Won't be cheap.

"Did he get a reply to this?" Lance said, though he couldn't see any.

"If he did, he must have deleted it."

"Check the deleted folder," Lance said.

She did, but there was nothing there.

There was a pen and notepad on the desk, and Lance wrote down the address the message had been sent to. It looked like random characters—a throwaway address from an encryption service—but it might be traceable. "How long has this been going on?" he said.

She shook her head. "Since as long as I've been around, that's for sure. Probably a lot longer."

"And any idea who the buyer is?"

"Well," the woman said, "I'd be speculating—"

"Anything you can tell me, I'd be grateful to hear it."

"We've got a few theories, me and the girls. We might not have actually seen a murder happen, but there have been other things."

"What sorts of things?"

"Let's call them *near misses*," she said. "Let's go back out to the bar. The others can tell you."

20

When they got back to the bar, the bartender said, "Are you sure we can't get you something to drink? It's the least we could do."

"Do you have coffee?" Lance said.

She glanced at one of the other women, then said, "We can make some coffee. Susie, there's coffee in the motel office, isn't there?"

Someone ran off to get the coffee, and Lance said, "Is that a siren?" Everyone listened. It was. "Did anyone call the cops?"

No one had. Lance went over to the window and looked out at the road. He couldn't see the police cars yet and wanted to get going before they arrived.

"I've got something for you," the sixteen-year-old who'd spoken earlier said.

Lance looked at her. If he didn't leave now, he'd

have to talk to the cops. He hoped it wasn't Belcher. "All right," he said.

Her dark eyes looked around the room, at him, at the other women, gathering her words. "It was when I first got here," she said, "about a year ago." Her voice was frail but steady. "I never talked about it."

Everyone waited for her to go on.

"It was at the house. Millsy woke me."

"Millsy?"

"One of the goons you shot outside," the bartender said.

"I didn't know where I was," the girl continued. "I was pretty out of it back then. High most of the time. Anyway, Millsy woke me in the middle of the night. No one had ever come into my room there, but I'd figured it was only a matter of time. I thought he was going to get into my bed."

"But he didn't?"

"No. He shook me awake and told me to get up. To hurry. It took me a minute to come to my senses, and when I did, I could tell he was in a panic. I didn't ask what was going on. I just put on some clothes and followed him out of the house."

"The house where you still stay?" Lance said.

She nodded. "There was a Jeep in the driveway, and I got in the back. Someone was in the passenger seat. When I saw his face, I realized it was the boss."

"The one I killed?"

"Yes," she said. "He didn't say anything. Never

looked at me. On the drive, neither of them said anything, and when I asked where we were going, they told me to shut up."

Lance kept watch of the highway through the window. A single police cruiser came into view, its lights flashing. "Where did they take you?" he said, sensing where the story was going.

"I knew it was no place good," she said. "The road seemed to go on forever. I lost track."

Outside, the police car pulled into the parking lot. Lance watched it.

"First, we drove through town, then north along the lake."

"Past the old mill?" the bartender said.

"Yeah. Into the mountains. It's all forest and logging roads out there."

The bartender nodded.

"At some point, we turned off the paved road and got onto a logging track."

"Could you find your way back there?" Lance said.

She shook her head.

Outside, the door of the cruiser opened, and a cop stepped out. It took Lance a moment to see that it was Lola. She was alone. That was a relief.

"We were on the logging track for a long time. At points, the Jeep struggled to get over obstacles. It was tough going. We kept at it, and eventually, we came to a house," the girl continued. "It was a strange house. It looked like a Swiss cottage from a storybook. A children's storybook. I didn't know what it was doing up there, very big, with a wrap-around porch on two levels. It reminded me of a picture of an old inn in the Alps or something."

Lance went to the door and opened it. Lola didn't seem surprised to find him there, though she did have a hand on the pistol at her waist. "Officer Quinn," he said.

She looked at him, and he could tell she was still angry about what had happened earlier. "Mr Spector," she said frostily.

"You'd better come inside," he said before she had time to look around the parking lot. It was dark but it wouldn't take long for her to stumble across the bodies if she started looking.

"What happened here?" she said, eyeing the tarp behind the Escalade.

"Do me a favor," Lance said, ushering her into the bar. "Don't ask until after I'm gone."

"What have you gotten yourself into?"

"Housecleaning," a voice from behind him said. It was the bartender.

Lola looked at them sternly, her jaw set in a way that Lance already knew meant business. "There was a report of gunshots," she said. "I took the call and responded before anyone else could, but they won't be far behind me."

"Does the chief know?" Lance said, instantly regretting it.

Lola gave him a withering look, then pointed at a stain on the floor. "That's blood, isn't it?" she said.

"This won't take long," Lance said, leading her to where the rest of the women were seated.

She followed him, eyeing the women. "Is anyone hurt?"

"No one's hurt," the bartender said.

"Do you know a house north of town?" Lance said to her before she had time to ask any more questions. "In the forest? Looks like a Swiss cottage?"

"The Breckenridge? I know it."

"Breckenridge?"

She shrugged. "That's what they call it. It's an old hunting lodge. Unused. It's been searched before. Why?"

Lance turned to the girl. "Why don't you continue what you were telling us? They brought you to the house."

The girl eyed Lola in her uniform, then said, "They went inside, the boss and Millsy, and left me in the car. There were other vehicles parked outside. Heavy duty, like what you'd take off-roading."

"Okay," Lance said.

"That place is deserted," Lola said. "Some company owns it, but they haven't used it in decades, as far as I know."

The girl nodded but said, "There was someone there that night. There were lights on inside. Leading up to it, there were torches, like you might have for a wedding or something. It creeped me out. And there were guards there, too, with dogs."

"How many guards?"

"At least two."

"You heard of that happening up there?" Lance said to Lola.

She shook her head. "It's pretty secluded, though. You could set off fireworks, and no one would be the wiser."

"It looked like they were waiting for someone," the girl said. "I began to steel myself to go inside. I wasn't wearing fancy clothes or makeup or anything. I didn't see any other girls."

"You were afraid?" Lola said.

"You bet your ass I was afraid."

"But they didn't take you in?" Lance said.

She shook her head. "I was sure they would. Why else bring me there? But then another vehicle arrived, a Jeep with big tires like the rest of them, and some men pulled another woman out of the back seat. She was struggling, crying, trying to fight them off, but she couldn't."

"Did you see who she was?" Lola said.

"I should have helped her," the girl said as if she hadn't heard the question.

"What could you have done?" the bartender said, putting a hand on her shoulder.

The girl shook her head. "I should have tried," she said, then looked around the room. "I didn't know the woman, but she looked native. Straight black hair. A few years older than me. Maybe twenty. They pulled her by the hair, kicking and screaming, the dogs on the leashes barking like they wanted to eat her."

"Into the house?" Lola said. She'd taken out a notebook and was scribbling down notes.

The girl nodded.

"And this was when?"

"A year ago."

"Was it Cavalier?" Lola said. "Gloria Cavalier? Was it around when she went missing?"

The girl looked at Lola, then said, "I knew I should have done something, but I couldn't move. I couldn't think. It was cold and I was shivering. But I knew. I knew." She started to cry.

"Knew what?" Lola said.

"In my heart," the girl said, wiping her face on her sleeve, "I knew something very bad was going on. I knew it was connected to the disappearances. I knew that woman was never going to be seen again."

"It was Cavalier, then?" Lola pressed, furiously scribbling in her notebook.

"She disappeared into the house," the girl continued. "And the boss and Millsy came hurrying out, almost running down the steps. Their faces were pale, and I noticed a helicopter in the air. Everyone was clearly frightened. I said something, I don't remember what, and Millsy told me to shut up. He told me to lie down. The windows were tinted, but he wanted me down, so I got down on the floor. No one spoke on the drive back to the house, but when we got there, the boss told me if I ever breathed a word of what I'd seen, I would die. And I believed him."

"The woman you saw?" Lance said.

"It was Cavalier," the girl said. "I saw the story in the newspaper a few days later. Another disappeared woman. There was a photo. It was the same woman."

Lance looked at Lola, motioning for her to follow him. He led her back to the room where the computer was and said, "Can you give me directions to that house?"

"You want to go up there alone?"

He nodded. "From what you said, it sounds like no one's going to be up there anyway."

"From what the girl said, it sounds like it's a lair for some murder cult."

"I'll be careful."

"How are you even going to get up there?"

Lance shrugged. "I'll take one of the cars from the lot."

"The road's pretty bad."

"I'll manage."

She sketched out some directions in the notebook and tore out the page. The map she'd drawn was surprisingly detailed. He looked at her. "Where is this taking me?"

"You'll see," she said. "The important thing is not to take the turnoffs into the valley. You'll get stuck down there. Keep climbing."

"Thanks," he said. "Do you know who owns the place?"

"Some corporation," she said, shrugging. "We looked at the place. At least, I was told we had. I haven't been there personally, but it's been written off as empty. It was cleared."

"The ownership should be a public record."

She nodded. "I'll get on that as soon as I get back to the station."

"This computer, too," Lance said. "It's important."

"What's on it?"

"Emails. You'll see when you take a look."

"We don't exactly have a crack forensics team back at the lab, if you know what I mean. I can send it to the state facility in—"

"No," Lance said, taking her notepad and writing down a name and number. "Call this woman."

Lola looked at the paper. "Laurel Everlane? Who's that?"

"A colleague."

"This is a DC number."

"Yes," Lance said. "She'll tell you who sent the emails."

"How's she going to do that from DC?"

Lance went over to the computer and switched it off. Then he moved the monitor aside, opened the desktop case, and pulled the hard disk from the drive bay. It was metal and rectangular, a little smaller in size than a VHS cassette.

"What are you doing?" Lola gasped. "That's—"

"Evidence," Lance said, handing it to her. "You tell Laurel you have it, and she'll tell you what to do with it."

"Simple as that?" Lola said skeptically.

Outside, a wolf was howling. The smell of blood was attracting them already. He said, "What's going to happen with the women?"

Lola shook her head. "I don't know. There's a community organization back in town, it helps women in crisis but...."

"But?" Lance said.

"They have to want to be helped."

Lance nodded.

"I bet most of them get a bus to the city tomorrow," Lola said.

Lance made for the door, and Lola said, "So that's it, then? That's how you roll?"

"What do you mean?"

"Come in and make a mess, then leave it for others to clean up?"

"Mess?" Lance said. "I'm just getting started."

21

Lola stood at the door of the bar and watched Lance drive off. He'd taken an SUV that must have belonged to the thugs and she planned on giving him a few more minutes before calling for backup. She watched his taillights disappear into the darkness then went back into the bar.

Inside, the women looked like they were getting ready to leave. By rights, Lola shouldn't let them, but technically, she hadn't found any bodies yet. No crime had been committed. She was just checking out a report of gunshots. "Where are you going to stay tonight?" she said to them.

"The house will do us for a while longer," a woman in a tracksuit with a blanket over her shoulders said.

"You're not worried something will happen there?"

"Like what? Your friend killed the whole gang."

Lola nodded, but she knew nothing was ever that simple. Gangsters had friends. They had business associates. They had creditors. "I'll be needing to take statements tomorrow," she said.

"Are you telling us not to leave the state?"

"I think that would be for the best."

"The bodies are out by the Escalade," one of the other women said. "Beneath the tarp."

"I'll pretend you didn't say that," Lola said. "Mind if I have a look around after you leave?"

"Knock yourself out," the woman in the blanket said.

"Computer's in the office," the woman behind the bar said. "The cages are in the basement."

"Cages?" Lola said, eyes widening.

"You'll see," the woman said.

They had keys for the Escalade outside and seemed to have a pretty good idea of where they were going, so Lola left them to it. There was some cash in the till and some more in a safe behind the bar, and when the women took it, Lola pretended not to notice that either.

"There's an organization in town," she said before they left.

"The shelter?" the woman in the blanket said.

"It's a good place," Lola said. "They can help you get back on your feet."

"We're not on our feet now?"

"She thinks we're on our backs," one of the younger girls said. "With our legs spread."

"I didn't say that," Lola said.

"You didn't have to."

"Look, I don't care what you do. Go there. Go somewhere else. But that house you're going back to tonight? It's not going to be safe once word of this bloodbath gets out."

The women said nothing then. They knew she was right.

"Come to the station tomorrow," she said. "First thing. I'll need statements. If anyone's interested in the crisis center, you can tell me then, and I'll get something set up."

She watched them leave in the Escalade, pulling away carefully from the tarp that she was already dreading looking under. Another wolf howled, nearer than before, and she glanced at her watch. It was almost twenty minutes since she'd been sent out. If she didn't call dispatch soon, someone would come looking for her.

She reached into her pocket and felt the cold metal of the hard disk. She was breaking the law by removing it from the scene, but all she had to do was think of the missing evidence in the shed to know it was worth whatever consequences it might entail.

The place was dead silent, then another wolf howl, louder again, filling the air with its mournful, lonesome wail. She felt an involuntary shudder run down her spine. She was about to make for the cruiser and call dispatch when she heard a door creak loudly from behind the bar. Instinctively, she put her hand on her pistol.

She turned around and moved slowly toward the bar. When she got there, she saw that the creaking had come from a heavy steel door in the room behind. It hadn't been fully shut. At first, she thought it led to a walk-in cooler, but then she saw that there were steps behind it.

She remembered what had been said of cages. They were in the basement. She glanced over her shoulder, suddenly afraid someone might still be there, then swung open the heavy steel door and checked the lock. She did not want that door slamming shut behind her, but she could see it didn't have the kind of latch that would lock if it did.

She pulled a keg over to hold the door open, then, taking a deep breath, stepped through. She hit the light switch and began descending the stairs. The first thing to hit her was the stench. Fear welled up inside her, and she pushed forward. She wasn't sure what was driving her, but she knew she had to see what was at the bottom of those steps. *Cages*, the women had said. How was that possible? Her heart pounding, she continued putting one foot in front of the other. When she reached the bottom, there was another door, and again, she felt the impulse to go back, to get the hell out of there, to run as fast as she could. But something stopped her. Women had been disappearing from that town her entire life. For as long as she could remember. And now it was her job to do something about it. She needed to see what was beyond that door. She needed to look that evil in the eye.

She opened the door. There was another light switch, and she hesitated before touching it. Already, the overwhelming stench told her that whatever she was about to see wasn't anything pretty. She'd volunteered at an animal shelter when she was younger. The stench now was far worse than anything she'd ever smelled there.

She forced herself to keep her eyes open, flicked the switch, and saw it. Cages.

She stared at them for a second, almost unable to believe what she knew was the truth. Women had been kept in them. Women and girls.

What kind of world was it, she thought? What kind of God looked down on it if such things were allowed to happen?

She heard a sound then, something back upstairs in the bar, and suddenly felt very afraid. She turned and ran back the way she'd come, back up the steps, back through the heavy door. With her gun drawn, she went straight through the storeroom, through the bar, and out onto the porch.

There was no one there. There was no one anywhere. Everything was as she'd left it, the same vehicles, the same tarp, its edges flapping in the wind. The cruiser was there. And then she saw it, a lone wolf staring at her from the middle of the lot. It was about twenty yards from where she stood, exactly between her and the cruiser, as if it knew where she wanted to go.

“Go on,” she yelled. “Get.”

It didn’t move. It just looked back, and in its gaze, it was almost as if the wolf knew. It was as if what Lola had just seen, the wolf had seen too and knew it was evil.

Lola drew her gun and pointed it at the wolf. It stared back. She raised it into the air then and let off a single shot. The wolf continued staring at her, then turned and loped away back into the forest.

Lola didn’t waste any more time. She walked straight over to the tarp and pulled it off the pile it covered. Just as she’d known, the bodies of the thugs that ran the club were piled up beneath it like lumber being stored for winter. She grimaced, then walked over to her cruiser and picked up the radio.

“This is Quinn. I need backup out at the strip club on eight. There’s been some sort of shoot-out.”

22

Lola, back at her desk at the station, looked at the phone number Lance had given her.

Laurel Everlane, Washington DC.

Lance called her a colleague. She typed the number into a database query and ran it through the system. Nothing. She entered it into Google. Nothing there either—for the number or the name. Mysterious, she thought, though what could she expect? Everything Lance Spector had done since his arrival was mysterious.

She picked up the phone and dialed.

A female voice answered. "Operator."

Lola cleared her throat.

"Lance?" the voice said.

"No."

"Who is this?" the woman said in a tone that suggested she was used to getting her way. "This is a controlled line."

"A controlled line?"

"You've dialed the wrong number."

"Laurel Everlane?" Lola said.

The woman said nothing for a second, then "Your location's being locked. Black Swan, Washington. If you don't start—"

"Hold on, hold on," Lola said. "I'm a police officer in Black Swan. My name is Lola Quinn."

"How did you get this number?"

"Someone gave it to me."

"*Someone*?"

"A friend," Lola said, and, for the life of her, couldn't fathom what had possessed her to say that. Lance Spector was not her *friend*. He wasn't her *anything*. What was she thinking?

"*Friend*?" the woman said.

"Acquaintance."

"Listen," the woman said. "You better start making sense right—"

"I got it from Lance Spector."

"You—" she stopped mid-sentence. That got her attention, Lola thought. The woman said nothing for a moment, then, "He wouldn't give you this number."

"Well he *did* give me this number. He said you'd be able to help."

"Help? Help with what, exactly?"

"A hard drive."

"Okay," the woman said skeptically, speaking now as if Lola were a three-year-old. "And did he say *how* I was going to help with this hard drive?"

"I'm sorry," Lola said. "You know what? Why don't you just forget it? Forget I called."

"Wait," the woman said instantly, and Lola realized she had the upper hand. The woman wanted to know what this was about. She was curious. "If he said I could help—"

"No, no," Lola said. "I'll figure it out on my own. Have a real great night."

She hung up and sat there then, staring the phone. It took all of three seconds for the woman to call back. Lola smiled, took a sip of her coffee, took her sweet time picking up, then, in her chirpiest receptionist voice, said, "Black Swan Police."

"We got off on the wrong foot."

"I'm sorry," Lola said. "Who's calling?"

"Very funny."

"It's not, actually," Lola said. "It's not funny at all."

"I know," the woman said. "Black Swan, Washington. I'm reading it now. You have a disappearance. A woman who was identified as Raven Spector. Now she's been reclassified as a Jane Doe."

"Right," Lola said, pleased to finally be taken seriously. "There was a mix-up with the identification."

"A mix-up?"

Lola wondered how the woman had managed

to find out so much so quickly. She wondered what else she could do. "Someone's fucking with us," she said.

"Someone misidentified your Jane Doe on purpose?"

"I think so," Lola said, then, "how did you access our file so quickly?"

"I'm not at liberty to say."

"Right, but I suppose you want me to trust you with every single little—"

"I'm CIA," the woman blurted.

"CIA?"

The woman cleared her throat. "And I probably shouldn't be talking to someone like you."

"But you are."

"If Lance told you to call, well...."

"Well," Lola echoed, picking up the hard drive on her desk. "All right. I've got a hard drive here. Lance said you'd be able to find out what's on it."

"I think that's something we could handle. Are you sitting at a computer?"

Lola glanced out the window. A cruiser was pulling up, its lights flashing. It was Belcher's car. "Hang on a second," she said. "Someone's coming. I don't want them to see me doing this."

Belcher barged in, rushing past Lola's desk. He looked ridiculous, with a big bandage covering his nose and half his face.

"Aren't you supposed to be off?" Lola said.

"Haven't you heard?" Belcher gasped, breathless from his haste. "Multiple homicides up by the strip club. Looks like some wack job went on a shooting spree."

"I was already up there," Lola said. "It was awful."

Belcher grabbed something from his office, then barged back out to his car and sped off. Lola watched him go, then picked up the phone. "Okay," she said. "Still there?"

"Still here," Laurel said. "I'm going to send you a link. It will give me control of your computer and access to the hard drive once we have it connected. Do you know your IP address?"

Lola quickly Googled how to check her own IP address—she'd be damned if she was going to give this woman the pleasure of explaining it to her—then followed her instructions for connecting the hard drive to her machine. Once it was done, Laurel downloaded the drive's contents. "What am I looking for?" she said.

"Emails, apparently. The drive came from a strip club. The owner was involved in trafficking the women."

"On it," Laurel said. "I'll call you back in a few."

Lola put down the phone and went over to the window. The lot was empty and she went outside for some air. The night was as still as any she'd ever seen. The sky was so clear she felt as if she could almost reach up and touch the moon. Lance had given her a cell number before leaving the brothel, and she tried calling it now. It went straight to voicemail. He wouldn't get signal where he was going anyway.

She went back inside, back to her computer, and logged in to the local property registry. She wanted to find out who owned the Breckenridge, but when she looked it up, it just gave her a numbered corporation based out of Delaware. She took down the number, then went to the federal companies registry and typed it in there. She wasn't expecting much of an answer, and sure enough, the owner of the Delaware company was another nameless, faceless entity, this time registered in Nevis. A quick Google search told her the place was an island nation in the Caribbean, known for its beaches and sugar plantations, and also its super-lax tax laws. She took down the details of the Nevis company and waited for Laurel to call her back.

She didn't have long to wait and was just refilling her coffee when the phone on her desk started to ring.

"Laurel?" she said.

"Yes. I got what you wanted. All the emails. Full access."

"Can you track down the owner of an overseas company?"

"Sure," Laurel said. "What's the company."

"It's the owner of a property out here. The one that Lance has gone to investigate."

"Shouldn't be a problem," Laurel said. "We can hack any foreign corporate database."

"Okay, it's a numbered corporation based in Nevis."

"Nevis?"

"Yes, it's an island," Lola said, looking at her computer screen. "Saint Kitts and Nevis. Two islands, I guess."

"That's a problem," Laurel said.

"Why?"

"It's a tax haven. One of the worst. I don't think I'm going to be able to tell you who owns that property."

"But you said you could hack any foreign database."

"Oh, I can hack it," Laurel said, "but the unique thing about the legal system in Nevis, and the reason global crooks like it so much, is that it allows you to register a corporation without telling anyone who you are."

"What does that mean?"

"It means Nevis doesn't keep track of the owners of the corporations registered there."

"How does that make sense?"

"It doesn't, unless you're trying to hide your tracks."

"You mean like—"

"Like tax evasion, sanctions busting, drug cartels—"

"And that's allowed?"

"It is in Nevis."

"They don't know who owns a company they registered?"

"They don't know, they don't want to know."

"But how does that even work? I mean, practically?"

"If you want a corporation in Nevis, you register, you pay the fee, but you don't ever tell them who you are. When you need to, you have documents that prove you're the owner of the company, but the registrar in Nevis doesn't keep any record of who *you* are. Nor do they keep track of the assets owned by the corporation."

"So it's completely anonymous?"

"Completely."

"And that corporation is allowed to hold property here in Washington?"

"In Washington State, in New York State, in California, in any state in the union. In any country, in fact."

"But we don't allow anonymous ownership of real estate here?"

"That's true," Laurel said, "but the global legal order tolerates this. There's nothing we can do about it."

"So it's a dead end?"

"Look, I'll hack the Nevis database for you, but I can virtually guarantee there'll be no owner listed. It's the whole point."

Lola sighed. "That leaves the emails then. The emails and whatever Lance finds while he's out at the property."

"The emails are a lot," Laurel said. "I'm sending the reorganized folders to you now. The owner of the account was definitely up to something nasty. Trafficking women, definitely. *Selling* them, by the looks of it."

"And can you tell who he was selling them to?"

"Afraid not. It's another dead end. A completely anonymous email service. Even the Pentagon couldn't crack the type of encryption it's based on."

"So we're stuck?"

"Not exactly," Laurel said. "There's one thing I can do."

"What's that?"

"I can send a message back."

"From the pimp?"

"From the pimp to whoever he's been talking to on the other end. Whoever's buying these women from him."

"But the pimp's dead."

"Does the person he was communicating with know that?"

Lola thought. She wouldn't be able to keep the shootings out of the news for long. Too many people already knew what had happened. But the identities of the victims, that she could probably swing with the help of the chief. "We'll have to be fast," she said.

"What do you want me to say?"

"In the message? Tell them there's a problem. An emergency. Tell them you need to meet face to face."

23

Lance read Lola's directions by the glow of the dashboard light. He was driving the BMW X5 the goons had left at the brothel and could smell the piss in the backseat. *Animals*, he thought, turning from the highway onto an unpaved logging road. The death he'd given them was more than they'd deserved. He should have made them suffer.

The road wound its way upward into the mountains and got progressively more difficult to follow. The fact that it was night didn't help any. If it wasn't for the map Lola had given him, he'd surely have taken a wrong turn somewhere along the way. At a few particularly steep points, the vehicle skidded on the wet ground, and he thought he'd have to continue on foot, but eventually, he managed to keep going.

It was after midnight when he finally spotted

the property, *The Breckenridge,* as Lola had called it. It truly did look like something out of a storybook and had absolutely no business being up there at the end of a remote logging road in Washington. How it had been built and by whom, he couldn't imagine, though it was certainly old.

As more of the property came into view, he saw that there was an old, disused railway track running behind the lodge. There were a few scattered lights too, some along the driveway on the approach, others spread around the grounds or mounted on the side of the lodge itself. Presumably they were powered by a generator but the place was eerily quiet.

The lodge, what he could make of it, was grand, two stories in height with a broad wrap-around porch on both levels. He counted six doors opening onto the porch on the second floor, and that was just on the side he could see. The ground floor was similar, and he estimated the building to be about the size of a twenty-room inn.

There was a clearing off to one side, the land flat and laid with grass. It was the only lawned area on the property, and if he had to guess, he'd have said it was the helipad. Presumably, it was how the building's occupants came and left. They must have flown in the supplies they needed, too, given the state of the road he'd just come up. He couldn't imagine too many local businesses driving up that way with groceries and the like. Beyond the helipad was a small utility building and what looked to be a well. There were solar panels on the roof of the utility building, a wind turbine, and probably the generator inside.

The whole place looked to be about as self-contained a compound as you could get. It also looked empty. There were no vehicles outside, no helicopter. Inside the building, there were no lights on. Lance had pulled up about a hundred yards from the entrance, and judging from the lack of response, he didn't think there were any guards present either.

The security system was something else, however. He could already see some of the cameras, and he had no doubt there were sensors, too. If he hadn't triggered them already, he would soon. He got back into the car and drove as far as a tree that had an industrial-grade camera mounted to it. He couldn't see where it was getting its power, but on the side of the tree was a sensor that certainly wasn't civilian. It could detect motion, heat, vibrations, the works. Definitely not the kind of thing you could pick up at the local hardware store. When he found the power lines, he followed them through the woods to a fast-flowing brook. There was a turbine there, supplying power, and for comms, they didn't connect to a phone line but to a dedicated, military-grade satellite uplink. It was not the type of setup used to contact a call center or the local police station. This was heavy-duty security. Lance half-expected to see a phalanx of attack helicopters coming through the sky. He listened. Other than the wind, there was nothing.

Whoever owned this building, he thought, whoever had set up the security system, was connected. They had access to hardware that was not easy to access. They might even have had a security clearance, he thought. It was even possible the taxpayer had paid for it.

Lance walked up to the front door of the lodge, tripping multiple sensors and cameras as he did. It didn't worry him. No one would use that kind of security to protect a property. A system like that was a warning system. It was for when the lodge was occupied, not when it was empty.

The door was a solid oak monstrosity that looked like it had been taken from a medieval German church, and he gave it a hard kick with the heel of his boot. It took a few more tries before the frame split, then he pushed it open with a loud creak. He had the flashlight with him and he turned it on and stood in the doorway listening. Everything had been so quiet until he'd kicked open the door, and he waited now to see if the noise had roused any sleeping monsters. Everything was eerily silent as if even the birds knew to stay away from the place.

He inhaled the musty air, thick with the smell of wood polish and mahogany paneling. Whoever had done the decorating certainly had a specific style in mind. He scanned the entrance hall, the beam of the flashlight extending out from him like a physical object, and saw thirty-foot walls hung with old hunting trophies. The preserved animals —stags, bears, wolves—stared back at him accusingly as if the taxidermist had intended them to ward off trespassers. A gun rack held old rifles and above it was a shield bearing a coat of arms—two minotaurs holding lances pointed at a dead snake. Between the minotaurs was a black inverted crucifix. Beneath the cross was a single letter 'A' in a Caslon serif font.

To his left, a door led to a library where shelves were laden with old leather-bound tomes. There was a brass bar cart next to a pool table, and on the cart were crystal snifters and bottles of fine brandy and cognac. One of the bottles was a Hennessy Ellipse, worth more than a small-sized family car. The whole place reminded him of a Bavarian hunting lodge.

To his right was a dining hall with a massive stone fireplace on one end, still full of ash. Lance examined the ash. It seemed recent, though not recent enough to be still warm. He tried the beer taps at the bar. They worked, though the beer was stale and foamy. It came out like soapy water. There was a large leather chair in front of the hearth, and the place hadn't been cleaned since it was last used. Lance could tell by the snifter resting on one of the arms, which still smelled of brandy, perhaps even the Hennessy, and an ashtray with cigar butts stubbed out in it. He recognized the yellow paper cigar bands as Cohiba.

He looked around and wondered who served the occupant, who cleaned up his mess and brought him ice while he sipped his cognac and smoked his Cohibas? Who cooked his meals? Did he fly someone in with him, or did he come alone? Did he do his own housekeeping, his own laundry? If someone came with him, did they know what happened there? Because it sure as shit wasn't deer hunting.

Lance continued moving through the lodge, aware that he was tripping motion detectors and heat and sound sensors in virtually every room he entered. There were cameras, too, and they turned to follow him as he moved, staring after him like curious onlookers. No one would come, he thought, and if they did, well, so much the better. They would lead him to whoever he was looking for.

He took his time going through the lodge, starting methodically on the ground floor, going room to room, turning on and off lights as he went. The place looked like it had been set up as a sort of frat house—with bars and ashtrays, leather chairs by fires, pool and table tennis tables, dart boards, big screen TVs—but it didn't look like any of it, other than the one chair by the hearth, had been used any time lately. There was a full commercial kitchen, as well as a formal dining room with an enormous oak table over twenty feet in length. It could easily seat forty or more people at once. But again, even the freezers in the kitchen were empty, and many of the appliances, including the ovens, didn't look like they'd ever been used. They weren't new by any means, they'd been there for years, but they still had the manufacturer's stickers on the doors. The microwaves had warranty paperwork inside them in little plastic sleeves.

Through the kitchen was a small staff area, again unused apart from a single place setting on a little table in front of the sink. The setting consisted of a porcelain dinner plate and silver tableware, but on the plate was a paper bag from a fast food restaurant. Someone had eaten takeout there, a burger and fries, using ketchup and salt from paper packets and, presumably, their hands because the silverware hadn't been used either. There was a half-empty wine bottle, something expensive, and a used wine glass, and above the wine bottle, some minuscule fruit flies had spawned and buzzed around silently.

Lance searched for any sign of a basement—stairs, or a trapdoor leading to a lower level—but there was none. He went outside and confirmed that the building was perched on solid rock. There would be no basement in that.

Back inside, he climbed the stairs to the second floor and began going through the bedrooms. He counted twenty-six of them, all anonymous-looking, nothing that would have been out of place in a German country inn with their double beds, dated lampshades, and oversoft mattresses. All the rooms but one were pristine. They didn't look like they'd been slept in for years. Only in the final room was a bed unmade. There was also another wine bottle there, empty, and a glass, as well as an ashtray and more Cohiba butts.

Lance spent time in the room. He sat on the bed. He looked at the rustic furniture, the bedding. Everything was rich but dated. The blanket was expensive but had faded where the light caught it near the window. It would have taken time for that to happen—years, probably. There was a bathroom attached to the room—functional, with an old porcelain sink and bathtub. Lance checked the water. It took a while but eventually ran hot. There was a used towel on the floor and a hand towel next to the sink that had also been used. In the garbage can was more evidence of use—an empty floss container, some cotton swabs. In the bath was a small piece of soap. Embedded in it was what looked like a black pubic hair.

The place, if it were a hotel, would have struggled to maintain a four-star rating.

He left the room and sat down on the bench at the end of the hall, looking back down the long corridor toward the stairs.

That was it. He'd seen the whole place. He'd found no hidden lair, no secret torture chamber. If the woman had been murdered there, even if she'd been taken there, he saw no evidence of it. The mutilation he'd seen at the morgue, that sort of depravity, that level of violence, it left a mess. There was no mess here.

But the place was creepy, no doubt about that, and Lance had no doubt terrible things had occurred there. He just hadn't found proof.

It was possible someone had cleaned up the mess of a murder, but then, why hadn't they cleaned up the food? The McDonald's bag downstairs in the kitchen? The ashtrays and empty wine glasses? Why not make the bed and take out the trash from the bathroom?

It didn't feel right.

He was about to go back down the stairs and begin the search all over again when he noticed something beneath the bench he was sitting on. There was a handle, a little metal lever, built into the underside of the seat. He pulled it and heard the clack of a latch, followed by a creaking sound. He turned to see a false door in the wall behind him. He tried to move the bench, but it was fixed in position, so he stepped over it and through the door. It led to some wooden steps, and he climbed them up to a small attic area directly between the gables. It was dark, and he felt along the wall for a light switch, but there was none, so he scanned the interior with his flashlight.

The peaked roof rose up above him, its beams and timber exposed like in an old barn. The walls were the same solid logs as the rest of the building. There didn't seem to be any electrical lighting, but there were torches in a metal bracket next to the door. They smelled of paraffin wax. There was a box of matches next to them, and Lance picked up a torch and struck a match. The torch took flame in a quick burst, filling the space with light and immediately illuminating a raised dais in the middle of the attic.

Before his eyes even focused on it, he knew what it was, and he resisted going straight to it. He resisted even the urge to look at it, looking instead at the walls, where enormous oil portraits hung in intricate gilded frames. He counted forty-four paintings in total, each one at least three feet by eight in size. All were of women. All young. Many were Native American. Were they the victims, Lance wondered. Had someone been keeping a record of sorts with these portraits? If so, when? It was impossible to date them by the women's dress —all were nude. Were they, Lance wondered, a macabre analog to the taxidermy hunting trophies on the ground floor? Had someone graduated from hunting game to hunting women?

Swallowing, he turned to the altar. It was made of stone and wood, a raised platform about the size and height of a professional billiards table. Iron rings were fixed to the corners, and a chain with a wrist or ankle cuff was connected to each ring.

There were feathers everywhere. Feathers and blood.

The image of the woman he'd seen in the morgue, naked, afraid, chained to the altar, seared into his mind. The agony, the raw flesh, the disfigurement, and the torture. He could see it all.

This was where it had been done.

This was where the woman had been murdered. There was no doubt in his mind.

And not just her, but many women over many years.

He could sense it. This was a place of evil and had been for a very long time.

24

Laurel reviewed the final text of the message drafted by Lola, double-checked the headers and flags, and hit send. It was a long shot, but it was the best chance they had. She sent an email to Lola telling her it was done, then shut down her computer.

It had been a long day.

She looked out over the sixth-floor office and couldn't help but be overwhelmed with a feeling of melancholy. The desks were empty, the terminals shut down, and even the chairs had been gathered up and placed in a big pile by the service elevator. It was the end of an era. The portrait of Roth, put up when he was appointed director, had been removed by the custodial staff earlier in the day. They were already preparing for his, as yet unnamed, successor. The world stopped for no man, even the director of the CIA. Laurel knew that, but it still all felt very perfunctory, very *unceremonious*. They could at least have waited until after the funeral, she thought, looking at the spot on the wall where the portrait had been.

She walked over to her coat and put it on. Time for her to go home to her cold, empty apartment. She gazed out the window and thought about the first time Roth had shown the view to her. The CIA campus, the leafy bank of the Potomac, the white and red lights of the traffic flowing along the parkway. More than anywhere else, this had been his home. This had been where he'd planted his roots and made his mark on the world. Even after he made director, he'd never really left the Special Operations Group. Until now.

And without him, it just wasn't quite right. For the first time since joining the CIA, Laurel felt... *untethered*. She felt alone.

She pushed the button for the elevator and while waiting for it, the phone on her desk started to ring. In the empty room, it rang out in the silence like a fire alarm. She looked at her watch. It was very late. Unless it was Lola Quinn calling back, she couldn't imagine who it would be.

Nevertheless, she hurried over and picked up. "Everlane."

"Laurel," a whiny, slightly nasal voice said. "It's Jared."

"Jared?"

"Cutler. Have I caught you at a bad time?"

Jared Cutler was the president's National Security Advisor. He wasn't Laurel's first choice for a late-night phone call just as she was about to clock off, but there it was. "I was just heading out, actually."

"Right," Cutler said. "It's late. I wasn't sure you'd be there."

"Yes," she said, certain that he would have rustled up her cell number in any case. She got the sense that he was stalling for some reason and said, "In any case, you caught me now."

"I did...."

"*And*?"

"Well, it's not the best news I've been tasked with delivering."

"When is it ever?"

"Right. Well...."

"Don't hold back, Jared. I promise it won't be the hardest conversation I've had today."

"No," he said. "I don't suppose it will."

She waited for him, but he was still hesitating. *Imbecile* was the word she would have used if she'd been asked to describe him. "Is it about Roth?" she said. "Have they recovered a body?"

"It's not about Roth," Cutler said. "Not directly, at least, though I do recall how close you two were. You have my condolences."

It was strange to be receiving condolences over Roth, she thought. What was she to him? But then, who else was there to give condolences to? Not a wife. Not a family. It was a preview of what her own future might look like, she thought. "He'll be missed," she said. "He was...."

"He was, yes—"

"A good man."

"Quite," Cutler said, then continued. "Now, I'm aware the timing might be off for this, but I do need to inform you that there are going to be some changes."

"No kidding," she said, eyeing the piled-up chairs by the elevator.

"Yes, and you're aware the president wasn't entirely happy with some of the most recent decisions Roth made?"

"I'm aware."

"That business in Russia. It was very... *touch and go.*"

"That's one way of putting it."

"It could have sparked war."

She said nothing to that. By some counts, Russia and the US were already at war, they just weren't admitting it, but she did take his point. What Roth had done came very close to disaster.

"Anyway, the incoming director has made it clear—"

"The incoming director?"

"Yes."

"Who is it?"

"I'm not at liberty to say, Laurel, but suffice to say the Special Operations Group is not a program that's going to continue enjoying support."

"I see."

"Yes, well...."

"You're pulling the plug on us?"

"We're winding you down, yes. It's pretty much just you and the Russian woman at this point anyway, isn't it?"

"Tatyana Aleksandrova."

"Right. You'll be reassigned. Together if you wish."

"Okay."

"We'll be bringing you back into gen pop, so to speak. Bringing you in from the cold."

"We haven't been cold up here," Laurel said, though she wasn't sure what the point of arguing was. This was a decision that had been made at the highest level. It wasn't something that was up for debate now, with her. Roth had put his weight behind a Kremlin coup. Worse, he'd put his weight behind a *failed* Kremlin coup. It was probably the closest Moscow and Washington had come to nuclear war since the Cuban Missile Crisis. You didn't come back from that.

"The decision's been made, and, well...."

"Let me ask you one question," Laurel said. "Before you go."

"Okay," Cutler said.

"Are you the new director?"

There was a moment's silence before he said, "I really can't give you any information right now. Suffice to say, an announcement will be made in due course."

"And Tatyana and I—"

"You can take the rest of the week off while we figure things out."

"Figure things out?"

"Get you reassigned, I mean."

"Are our clearances being revoked?"

"What? No. Of course not."

"Not *yet*."

"Look, if you want to be blunt, Laurel—"

"Sorry," she said, checking herself. What was she thinking? She wasn't doing herself or Tatyana any favors picking a fight now. Not with the crosshairs on their backs. Roth had been their patron. He'd been their protector. And now, he was gone.

"It's been a tough week," Cutler said. "Let's just take some time to let the dust settle."

"All right," she said, knowing in her heart that it was already too late. She and Tatyana were dead in the water. They were going to be axed. Their necks were on the block. "Well, thank you for the call," she said. "I do appreciate it."

And he was gone.

25

Tatyana was sitting at the end of the bar at the Old Ebbitt Grill, out of sight from the main dining room, when she received Laurel's message asking where she was.

Great, she thought. If she'd wanted to agonize over every detail of the future with Laurel, she'd have gone in to the office. Instead, she'd purposefully avoided the place and come here, where she had a top-shelf vodka soda in front of her and a bartender who could have modeled underwear for Calvin Klein.

The bartender came over. "How's the drink?"

"Oh," Tatyana said, looking up from her phone. If she was going to have any chance tonight, she would have to act quick. Laurel was already in a cab at Dupont Circle. She'd be there in a matter of minutes. "Could use some lime," she said.

The bartender smiled, cut a lime wedge, then

put it into her glass, making sure to let his fingers get wet in her drink.

Tatyana arched an eyebrow. He was bold, she'd give him that much. He was also well over six foot and well over two hundred pounds of pure muscle. She pictured all the things he could do to her as she raised the glass to her lips.

"Better?" he said.

"A little," she said, "though it could definitely do with something else."

"Something else like what?"

She shrugged. "Hard to put my finger on it. Maybe another garnish?"

"A garnish," he said. "Sure. That's one word for it."

She smirked shamelessly.

"I think I have one in the storeroom," he said. "We could go back and take a look together."

She made a face like she was trying to make up her mind, which is exactly what she was doing when Laurel arrived and killed the vibe with a single word.

"Hey," she said, hopping onto a stool and putting a decidedly unfashionable purse up onto the bar, exactly where it didn't belong. "This place is starting to empty," she said to Tatyana. To the bartender, she said, "Have you made last call?"

The bartender glanced at Tatyana, and Laurel must have picked up on the energy between them because she said, "Oh! Oh my God. I'm sorry. Did I just interrupt something?"

“We may never find out,” Tatyana said dryly, taking another sip of her drink.

“You’re unbelievable,” Laurel said, hitting her on the arm. “Roth’s body isn’t even cold.”

“We all process grief in different ways,” Tatyana said with a shrug. “Which reminds me. Can I borrow some black gloves for the funeral? Mine never made it from Russia.”

“I don’t know what kind of wardrobe you think I have,” Laurel said, “but I assure you, there are no black gloves in it.” Then, to the bartender, she said, “Can I have whatever she’s having, if that’s not too much trouble.”

“And I’ll have another,” Tatyana said, finishing her glass. “We’re in mourning.”

“You don’t look like you’re in mourning,” the bartender said.

“And what would mourning look like?” Laurel said.

The bartender eyed her cautiously, then, gauging her mood, backed off to get the drinks.

“Nice,” Tatyana said. “Real helpful.”

“I wasn’t trying to be helpful.”

“*Really*?”

The bartender was back, and, this time, Tatyana put her hand on Laurel’s leg to keep her from sabotaging anything. It worked because, for once, she held her tongue.

“Anything else, ladies?” the bartender said.

“No,” Laurel said curtly.

"Yes," Tatyana said. "What about some food? Is the kitchen still open?"

"It's open for you."

"*Nice,*" Laurel said sarcastically.

"Yes, nice," Tatyana said. "I have an appetite."

"I think he can see that," Laurel said.

Tatyana squeezed her leg just above the knee, hard enough to hurt. She said, "Anything you'd recommend?"

"Have you tried our oysters?"

"Yes," Tatyana said, "of course, but I was thinking of something more…."

"*Meaty*?" Laurel said, rolling her eyes.

"Oh, you've got to try the oysters," the bartender said. "Today's feature is called *Belle du Jour.*"

"*Belle du Jour*?" Laurel repeated. "How appropriate."

"From Boutouche Bay, New Brunswick," the bartender said, ignoring Laurel now. "Very subtle. Very sweet."

Laurel rolled her eyes again and Tatyana decided it was time to seal the deal, if only to rub it in Laurel's face. "I do love oysters," she said. "The way they slide down my throat."

Laurel almost spat out her drink. "Excuse me," she said, covering her mouth with a napkin and getting down from her seat. She hurried toward the washroom, and Tatyana caught the bartender's eye and held it. He had a pen in his breast pocket, and she reached over and took it from him, writing her number on a napkin. "Call me after your shift," she said.

"I won't be out of here until after two," he said.

"That's fine. I'll be up."

He looked like he was going to say something else, but Laurel was returning, so he cut a hasty retreat.

"What are you looking so smug about?" Laurel said, taking her seat.

"Why don't you quit pretending to be a prude and tell me what you're in such a bad mood about? What was so urgent it wouldn't wait until tomorrow?"

"They're wrapping us up."

"The Group?"

"Yes. Cutler told me an hour ago."

"They're not making *him* director?"

"He didn't confirm or deny."

"That's just what we need. A strident China, a panicked Kremlin, and Jared Cutler at the head of the Agency. We might as well fold up the flag now and call it quits."

"Well, they're not asking our opinion, so there's not a lot we can do about it."

"What are they going to do with us?"

"He said we'd be reassigned."

"*Reassigned*?" Tatyana said. "There's a euphemism if ever I heard one."

Laurel nodded. "I know," she said quietly.

"Have you heard from Lance?" Tatyana said.

Laurel's entire demeanor changed at the

mention of Lance. It was almost as if Tatyana had brought up an old lover. It was always that way with Laurel. "I've spoken to him," she said stiffly.

"About this?"

She shrugged. "I don't think he's going to be much help. I don't think he's even planning on coming back for the funeral."

"You're kidding."

"He's gotten himself mixed up in another thing."

"What other thing?"

"What is it always with him?"

"A rescue of some kind?"

"Exactly."

"A pretty girl? A damsel in distress?"

Laurel nodded.

"He never could say no to a pretty girl who needed his help."

"Worked out okay for you," Laurel said.

Tatyana couldn't help but notice a sharpness to the words that wouldn't ordinarily have been there. "Yes, well," she said. "We all had our own path to getting here, didn't we, Laurel?"

"Anyway," Laurel added, "this case looked like it had a possible connection to his sister."

"His sister?"

"She disappeared when he was a kid. She and the mother."

Tatyana nodded. She was about to say more when the waiter came over with her oysters. They were laid out perfectly on a tray of crushed ice, with horseradish and mignonette in little dishes on the side.

"Lemon juice?" the waiter said, holding a wedge in his fingers that he seemed intent on squeezing for her.

"I'll leave you two to it," Laurel said, finishing her drink. She was gone before Tatyana could stop her.

26

When Lola finally got home for the night, she opened a can of food for her tabby, Hieronymus, then put a frozen Weight Watchers Thai chicken curry into the microwave for herself. She sat at the counter then and dozed off before the ding roused her back to her senses. She brought the plastic container—she was too tired for a plate—into the living room and turned on the TV. A rerun of *Friends* was playing, and she sat down on the sofa and fell asleep instantly.

When she woke up, she saw that Hieronymus had taken it upon himself to finish the chicken for her. *Friends* was still playing on the TV, and her phone was ringing.

"Hello?"

"It's me."

"I'm sorry, who?"

"Spector."

"Of course," she said, rubbing the sleep from her eyes. "Right."

"Did I wake you?"

"What? No."

"It's two in the morning."

"I was just... two, is it?"

"Listen, I'm calling from the pay phone at the gas station. I wanted to ask if the local police are looking for me."

"Because of what happened at the strip club? No. The chief made sure you weren't in the report. I wouldn't go by there, though. It's crawling with investigators."

"I was thinking I should probably get out of town. It's only a matter of time before I'm connected to it."

"You could come here," Lola said, though she wasn't sure what had inspired her to say it.

"Do you have a garage?"

"Yes," she said. "Let me give you the address."

She gave him the address and hung up, then grabbed the microwave meal and brought it back to the kitchen, where she threw it in the sink. She went to the bathroom and gave herself a quick look-over. She'd fallen asleep in her makeup, and the result was frightful. Her hair was sticking up at the back of her head and she was trying to pat it down with water when she heard the car in her driveway.

She ran through to the garage and opened it, then shut it behind Lance's vehicle.

"Hi," she said when he stepped out, feeling like a high schooler greeting a date.

"Hi," he said. "Sorry to come by so late."

"It's no problem," she said too quickly.

"Do you know if the vehicle's been reported stolen?"

"Why don't you come inside?" she said, hugging herself. The garage was as cold as an icebox.

He followed her to the kitchen and she put on a pot of coffee. Lance sat at the table and the cat jumped instantly to his lap.

"Hieronymus!"

"It's all right," Lance said, patting the cat before it jumped back to the floor.

"Sorry about that." She finished making the coffee and poured two cups, feeling his eyes on her while she worked. "You take it black, right?"

He nodded and took one of the cups from her. "Thanks."

"Of course."

She sat across from him, and the two cradled the cups in their hands. He said nothing and she cast her mind for something she could say to get rid of the silence. "No one's looking for you," she said. "Not here in Black Swan, in any case. You weren't mentioned in any of the reports from the shoot-out. The car you're driving hasn't been reported missing and won't be any time soon. Also, none of the bodies has been identified officially."

"Thanks for that," Lance said, taking a sip of the coffee.

"No need to ride off into the night," she added and again bit her tongue. What had gotten into her?

He looked at her closely, and she began playing with her hair.

"You live here alone?" he said.

"Oh," she said. "Yeah." That embarrassed her as well. "Unless you count Hieronymus."

"He counts," Lance said, smiling at the cat rubbing against his leg.

Lola took a sip of coffee and mentally chided herself for feeling so girlish. Something about him being here, in her home, at this time of night, it put her off balance. "Well," she said, "I take it you're not here on a purely social visit. What did you find up at that lodge?"

Lance's expression grew grave. He shook his head and said, "It wasn't pretty."

"I take it I should get a team up there?"

"Yeah. The place you're looking for is in the attic. There's a hidden passageway at the end of the second-floor corridor. I left it open."

"That's where the murders happened?"

"That's where they happened."

"You're sure of that?"

"You will be, too, when you see the place. An altar for ritual sacrifices. Untold evil. There are pictures on the walls, paintings of women."

"Paintings?"

He nodded. "I think you'll find many of your victims among those portraits."

Lola swallowed. The thought of it was making her emotional. To finally know what had happened, what had been happening. So many women. So many years. It was overwhelming. "The chief," she said, her voice cracking, "he won't be able to believe it. He won't believe it's over."

"It's not over until we have the person at the top."

"Which might be a problem," Lola said. "Getting a warrant, tying this to one man, I don't know how we'll do it."

"I take it the property register was a bust."

She nodded. "Your friend in Washington was able to enlighten me on some vagaries of the legal system." As she said the words, she found herself wondering if Laurel was more than just a colleague to Lance. She'd certainly acted like she was.

"She couldn't find the owner?"

Lola shook her head. "I'm afraid not. It's held in the name of a numbered company."

"Even numbered companies have owners."

"Have you heard of the jurisdiction of Nevis and Saint Kitts?"

Lance nodded. "I have," he said.

"Then you know their government allows for corporations without listing the owners."

"That's what Laurel said?"

"Yes," Lola said, keeping her face blank at the mention of the other woman.

"Was she able to find out where the emails were going?"

"Not exactly," Lola said, "but we were able to send one back. We said we needed a meeting. A face-to-face."

"And they bought it?" Lance said, suddenly energized.

"It could be a trap," Lola said.

"Sure," Lance said, but she got the strong impression that wasn't going to be a factor in what happened next. She pulled a piece of paper from her pocket and he was so eager to have it that, despite herself, she couldn't help smiling at him.

She handed it to him, and their fingers touched.

> Nisqually Cut Off. 9 am. Come alone and unarmed.

27

Lance sighed as he pulled onto the Interstate, weaving between the cars as he gained speed. He'd snatched a few hours of sleep on Lola's couch and let himself out before dawn, headed for the meet at the Nisqually Cut Off. His mind kept going back to Lola, he knew she would have let him into her bed, but he'd resisted the temptation. She deserved better than a one-night stand with the likes of him.

To give himself something else to think about, he began going over the details of the case. The impression he'd gotten when he first arrived in Black Swan was that the murders were the work of some hidden group. Some all-powerful, all-seeing sect of some kind. But after what he'd seen at the lodge, he was beginning to think that this evil, the murder and mutilation, was ultimately the work of a single man. Certainly, he had help. It seemed that he could afford all the help in the world, stooges and thugs, fixers and pilots, but only one man had stayed at that lodge. Only one man had slept in that bedroom. Only one man had eaten at that table.

The woman, still unidentified, had left the trailer park on foot and headed for the grocery store. Someone from the brothel, either the pimp himself or one of his heavies, had picked her up off the highway. That had probably been a random sighting. Wrong place, wrong time. Simple as that. Maybe there'd been a struggle. Maybe they'd offered her a ride. In any case, they succeeded in getting her into the car.

From there, things went south for the woman fast. She was brought to the brothel, kept out of sight, and smuggled down to the basement, where she'd ended up in one of those horrible cages. Had she been kept in the dark there, or had someone left on a light for her? Had they hurt her while she was in the cage? Had they molested her? Lance shook his head. He'd killed every man involved in that place. He would never know what had happened there, and whatever it was, it was over. He couldn't say justice had been done, there was no justice in a thing like this, but the score had been settled. There was no one left to kill.

What he did know was that they'd sold her like a piece of meat, like a piece of livestock, to whoever owned that hunting lodge.

And that was when things moved quickly. The buyer got word there was a woman and moved quickly. There'd been an offer and acceptance. A simple email exchange. The buyer and the pimp knew each other. They'd done business together in the past. There'd been no haggling, no bargaining, the asking price was paid, and the girl had been delivered, either by the pimp himself or one of his goons. According to the pimp, the deliveries were made at the buyer's instruction. He sent coordinates, and the women were left at the coordinates, in the forest, at night, naked, bound, gagged, and terrified.

But as terrifying as all that was, worse was yet to follow. Because the real evil happened at the lodge. The buyer or his agent came and picked up the merchandise, brought her up to the Breckenridge, and chained her to the altar, ready for the final act of sacrilege.

It was to find out who'd done that final work that Lance was driving past Olympia now. The cut off wasn't far and he'd be there early. He wanted to get there first. Whoever arrived first would have the upper hand.

He had with him in the car the rifle and scope, the hunting knife, and two handguns he'd taken from dead bodies at the brothel.

He'd be meeting a handler, he imagined. Some sort of gopher who ran errands, moved money around, made deliveries. Someone who got his hands dirty. Whoever he was meeting had maybe even seen the woman, picked her up in the woods, and brought her back to the Breckenridge, but he wasn't the one who'd done the deed. If there were helicopters and private planes and secret offshore companies, then this meeting wasn't with the head honcho.

Which meant Lance couldn't kill him outright.

He needed to talk to him.

He needed to find out who'd sent him.

The Nisqually Cut Off led straight into a wildlife refuge, and Lance could see why it had been chosen as the meeting place. There must have been a public entrance to the park somewhere, but this wasn't it. This road was unused. Weeds grew through the asphalt. He followed it for a half mile into the forest and saw the flattened grass where a vehicle had gone off the road.

So he wasn't first.

Someone was laying a trap.

Someone who didn't know jack shit about hiding his tracks.

Lance hadn't imagined that the email Lola and Laurel sent would have tricked anyone. And it hadn't.

But it didn't matter. A trap was still a lead. He'd walk into it and see who showed their face.

Another half-mile and the road ended at a small lot, barely big enough for a car to turn around in. There was also a trail for bikes or hikers with a barrier to stop cars from entering.

There were no street lights. At night, the place would have been pitch black.

Lance looked at his watch. It was just before

seven in the morning, two hours early for the meet, but not early enough.

He shut off the engine and took the handgun that was in his waistband and shoved it into his boot. An ankle holster would have been nice but he didn't have one. The other handgun and the knife were in the carryall in the trunk, along with the rifle.

He got out of the vehicle, walked around to the back, and popped the trunk. Then he slung the rifle over his shoulder and took the second handgun and the hunting knife from the carryall. He slid them conspicuously into his waistband, making sure that whoever was watching would see him do it. Then he made as if he was going to hike up the trail. He hadn't taken five steps toward it when a gunshot rang out in the stillness and hit the ground by his feet.

Lance swung wildly in the direction of the sound, putting on a show for the shooter.

"Next shot's in your chest, tough guy," a voice called out. "Drop the rifle."

"Shit," Lance said.

"Do it!"

Lance let the rifle fall from his shoulder.

"And the gun in your pants, fucko. Drop it slowly, or it's lights out."

Lance let the handgun fall, too.

"And the knife, dipshit. Come on. You know the drill."

Lance hesitated a moment, like it was the last

weapon between himself and certain death. Another bullet hit the dirt by his feet.

"Okay, okay," he called out.

He pulled out the knife and threw it on the ground next to the handgun.

"Now," the man said, coming out of the brush and onto the road. "Who the fuck are you?"

"Who's asking?"

Another bullet in the ground by Lance's feet. "Answer, dipshit."

"Lance Spector."

"That's your name?"

"Yes, sir."

"And who the fuck are you?"

"I thought the woman who disappeared—"

"You thought that cunt was your sister, but she wasn't, so why are you still coming at us?"

Lance wondered where the guy was getting his information. He seemed to know a lot about a supposedly ongoing investigation in Black Swan. "Were you the one who altered the record?" Lance said.

"What are you talking about?" The man said, getting closer and closer.

"It was the police computer that said they'd found my sister, but the entry was false."

"I don't know nothing about that," the man said, and Lance believed him.

The man was tall, athletic, about Lance's size and build. He looked like exactly the kind of guy someone would want to hire for this kind of work. Competent enough. Nothing fancy.

"So let me get this straight," the man said. "You found out it wasn't even your sister who'd been killed, but instead of walking away, you kept digging and digging until now, here you are, about to die in a forest and become food for ants."

"Who says I'm about to die?" Lance said.

"That's very funny."

"I just needed to know the truth," Lance said.

"And you feel better now? Now that you know? Did it put your curiosity to rest?"

Lance didn't say anything. He might be able to get information from this guy while he still thought he had the upper hand.

"You know what all your digging around's done?" the man said. "It's just gone and created a bigger mess."

"If you call a bunch of dead thugs a mess," Lance said. "Some would call that cleaning up."

The man grinned. "Cleaning up? Is that what it is? Well, we've been doing a little cleaning up of our own. Thanks to you."

Lance felt a shiver run down his spine. Lola's face flashed through his mind. If something had happened to her, he'd never forgive himself. "What cleaning up?" he said.

"Just a few loose ends back in Black Swan."

He was still coming closer. He was coming too close. The barrel of his military-issue M4 carbine was almost within Lance's reach. Lance doubted this guy was stupid enough to get any closer, but he was open to the possibility. "What loose ends?"

The man wasn't stupid enough to come any closer. He was six feet away. From that distance, the gun would tear Lance to shreds. The strap was slung on the man's shoulder, and the nose was pointing downward, unguided. The man had one hand on the stock, and the other was holding a pack of cigarettes.

He shook a cigarette from the pack and plucked it out with his mouth. Lance took that moment to make his move.

He dove to his left and had the handgun from his boot aimed and fired before he hit the ground. He hit the guy somewhere around the shoulder and rolled as he landed. Then he leaped forward at the man who was still standing, spraying bullets in an arc that followed Lance's path just a fraction of a second too slowly.

Lance grabbed him around the legs and pulled him to the ground. The man had drawn a blade, but Lance grabbed his wrist and forced it to the ground. He still had his pistol in his hand, and he put two more bullets in the man's left thigh.

He stayed on the man, his gun still jamming into his thigh where the two bullets had just gone. "Tell me who told you to be here, or I'll scrawl your eyes out with my nails, I swear to God."

"Okay, okay."

Lance jammed the gun into the bullet wound.

"I don't have a name."

"Just tell me what you've got," Lance said. He put a hand on the man's face, his thumb over one eye and his index finger over the other. "Tell me, or I'll crush them."

The man knew he was beat. His only choice now was between agony and death.

"The guy texts me. The messages are on my phone. They come from a withheld number."

"Okay."

"I don't know who he is, but he told me to park my car on the roof of the long-stay parking lot at the airport."

"Seattle airport?"

"Yeah. I'm supposed to go there right after this meeting. Right after I killed you."

"The long-stay lot?"

"Yeah, the roof. Leave the car there with you in the trunk. There's another car for me there. That's all I was supposed to do. I swear to God."

"Okay," Lance said. "And what was all that talk about cleaning house back in Black Swan? When were you there?"

"Last night," the man said.

"You were in Black Swan last night?"

"It was just cleaning our own house. It was nothing."

"Who did you kill?"

The man looked away and then looked back. Lance knew the next words from his mouth would be more lies. He was about to ram the gun farther into the wound in his thigh when he felt a sudden pain in his ribs. Somehow, the man had slipped a second knife from somewhere on his person and stuck it in him.

Lance pulled the trigger three times, killing the son of a bitch. He gurgled and shook his head as he died, like he was scared of where he was going.

Lance checked his pulse, then got to his feet and checked the stab wound. It wasn't deep, but there was a decent amount of blood soaking into his black shirt. He put his hand on it and searched the man's corpse for his car keys. He found two sets in his pocket, Dodge and Mazda, and took them both. Then he gathered up the handguns, the knife, and the man's M4 and loaded them all into the canvas carryall in the trunk of his car. He took off his coat and put on the dead man's coat. It was a peacoat, like what a sailor would wear, and the right size for Lance. He also swapped boots with the dead guy, intending to make himself look vaguely like him in case someone was watching the roof of the long-stay parking lot. Then, taking the carryall and maintaining pressure on the stab wound, he walked back down the road to where he'd seen the flattened grass.

The man's car was an old Dodge sedan, parked out of sight behind some brush. Lance searched the trunk and the glove box. He found a first aid kit in the glove box and bandaged the stab wound by his ribs. It wasn't too bad.

Then he got in the Dodge, got back on the Interstate, and made his way toward Seattle airport.

28

Lance called Lola while *en route* to Seattle.

"Yes?" she said.

"You okay?"

"I'm fine, but Belcher isn't."

"What do you mean?"

"He was shot dead last night."

"Hmm," Lance said. "Where was he when it happened? What was he doing?"

"He was in an alleyway behind the old theater. Off duty."

"What was he doing in an alleyway off duty?"

"My guess?" Lola said. "Meeting someone he shouldn't have been."

"I think you're right," Lance said. "And I think the guy I just met with is the one who killed him. He said something about cleaning house."

"You think Belcher was dirty?"

"I'd be willing to stake money on it," Lance said.

"And the fact they're killing their own means they're scared."

"The filthy son of a bitch," Lola said. "I always knew he was no good."

"Well, you just watch your back. Who knows how many tentacles this thing has? They might not be finished making amends. Might even be worth leaving town for a day or two."

"I'll watch my back," Lola said, "but I'm not leaving town, not now when they need me most. I've got to interview those women from the club today and convince as many of them as possible to give the shelter here in town a try."

"Well, just make sure nothing goes down in the record that might put them in harm's way. We don't want anyone thinking they need to come back and do more house cleaning."

"All right," she said. "And what about you? What happened at the meet?"

"The guy was a lackey. I killed him."

"Just like that?"

"We're ripping this thing out by the roots, Lola. I'm killing everyone involved. I'm on my way to Seattle now to meet the guy who was giving him his orders."

"Will that be the end of it? The head honcho?"

"I doubt it," Lance said.

"Well, be careful. You know what they say about killing monsters."

"What's that?"

"You need to be careful you don't become one."

He said goodbye and hung up. As he drove on, his mind focused on the trail of blood he was following. He was working his way up, but something told him he wasn't at the top yet. This thing didn't end in Seattle.

He drove for a while, then took the exit for the airport. He followed the signs for long-stay parking, which was a concrete multilevel lot. He missed it on his first pass and had to loop back around. Second time, he pulled in, grabbed a ticket, and drove through the barrier. He was tense as he ascended the concrete ramps in the Dodge, up six levels, painfully aware that if he spooked whoever was coming to pick up the car, the trail would end, perhaps permanently. One wrong move and that was it, the fish could slip the hook.

When he got to the roof, he saw a single parked car at the far corner. It was a Mazda, and a Mazda key was among the things he'd taken from the dead guy's body. Lance rolled up next to it, came to a halt, and killed the engine.

The roof was a vulnerable position, to be sure, the entire area completely exposed to the taller hotels and high-rises around it. There were literally a thousand spots a sniper could have set up shop. There was a wool hat on the back seat of the car and he grabbed it and pulled it onto his head. Then he took a deep breath and stepped out of the car, certain that he was being observed, praying that whoever was watching wouldn't realize he wasn't the right guy.

He opened the back door of the Dodge and pulled out the carryall containing the weapons, slinging it over his shoulder. Then, he stepped up to the driver's door of the Mazda and tried the key. It worked. He breathed a sigh of relief, then threw the carryall into the trunk, got into the driver's seat, turned the ignition, and drove off. He still had the ticket from when he'd entered the lot and used it to exit. He didn't have to pay anything. All this was for the benefit of whoever may or may not have been watching him.

Out of the lot, he drove back around the loop, past the terminal and the other parking lots, coming right back around to the same long-stay entrance. The roof was the sixth level so this time he drove to the fifth and parked where he had a clear view of the ramp.

Taking a handgun from the carryall, he walked to the ramp and slowly made his way up until he could see across the roof to the far end of the lot. The Dodge was still there. He went back to the Mazda and waited in the driver's seat, ready to duck at a moment's notice. If anyone went up to the roof, he'd see them. And given the weather, and the fact that there were a lot of spaces available on the lower levels, no one was likely to go up to the roof unless they were his man.

Fifteen minutes passed. Then thirty. Then an hour.

Lance turned on the radio.

He looked through the glovebox and the

pockets in the backseats. He found a map and some insurance paperwork. There was a name on the papers, and he took a picture of it with his phone.

There was a pack of gum in a cupholder and he chewed through the whole thing. There was a box of cigarettes, but he resisted the urge to light up. After the third hour, he began to worry that he'd fall asleep and miss the whole thing. The day dragged on and by the time it started to get dark, still no one had shown up. He began to wonder if anyone was coming at all? What if they'd realized he was the wrong guy? What if they knew their own guy was dead? What if the guy had lied, or was supposed to make a phone call or some kind of signal? Lance hadn't found a phone, either on the man or in either of the cars.

The only thing he had going for him was that he knew he was in the right place.

He continued waiting. He had nowhere better to be, he told himself. He called Laurel and got the details for Roth's funeral. He called Tatyana and got details about Laurel. He called Lola and made sure there'd been no further happenings in Black Swan. Mostly, he waited. Waited and thought. And remembered.

He remembered Roth. Clarice. Sam. His sister and mother. He remembered the first time he'd met Tatyana, almost strangled to death. And Laurel, when she and Roth came out to Deweyville to bring him back into the fold. He couldn't believe his eyes the first time he'd seen her. He usually tried not to think about the past, but he felt now like he was reaching some kind of an ending. If Roth was out, the Group would be disbanded, and if the Group was disbanded, well, he didn't quite know what that would mean for him, but it would definitely be an ending. And endings called for recollection of beginnings.

He must have dozed off because suddenly it was nine at night, and a car was driving by him, onto the ramp and up onto the roof. A blue Mercedes sedan. The lights had roused him, otherwise he'd have missed it.

He grabbed the M4. He'd checked it earlier and it was ready to go. He took off his coat and draped it over the gun so that if anyone happened to be around, they wouldn't see the gun. He put a handgun inside his belt.

Then he got out of the car and walked up the ramp. He climbed it at a crouch, watching the Mercedes as it parked right next to the Dodge. It looked like there was only one person in the car. It stopped, the engine cut, the lights went out. All was quiet and dark for a moment, then the door opened and a man in a suit stepped out and made for the trunk of the Dodge.

Lance let him open it. He let him realize his mistake. The man stood there for a second, staring into the empty trunk, then slammed it shut. When he turned around, he saw Lance walking toward him. The man froze—if he was armed, he didn't reach for his gun—then he came to his senses and started to run. He was going for the Mercedes, and Lance dropped to one knee, threw away the coat, raised the M4, and put a bullet in the man's shin.

The bang rang out in the night air like a thunderclap, and the man broke stride and stumbled. If anyone in the overlooking buildings had seen the muzzle flash or heard the shot, then it would be only a matter of minutes before the police showed up.

Minutes would have to do.

The man writhed on the ground, whimpering in pain, still struggling to get to his car.

Lance approached cautiously. He didn't want to be surprised by a pistol shot to the gut. "I'm going to give you one chance to save your sorry ass," Lance said.

"Who are you?" the man gasped.

"Give me the name of whoever you work for or I'll take two of your fingers and start ripping them apart until your hand splits."

"I don't know what you're talking about."

Lance didn't have time for the usual back and forth. He put the gun on the ground, out of the man's reach, walked over to him, and grabbed his hand.

"Please, no," the man cried. "I'll talk."

Lance grabbed a pinkie in one fist and a thumb in the other and pulled them away from each other. The fingers dislocated, and the man's screams were deafening. The pinkie began to tear loose from the rest of the hand like a chicken leg, and Lance said, "I gave you the chance to talk without all this."

The man couldn't believe what had happened. He looked at Lance uncomprehendingly, then looked at his mangled hand. In a minute, he'd be in shock, and it would be difficult to get sense out of him.

"Next, I'm going to rip open your mouth until I have two cheeks in my fists," Lance said.

The man was terrified. "I wasn't there," he stammered.

"I really don't mind ripping your face open. It'll make it harder to talk but I'll give you a pencil. You can write down the answers with your other hand."

"No," the man cried. "I'll talk. I'll talk."

"Who was at the lodge? Who did that to the woman?"

"The client."

"The client? What's his name?"

"His name is Arps. Skadden Arps. He's a big-time lawyer or something down in DC."

"Skadden Arps?" Lance said, testing the name in his mouth. He hadn't ever heard it before.

"These killings, they're a sport for him," the man continued. "He flies through here on his way to the lodge."

"And you? What part do you play?"

"I arrange things. I arrange the chopper. I arrange clean up. If he needs things, I bring them."

"How long have you been doing it?"

"Me?"

"Yes, you."

"I don't know. Years?"

"How many years?"

"Ten?"

"And him, how long's he been doing it. Arps?"

"Longer. Twenty years. Thirty maybe. Before him, someone else did the same thing out there. He passed it all to Arps when he died."

"What about others? Who else is involved?"

The man was shaking. He was beginning to go into shock. He looked at Lance then down at his ruined hand.

"Who else?" Lance repeated. He could hear police sirens and they were getting closer.

"No one," the man said. "He comes alone. It's just him."

Lance nodded. He had enough to go on. A name. A DC big shot. Skadden Arps would be dead in a matter of days. "Guess we're out of time," he said.

The man shook his head. "No, please," he gasped.

Lance reached for him and lifted him up, brought him to the edge of the building, and dropped him over the side. The scream was blood-curdling and then silence. Lance looked over the edge to see the man's body splayed across the pavement six stories below.

Whoever this Skadden Arps was, he'd know it was only a matter of time now. He'd know he was the one who was being hunted.

The keys to the Mercedes were in the ignition, and Lance climbed into it and drove away, back down the ramp, past the Mazda, and down another ramp. On the fourth level, he pulled into a parking spot and killed the engine and lights just in time for two police cars to speed by him on their way to the roof. He waited until they were out of sight, then pulled out of the spot and continued to the ground floor, where he saw two more police cruisers waiting by the exit to the lot. He left the Mercedes double parked at the far end of the lot, took off the hat and coat he was wearing, and put on a navy windbreaker that was draped over the back of the passenger seat.

A moment later, he was inside the terminal. He entered a public washroom and washed his hands and face. Then he walked back out through the arrivals concourse and got in a cab.

29

Two days later.

Lance sat back in the leather chair and exhaled the rich, fragrant tobacco. He was smoking a fifty dollar cigar outside a bar near Union Station and boy was it ever satisfying.

The job was done.

Skadden Arps was dead.

He'd been dead less than an hour, his body was barely cold, but it was done. Lance had shot him through a window of the Lafayette Hotel from the roof of his own office building. If that wasn't poetic, he didn't know what was.

It was done.

Over.

There wouldn't be any more disappearances in the town of Black Swan, at least not at the hands of Skadden Arps. And it turned out he wasn't a lawyer at all. Worse. He was a lobbyist. And a dirty one. With a lot of very powerful clients.

Which was why, now that he was dead, the question going through Lance's mind was, which of those clients had wanted Arps dead? And why had they zeroed in on him to pull the trigger? That he'd been manipulated, he was certain. Someone knew his psychology. They knew his history. They knew about his mother and sister. And they knew how to use it.

In the distance, he could hear police sirens, and some people even came out of the bar to see what was going on. Lance took his time with the cigar, and when it was finished, he went inside.

"Whatever's the best cognac you've got," he said to the bartender, taking a seat. "Neat. And make it a double."

The bartender brought his drink, and Lance swished it in the glass.

This was it, he thought, taking a sip. The taste of revenge. It wasn't a feeling he indulged often. When your job was assassin, you had to be careful which emotions you allowed yourself. You had to remain detached. He was used to thinking of himself as a tool of the president, a tool of the CIA. He didn't kill because he wanted to. But this one had been different. It was personal.

And it wasn't over.

He took out his cell and called Lola. "It's me," he said when she picked up.

"Lance?"

"It's done, Lola. It's over."

"Skadden Arps is dead?"

"He won't be paying any more visits to Black Swan."

There was silence on the other end of the line, and for a moment, he thought the call had dropped. Then he realized what it was. Lola was crying. "Are you all right?" he said.

"Yes," she said through the tears. "It's just, I can't believe it's really over."

"It's over. He's never coming back."

"I wonder what the chief's going to say."

"Good job, hopefully."

"It wasn't me that did this."

"Yes it was," Lance said. "This is because of you. You never gave up. And now, everyone who had a hand to play in it is dead."

"Even Belcher," she said quietly.

Lance took a sip from his glass and said, "Are you upset about that?"

"Not upset," she said. "I wouldn't say upset. It's just...."

"You knew him."

"Yeah."

They said their goodbyes, and Lance felt sorry that their time was coming to an end. He was enough of a realist to know it would probably be for good, and it would probably be for the best. For her, at least. "It's been an honor," he said before letting her go.

"You're one of the good ones, Lance Spector."

"I don't know about that."

"Don't doubt it," she said. "Whatever else you've done in your life, you did this, and this was good."

"It was a job—"

"That needed doing," she said, finishing the sentence for him.

He hung up and finished his drink.

"You want another?" the bartender said.

He was about to say no when the TV in the corner caught his eye. There was breaking news flashing across the bottom of the screen. The bartender picked up a remote and turned up the volume.

> DC was rocked just moments ago by the high-profile assassination of one of the city's most powerful lobbyists. Measures are being taken to evacuate the area around the Hotel Lafayette as we speak.

The news cut to footage of the scene. There was already police tape up around the hotel, and the reporters were peppering the police and hotel staff with questions. No one had any comment.

"All right," Lance said to the bartender. "Maybe just one more."

"Can you believe that shit?" the bartender said. "Right here in DC, not five blocks from where we're sitting."

Lance nodded. “What’s this country coming to?” he said.

30

Lance woke early and stared at the ceiling. He'd slept well. The mattress was good. He'd gotten a room at the Sofitel on Lafayette Square, a modern, five-star establishment with a decidedly art deco feel. It was scarcely two blocks from the Hotel Lafayette, and the heightened police presence was still evident outside when he'd checked in.

There was a phone by the bed and he picked up the receiver and called the lobby.

"Good morning, sir," the concierge said. "How can I help?"

"I spoke to someone last night," Lance said, "about a black suit."

"Room?"

"Two-thirty-two."

"Ah yes, you gave them your measurements."

"Were they able to find anything?"

"They were, sir. Yes. Everything you requested."

"Shoes?"

"Yes, of course, sir. Italian leather. White shirt. Burgundy tie. Everything top notch."

"Perfect," Lance said. "If they could have it brought up, that would be great."

"And will there be anything else, sir?"

Lance stretched out on the bed languorously. It really was a good mattress. "If they could send up a pot of coffee, too, that would be much appreciated."

He took a long, hot shower and shaved. As he stepped out of the bathroom, towel around his waist, there was a knock on the door. It was his coffee and suit. The maid set the suit on the bed and the coffee on the desk, and Lance tipped her fifty.

"Thank you, sir."

"You have a good day," he said.

There was a seating area by the window, and he sat down and poured some coffee. They'd brought Italian cookies with it, and he dipped one in his cup and took a bite. It was delicious.

The suit was nice, too. Nicer than he was used to. He was about to put it on when the hotel phone started to ring. He picked it up, expecting the concierge, but the voice that greeted him wasn't the concierge at all. It was someone else.

"Lance?"

Lance said nothing. In fact, he sat down on the side of the bed and took a long, deep breath. He'd expected this, or *suspected* was probably the word, but it was still something of a shock to actually hear the man's voice. "I was just dressing for your funeral," he said.

"Right. Sorry about that."

"Everyone thinks you're dead."

"A necessary ruse, I'm afraid."

"They announced they found a body."

"All for the Kremlin's benefit."

"Did you fake the whole thing?"

"No, no," Roth said. "The vehicle was definitely tampered with. They tried to have me killed for sure."

"Molotov's not going to take their word for it that they found the body. He's going to keep on it. I wouldn't be surprised if he has someone dig up the grave and look inside the coffin."

"I know, I know," Roth said. "It is what it is. I took a shot at the king, and I missed."

"And now you're paying the price."

"Enough about that," Roth said, putting on a brave face. "I thought you'd be more excited to hear my voice."

"I am excited."

"Your old friend hasn't kicked the can! That's good news, right?"

"Sure," Lance said. "I guess I'm just used to hiding my emotions from you."

The truth was, the sound of Roth's voice had struck Lance harder than he would have expected. He'd done a good job of ignoring the possibility the man was dead, or thought he had. Now, he realized he hadn't been as inured to that emotion as he'd given himself credit for. He was relieved. He was happy even. For the first time in days, he might even have been able to say that he was happy. "It's good to hear your voice, Levi."

"Yours too," Roth said. "I was worried what might happen to you if I was gone."

"Well," Lance said, "I'm sitting in a luxury chair in a luxury hotel room, dipping almond biscotti into my luxury coffee."

"That's a rosy picture."

"I'm a rosy guy."

"I hope so," Roth said, and from his tone, Lance could tell he meant it. "I'm going to have to disappear after this. I'm going to have to go for good."

"Or for as long as Molotov's in power," Lance said.

"At my age, that's likely to be the same thing."

"Does anyone else know you're alive? Tatyana? Laurel?"

"No," Roth said, "and I'd like it to stay that way."

Lance nodded, though he knew that without actually setting eyes on the body, there'd always be a piece of them that held out hope. "I take it you've prepared for this. A bank account somewhere. An identity? A wig and glasses or something?"

"You know me," Roth said. "Always ready."

"Well," Lance said. "I hope you at least write?"

Roth laughed. "I think this might be goodbye for good, son."

Son, Lance thought. It wasn't every day he got called that. "That's why you called then?" he said, his mind already running through possible alternative motives. "It's a sentimental move for a man who needs to disappear. They haven't even buried your coffin yet, and you're reaching out to old friends, making personal calls."

"Only to you, Lance."

"Well, Levi, that just makes me feel a little bit *too* special, know what I mean?"

"Can't a man say goodbye to his favorite assassin?"

"I just went from *son* to *Assassin*," Lance said. "You don't often call me that. It's usually operator, or asset, or—"

"You're killing people on President Molotov's hit list," Roth blurted.

"What are you talking about?"

"Don't pretend last night wasn't you."

"Skadden Arps?"

"Yes, Skadden Arps."

"That was me, but—"

"*But*? But he was placed on Molotov's hit list just a week ago."

"And how would I know a thing like that?"

"Maybe someone told you."

"Come on, Levi. You know me. You know that's not true."

"Then you tell me why you did it?"

"Have you been speaking to Laurel?"

"I told you, I haven't been speaking to anyone."

"I had my own reasons for killing Skadden Arps."

"If you did, that's mighty convenient timing, seeing as—"

"Why did Molotov want him killed?" Lance said.

"You're serious? You don't know?"

"Look. I know something's up. I know I was manipulated. Just tell me why Molotov wanted Arps dead so we can start making sense of it."

"The chatter is that Arps had acquired something on him."

"On Molotov?"

"Yes. Something embarrassing."

"*Kompromat*?"

"Yes, and it's big."

"You don't know what it is?"

"No, but I do know Skadden Arps kept a very secure safe in the basement of that new headquarters building of his. If the *kompromat's* anywhere, it's in that safe."

"I see," Lance said.

"Now, your turn," Roth said.

"All right. I killed Arps because he was involved in some murders in Black Swan?"

"Black Swan?"

"Black Swan, Washington. Disappearances. Women. Torture. Death."

"And how did you get pulled into a thing like that?"

"One of the victim's names came up as...."

"As what?"

Lance took a moment. He'd known, ever since

he'd realized the victim's name had been falsified, that someone had been pulling his strings. Now he was finding out who. "It came up as Raven Spector."

Roth said nothing for a moment, he had his own permutations to make, his own angles to assess. Then he said, "Oh, Lance."

"It was a false match," Lance said. "Someone tampered with the file. Purposefully pulled me in."

"Someone who knew a lot more about your history than anyone rightly should."

"But why go to all the trouble?"

"What do you mean?"

"Molotov has a thousand ways to kill someone like Skadden Arps. He didn't need me to get that job done."

"That's the right question," Roth said. "Why pull you into this? What's the fucker up to?"

"I intend to find out."

"I don't know if that's a good idea," Roth said.

"In all the time you've known me, Levi, when have I ever cared about good ideas?"

31

Tatyana stepped out of her front door and looked at the sky. Gray cloud, low and dark, perfect for a funeral, she thought. She went back inside and grabbed the umbrella by the door—there was no way she was letting this Christian Dior dress get ruined in the rain—then went back outside. It was early, and the street was quiet. There was no sign of her cab and she was about to call the company when she saw it round the corner.

"Good morning, ma'am," the driver said to her. He was a young guy in a Sikh turban.

Ma'am, Tatyana thought ruefully. That was harsh. She was still a few months shy of thirty. It wasn't that long ago that it would have certainly been *miss*. She got in the car and gave him the cemetery address.

"Funeral?" he said.

"What gave it away?" she said, looking down at

her black dress, black coat, black tights, black shoes.

"Oh," the driver said, "of course. Obvious."

Tatyana turned toward the window, hoping he would take the hint and stop talking to her, but he didn't. "Looks like rain," he said.

She nodded but didn't say anything, and after another few minutes of silence, he said, "Do you mind if I put on the radio?"

"Not at all," she said, then zoned out as a talk show host began speaking *ad nauseam* about someone quarterback's leg injury.

It wasn't until they reached the cemetery that the driver spoke up again. "Is that security?"

Tatyana looked ahead to see that the Secret Service was out in force. So the president had shown. That, she supposed, was an indicator that the death was real after all. Unless the president was assisting in a cover-up, which was a possibility.

"Who died?" the driver said as they pulled up to the gate.

"Hmm?"

"This funeral's for someone important or something?"

"My old boss," Tatyana said, leaving it at that.

Two secret service agents standing in the middle of the road waved them to a halt, and the driver opened his window.

"Who's in the back?" the agent said, poking his head in.

Tatyana lowered her window and flashed her credentials.

"You're going to have to walk from here, ma'am," the agent said.

There it was again, *ma'am*. This wouldn't do. She was going to need to change her hairstyle or something. She looked out at the gravel pathway leading into the cemetery and said, "I'm not walking on that in these shoes." As if on cue, a light rain began to fall.

"I'm sorry, ma'am, but I can't let the car through. The driver hasn't been cleared."

"He's a cab driver."

"I can't let him through," the agent said again flatly.

Tatyana looked around. "Is that your car?" she said to the agent, nodding at a black sedan with tinted windows parked behind him.

"It is, ma'am."

"Either he drives me, or you do."

The agent didn't look like he appreciated the joke, and Tatyana was wondering how she was going to navigate this hiccup when another car pulled up behind them. It was a fancy government Cadillac with flags on the front and a policeman on a motorcycle riding behind. Tatyana looked at the meter and handed her driver a fifty. "See ya," she said, stepping out.

She had no idea who was in the Cadillac but she figured she'd be able to wrangle a ride. As it turned out, it was Winnefeld, the Navy Chief of

Operations, without his wife. He was only too happy to make room on the spacious backseat for Tatyana. They made small talk on the short drive to the grave, some platitudes about Levi and how he would be missed, and Tatyana scrutinized his every word for evidence he knew something she didn't. She didn't see any.

When he got out, he held the door for her.

"Thank you, Frederick," she said, opening her umbrella. "You're a gentleman."

"Don't tell any of them that," Winnefeld said, nodding at the assemblage of somber black suits standing under umbrellas by the graveside.

She smiled and let him take her arm as they joined the group. When they got there, she immediately abandoned him to stand next to Laurel.

"Hi," she whispered.

Laurel nodded.

Tatyana looked around at the assembled faces. It was only officials in attendance, all with security clearances. No one had brought a wife or partner, and it seemed no one from Roth's family was there either. Perhaps it was true that he had no one outside the agency, she thought. That was certainly the impression he'd always given.

The president was there, standing under an enormous black umbrella next to Wally Schultz, his Chief of Staff. Sandra was there too, as well as Schlesinger and Cutler. There were more secret service agents than mourners.

The ceremony was a somber affair, dignified,

tasteful, and, most importantly, short. The rain got progressively heavier as the casket was lowered into the ground, and Tatyana wondered how many of those present knew what it really contained. She had no doubt the Russians were watching, though probably by satellite, given the location.

The rain grew heavier and heavier, and Tatyana worried about her shoes. She could feel her heels slowly sinking into the mud and wondered how much longer it would take. She was pulled from the thought by a light tap on the arm.

It was Laurel, and she pointed down the gravel path back toward the gates. There was a man approaching on foot, and she instantly recognized him as Lance. Her pulse quickened. There was something about that man, an effect he had on her that she'd never fully been able to come to terms with. On the one hand, he'd saved her life. On the other, he'd broken her heart. She was pretty sure he didn't know that.

"I didn't think he'd come," she whispered.

Laurel shook her head. "Neither did I," she said quietly.

The rain grew heavier still, and Tatyana could sense the eagerness of the assemblage to disperse. She couldn't be the only one worried about her outfit, she thought.

"Let's go," she whispered to Laurel.

"It's not over yet."

"I'm going," she said. "I'm getting soaked."

She hurried back down the slope to

Winnefeld's Cadillac and, a moment later, was joined by Winnefeld with Laurel in tow.

"You couldn't have given him thirty more seconds," Laurel said.

Tatyana held up her wet sleeve. "I think he'd have understood."

The other guests were abandoning ship, too. It seemed no one had too many qualms about cutting the ceremony short. As their car joined the procession of vehicles making its way back down the driveway, Tatyana looked out to see that Lance was the only person still standing by the grave.

He looked old, too, she thought.

32

Tatyana and Laurel got out of Winnefeld's car on Pennsylvania Avenue.

"It's still raining," Winnefeld protested. "I can get you closer to the bar."

"It's fine," Tatyana said, eager to be free of him. "You have your big meeting to attend." He'd let slip that the reason everyone was headed to the White House after the funeral was to discuss the fate of the Special Operations Group, and it had been a real dampener on the mood in the car. "Thanks for the ride."

The two women hurried through Pershing Park under their umbrellas and, a moment later, were entering Old Ebbitt's, the same bar they'd met at a few days earlier. They grabbed a secluded booth in the corner and asked for menus.

"This place feels different in the morning," Laurel said.

Tatyana nodded.

"I don't see your *friend*," Laurel said, looking toward the long oak bar.

Tatyana refused to take the bait. She was glad the bartender wasn't there, in any case. She'd gone back to his place that night, and they'd fooled around. It had been *fine*. But as soon as the guy fell asleep, she'd slipped out of the apartment without saying goodbye. She wasn't even sure she could remember his name. "These shoes are ruined," she said.

Laurel was wet, too, and doing her best to make herself comfortable. "The rain got through my coat," she said. "I would have worn something thicker, but this was the only black one I had."

A waiter in a white shirt and black suspenders came over with menus, and they both ordered coffee.

"Can I take those coats for you?" he said.

They gave him their coats, and Tatyana realized her dress was wet, too. "Great," she muttered.

Their coffee arrived, and they both ordered lox bagels with cream cheese. "They're good here," Tatyana said. It was more her place than Laurel's, though she'd only been there a handful of times.

"Better than the oysters?" Laurel said.

"Not *that* good," Tatyana said, letting a small smile crack an otherwise frosty exterior. "So?" she said. "Where do we stand? What are we going to do? They're talking about us right this second."

Laurel cleared her throat. "Well, I spoke to Cutler again."

"More good news?" Tatyana said sarcastically.

"He gave me the list of new assignments we're being considered for."

"So he's the one taking over?"

"He still didn't confirm or deny," Laurel said, fishing through her purse. She pulled out a sheet of paper on which the postings had been handwritten and passed it to Tatyana.

Tatyana scanned the list. "These are all in the Middle East. South East Asia. China."

"Yes, they are."

"I'm Russian," Tatyana said. "And your experience is Russian."

"He said the administration is reorienting our strategy."

"*Reorienting*?" Tatyana said. "What does that mean?"

"Less focus on Moscow."

"And more on Beijing?"

"To put it bluntly."

Tatyana chewed her lip. "All right," she said, "but that doesn't mean we forget about Russia."

"Of course not."

"So why move us? We haven't done anything wrong."

"It's not a punishment, Tatyana. The Middle East has been heating up for months. There's talk of putting boots on the ground. And long-term, China's obviously the new elephant in the room."

"Well, he can shove this up his ass," Tatyana

said, sliding the paper back to Laurel. "They're fucking us. In the ass."

"No use getting upset with me," Laurel said. "I'm just the messenger. This is what they've offered."

"Well, tell them to fuck off," Tatyana said, louder than was necessary.

"Keep your voice down," Laurel said. "People are looking."

The place was mostly deserted—there was a table of four women on the other side of the room drinking mimosas and a handful of lone businessmen scattered about—but Tatyana did moderate her tone. "I'm not saying those regions are unimportant, obviously."

"I know what you're saying."

"They're sidelining us. They're purposefully making us less valuable. It's a precursor to getting rid of us."

"Tatyana."

"Getting rid of us and dismantling everything Roth built."

"Well, Roth fucked up, okay," Laurel said, finally losing her composure. "He broke the cardinal rule. He went after Molotov and failed."

Tatyana shook her head. She couldn't believe this was happening, not after all that had happened.

"Look," Laurel said, her tone softening. "Times change. They move on. Things change."

"Some things don't change."

"Come on, Tatyana. Be reasonable."

"I'm serious. Some things don't change. Russia doesn't change."

"It feels like that—"

"It feels like that because it's true. When, in the last eighty years, has Russia not been the biggest geopolitical threat to the world? When did China try to take over half the world? How many nukes in the Middle East are pointed at America right now?"

"Look, I get it," Laurel said. "I do."

"Because it's true. No one threatens us like Russia. No one tries to."

"Well, what good is moaning about it?"

"You know, this is what they count on," Tatyana continued, slipping into a rant. "You know that, right? You know what they say in Moscow?"

"What?"

"They say America has no consistency. No staying power. No policy that outlasts the administration that brought it in. They say our time horizon for every strategic decision is four years. Eight years max. Then a new regime comes in and turns everything on its head."

"Yeah?" Laurel said. "And you're telling me this why?"

"I'm telling you because—"

"You're taking your frustration out on the wrong person," Laurel said. "You think I want to see everything we built get dismantled? You think I have the power to change it?"

"You're head of the Special Operations Group. You have the power to fight it."

"You're being naive."

"No, I'm not," Tatyana said. "Everything we've done. Everything we've fought for. Everything we've learned."

"Tatyana, I know."

"You think they're going to bring us in to at least advise the new Russia team?"

"That's not on the list," Laurel said, fingering the piece of paper.

"No," Tatyana said, leaning back in her seat and letting out a long sigh. "I can see that."

"We don't get to make the rules," Laurel said.

"So there's nothing we can do? No one we can speak to?"

"You want to speak to Cutler?"

"I want to speak to the president," Tatyana said.

"That's not going to happen."

"It happened before."

"Roth was around before. In case you haven't noticed, he's dead now."

"Roth's not dead. No one thinks that."

"It was his funeral we just attended, unless I'm mistaken."

"If he's dead, then show me the body."

"We just buried it."

"In a closed casket."

Laurel stared at her, her eyes like two fireballs, but said nothing. Tatyana could see she was as angry as she was. She was just hiding it better.

The waiter brought their food, and they both looked at the plates as if someone had just served them dog shit.

"Look," Laurel said, "whichever way you cut it, the old days are over. Things are going to be different. Roth's parting gift was to fuck us, and fuck the Group. No one wants our experience now. Our knowledge. You and me, we're damaged goods."

"Fuck!" Tatyana said, pushing away her plate.

This time, she really was too loud. She could see the waiter approaching.

"Ladies," he said, speaking in the loudest whisper imaginable. "I'm going to have to ask that you keep it down or leave."

"Sorry," Laurel said, eyeing Tatyana like the mother of a petulant child.

Tatyana looked away. She knew what she looked like. She knew Laurel thought she was being unreasonable. But the truth was, she wasn't overreacting. This was bad. As bad as she was saying. Russia was *her* country. *She'd* grown up there. *She* understood its system. This wasn't theoretical to her. It wasn't about strategy, and politics, and the long-term future of the global order. This was every single second of every single day of her entire life. Her life and the lives of over a hundred million other Russian citizens. Every minute that Vladimir Molotov remained in power was an agony to them. It was a minute lost. A minute that all those millions of people would never get back. Russia's people were not the source of Molotov's power, they were its victims. Every political prisoner, every émigré forced to flee, every soldier dying on the battlefield, every child in a classroom filled with propaganda and lies was paying the price for Molotov's crimes. This wasn't about geopolitics. This was personal. It was real life, all day, every day, from the moment she'd been born until the moment she died.

"I'm sorry," Laurel said, seeing the depth of Tatyana's emotion. "This is what a change of the guard looks like. It's not perfect."

"You can say that again."

"But the alternative is what Russia has," Laurel said. "A president for life. Someone who can never be ousted from power, no matter how corrupt, no matter how harmful he becomes."

"I'm beginning to see how that could have its advantages."

"You don't mean that."

Tatyana shook her head. "No," she said. "No, I don't."

33

Laurel didn't go home after her meeting with Tatyana at the Old Ebbitt. She still had her lease on a loft in the city, but it had been some time since she'd been back there. There was just something about the place now—the dead houseplants, the dead goldfish, the long-out-of-date food in the refrigerator—the thought of going back gave her an intense sense of anxiety. She'd also stopped sleeping at the office. When they'd told her Roth was dead and they were winding up the Group, the place had lost something for her. It's sense of security. It's permanence.

Instead, she was at run-of-the-mill Courtyard Marriott just off the Georgetown Pike in Langley. It was a stone's throw from the CIA compound, which was about the only thing it had going for it.

She'd been tired when she got back from the Old Ebbitt, she hadn't been sleeping, and the argument with Tatyana hadn't done anything to calm her nerves. But the hardest thing had been seeing Lance at the grave. They hadn't spoken, which was strange, but worse was what it augured for the future. Not that she'd ever expected Lance to be giving her phone calls on her birthday or inviting out her out to his place in Montana for Christmas. But to think it was really over, that they would no longer have a reason to talk to each other—that was hard.

She'd gotten out of her wet things when she got back—the rain had given her a chill—and run a hot bath. Afterward, quite unintentionally, she lay down on the bed and fell asleep. It was four in the afternoon when she woke up, it would be getting dark again soon, and the saddest thing about it was that it didn't even matter. No one was looking for her, no one was expecting her anywhere. She could have slept the rest of the week and there wasn't a person in the world who would have cared.

And it had all happened so quickly, so *unceremoniously*. She'd gone from sixty to zero in less time than it took to get a suit altered. She knew because her seamstress had just left a message that the three new business suits she'd dropped off to get taken in were ready. She'd bought them when Roth gave her the promotion.

She got out of bed and was seriously considering taking another bath when she heard a knock on the door. That was weird. Apart from housekeeping, no one ever came to that door, and housekeeping came in the morning. Instinctively, she reached for her gun.

"Laurel?" It was Tatyana's voice.

"Tatyana?" Laurel said, reaching for some yoga pants she'd flung on the floor earlier. "Hang on a second."

She pulled on the pants as well as a t-shirt and quickly tidied up a few other things she'd left lying on the floor. Then she opened the door.

And that was when she gasped. It wasn't just Tatyana standing there, still in her funeral outfit, looking like a supermodel, but Lance was with her. "What's going on?" she said.

"Can we come in?" Lance said.

"What are you doing here?"

"We'll tell you when you invite us in."

"How did you even know where to find me?"

"You updated your file with this address," Tatyana said. "I tried calling you five times on the way over. I was getting worried."

Laurel retreated into the room, cringing when she saw a pair of panties on the chair. She grabbed them, flinging them into the open suitcase in the corner, then hurriedly began gathering up the things she'd left on the desk. She'd been using the mirror and lamp there to apply her makeup in the mornings, and it looked like the counter at a cosmetics store.

"I like what you've done with the place," Tatyana said.

"Ha ha," Laurel said. "Is that why you came? To give decorating tips?"

Lance was over at the coffee maker, putting in one of the capsules. "Do you mind?" he said.

"Help yourself," Laurel said, glancing at Tatyana. "You might as well make her one too."

Lance made three coffees, one of them decaf because there weren't enough regular capsules, and Laurel wasn't sure which of them he'd given it to. She tasted hers, but it was all so bad that she couldn't tell the difference.

Tatyana sat down on the single chair in the room, leaving the bed for Laurel and Lance.

"Is someone going to tell me what's going on?" Laurel said, sitting next to Lance.

Tatyana nodded in Lance's direction and said, "Don't look at me. This is his show. I'm no wiser than you are."

Lance raised his cup and said, "Well, first off, here's to Levi."

"To Levi," Laurel and Tatyana said.

They each took a sip of watery hotel coffee in Roth's honor, and Lance said, "Best boss I ever had."

The women nodded, and Laurel watched Lance carefully. She figured none of them was fully convinced the old man was really gone for good, but now, looking at him closely, she wondered if he perhaps knew something that they didn't. Was she imagining it, or was there a certain levity to his toast that wouldn't have been there if he truly thought Roth was dead?

"Well," Lance said. "Look at us, the three musketeers, back together."

"Are we back together?" Tatyana said.

"It doesn't feel like it," Laurel added.

"Would it feel like it," Lance said, "if I said we had a job to do?"

"A job?" Laurel said. "What job?"

"A final waltz around the ballroom."

Laurel and Tatyana stared at him in silence, and he cleared his throat. "Right," he said. "Well, you two still have your clearances, right? You still have access to Group databases?"

"Last I checked," Laurel said, "though I wouldn't be surprised if Cutler cut them off without telling us."

"What's the job?" Tatyana said.

"Something that I think might make a difference for a common friend."

Tatyana glanced at Laurel and said, "A *common friend*?"

"Is that *common friend* alive?" Laurel said. Her eyes were glued on Lance. His face remained completely blank.

He said, "If this is the last thing we do together, at least it will be something worthwhile."

"Are you going to make us read between the lines the whole way?" Laurel said.

"Are you going to help?" Lance said.

Laurel took a sip of her coffee. Tatyana did the

same, then said, "We don't know what it is you're suggesting yet."

Laurel was still staring at Lance. He looked different, she thought. How, she wondered, had his mission in Black Swan turned out? She had no doubt he'd been involved in the spate of recent killings out that way. A pimp and a bunch of thugs gunned down. A man falling to his death from an airport parking lot. Had he gotten the closure he wanted? Somehow, she didn't think so. "Do you know he's still alive?" she said.

Lance looked at her. Again, he said nothing, but this time, she understood. There was no uncertainty. He knew.

"He is," she said.

"Let's just say," Lance said, "that without eyes on the body, without DNA, without their own witnesses and a fifteen-hundred-page lab report, the Kremlin's not going to stop looking for someone until they find him."

"And they will find him," Tatyana said.

Lance nodded. "We all know it. Sooner or later, maybe tomorrow, maybe twenty years down the road, they'll find him, and they'll finish the job."

"You want to make a trade?" Laurel said.

Lance nodded.

"Your life for his?" she said, shaking her head.

"No," Lance said.

Tatyana smiled.

"I mean," Lance said, "I like the guy...."

"But not that much," Tatyana said.

"I think I have something else to trade," Lance said.

Laurel took another sip of her coffee. She hadn't taken her eyes of Lance once. "And what's that?" she said.

Lance looked at them both, then said, "What do you two know about a man named Skadden Arps?"

34

Lance was the first to leave the hotel room. He already had the equipment he would need, packed into a canvas carryall in the trunk of a rented Ford Escape outside, and it was with a tinge of sadness that he said goodbye to the two women. They didn't know it yet, but they wouldn't be seeing him again. Maybe ever.

For their part, the women went back to Langley, back to the sixth-floor control center, where luckily their security passes were still good and they still had full access. It wasn't lost on any of them that this could well be the final operation they ran from it.

"One, two. One, two," Lance said into the mic attached to his earpiece. It was an ordinary-looking Bluetooth earpiece, though with upgraded security. "You picking me up all right?"

He was parked in a multistory lot two blocks from the Hotel Lafayette, and almost felt like he was tempting fate coming back there so soon. The hotel was still cordoned off by the police, and investigators had identified the Skadden Arps building across the street as the location used by the shooter. They were on the roof now, dusting for prints, testing for residue, looking for clues.

"We hear you," Tatyana said, her voice clear through his earpiece. "Stand by."

Lance had been standing by for four hours, waiting for the all-clear from Tatyana, who was monitoring the building. Laurel had been able to get full access to its security system and had done the same with City Police Dispatch. She'd know as soon as anything went wrong.

All according to plan, Lance thought, though Laurel had raised some concern that hacking the building had been easier than expected. "Almost as if they left the door open for us," she'd said. "It's suspect. We should abort."

"We're not aborting," Lance said.

"This smells like a trap," she'd said. "The main firewall was deactivated by an automatic, pre-programmed script."

"When did the script run?" Lance said.

"Last night. About an hour after you killed Arps."

"About the time his death was first reported by the media," Lance said. "I don't think that's a trap. I think it's a feature."

"A feature?"

"Arps had dirt on the most powerful people on

the planet. Throwing the lock in the event of an untimely death would be one way of dissuading them from killing him."

"There'd need to be more to it than that," Tatyana had said. "A script can't open an eighty-year-old mechanical safe."

That was true, and Lance had no idea if this was evidence of a trap or not, but it had been enough to convince Laurel to keep going. The only extra precaution she'd taken was to requisition a Keyhole Satellite, which allowed her to monitor the entire area around the building from above, giving her early warning of any potential ambush. "We'll have to be fast," she'd said. "If anyone else knows about this *feature*, we might not be the only people coming in hot for this safe."

"Fine by me," Lance said. "I'm ready to go now."

"Hold your horses," Laurel said. "Not until the police are gone."

That had been four hours ago, and Lance was starting to get antsy. "I think we need to move," he said into his mic. "It's almost midnight. They could be planning on staying up there all night, for all we know."

"Not until I say," Laurel said. "I mean it. I'll kill the mission before I send you in there half-baked."

"What's half-baked about a few detectives being on the roof?"

"Hush, both of you," Tatyana said. "They're packing up. Looks like they're clearing out."

"Finally, go time!" Lance said. He got out of the

car immediately, popped the trunk, and slung the heavy carryall over his shoulder. He was dressed in a generic set of worker's overalls and was going in unarmed. He hurried down the stairs and exited the lot onto K Street, then walked briskly the hundred yards to the Lafayette, where he crossed the street to avoid the police cordon. "Approaching entrance," he said into the mic. He could still see the police getting into their vehicles in front of the Skadden Arps building, but thought it lent him credibility to arrive while they were still on the scene.

"The guard's expecting you," Laurel said. "Just stick to the script."

"Oh, I'll stick the script," Lance said, pushing through the building's heavy swing doors. He did nothing to hide the fact he'd been speaking to someone as he entered the lobby, which was a vast, opulent space in the corporate, minimalist style—all glass and marble and untreated metal. There was a security desk about thirty yards from where he stood, and he cleared his throat as he approached. "Sorry, I think I'm expected," he said to the guard. "Rhino Cyber?"

The guard pulled his attention from his phone, where he was watching sports highlights, and looked at Lance skeptically. "I don't think so, pal."

"Check the log."

"No need. You're not on it."

"Are you sure? I've got you down for a full audit. Encryption, decryption, firewalls, the works.

From a cyber perspective, this place is on defcon one."

The guard lazily hit some keys on his computer. "Hmm," he said. "Strange."

"What's strange?"

"I guess you're on the list. Rhino Cyber. What did you say your name was?"

"Roth," Lance said as the guard started entering the name on the keyboard. "Levi Roth."

"What do you think you're playing at?" Laurel said into the earpiece.

Lance ignored her.

"Okay, Levi," the guard said. "Says here you've got lower level access only. Server room, comms hardware, computer room."

"Yes, sir. That's all I need. Might have to poke around a little, though. The server cables tend to snake around."

"All right," the guard said, handing him a visitor's lanyard and keycard. "You've been through the induction?"

"Oh yeah," Lance said. "We all have. You're our biggest client."

"Then you know the rules."

Lance nodded and put his bag up on a conveyor belt. It went through a scanner, and the guard said, "Whoa, whoa, whoa! What's all this shit?"

"Tools," Lance said, stepping through the metal detector. He was clean, but the carryall was a different story.

"I need to take a look at this," the guard said,

hauling the heavy bag onto the steel examination desk and opening it up. There was a camera inside, a tripod, and some pelican cases containing sensitive listening devices—all things Lance had picked up from a CIA stash in Bethesda earlier. There were no weapons in the bag.

"You sure you need all this crap?" the guard said.

"Oh, buddy, I wish I didn't, believe me, but you heard what happened last night, right?"

"Of course I heard. I was sitting right here when it went down."

"Then you understand."

"Understand?"

"Yes," Lance said.

The guard nodded knowingly then, though what it was that he knew was anyone's guess. He hit a buzzer, and Lance passed through a high-tech security turnstile. "You know where you're going?"

"These elevators right here, right?"

"Yup."

Lance pushed the button and waited. The guard watched him, both of them feeling slightly awkward in the silence, then the elevator arrived and Lance gave him a final nod. He stepped inside, scanned his keycard, and pressed the button for the lower maintenance level, two stories beneath street level. It was the only floor the keycard would allow him to access.

The moment the doors shut, Laurel said, "What the hell was that with the name?"

"I'm sending a message," Lance said.

"Levi's name? You're getting cocky," Laurel said. "You're playing with fire."

"Just sending a message," Lance said again.

The doors opened, revealing a blank, concrete corridor with vents and exposed ductwork running along the ceiling. There was no one there, and he walked the length of it, past numerous utility and storage rooms, until he reached a thick, steel fire door. There was a security scanner next to the door and a camera above it. Lance scanned the keycard and got a ding sound and a little red light.

"Tatyana?" he said under his breath.

"Just wait," she said. "Your card's good." The lock blinked three more times red, then turned green and dinged again at a higher pitch.

The door opened, leading to a large, climate-controlled service room. Inside, the air was frigidly cold, and there was a loud hum from the fans and ventilation equipment. On the far side of the room was a separate area, and that was where the famed Mosler vault was. The safe was the size of a small room, but Lance already knew that once the thickness of the steel was taken into account, the interior wasn't much larger than a regular refrigerator. On its door were three rotary dials.

Initially, when the safe was first installed by the government at the Oak Ridge National Laboratory, the controls were completely analog. Arps had kept them that way. While the rest of the building was digitized, which was what made it possible for

Laurel and Tatyana to hack it, the safe itself remained analog. It was a smart move from a man who knew the power of the nanocomputers that were on the horizon.

"All right," Lance said into his mic, walking over to the servers and pretending to examine them. "I see the safe."

"Good," Laurel said. "The guard's still at his post. Looks like you haven't raised any alarms."

"He was watching sports on his phone," Lance said, slinging the carryall to the ground and taking out the camera and tripod. He set them up in front of a server, but pointed its high-powered lens toward the safe. Then he turned it on and hit the transmission button on the camera.

"We have visual," Tatyana said.

"Good," Laurel said. "I see it. Can you attach the mics?"

Breaking the safe would involve a complicated coordination of visual data from the camera and audio data from a number of extremely sensitive electronic listening devices. Lance took a pelican case from the carryall and worked quickly to unpack the mics, which each looked, for all intents and purposes, like the heads of a doctor's stethoscope.

"You better do something with the server," Tatyana said. "The guard's looking at his computer screen."

Lance stopped what he was doing and went back to the server, fiddling with its control panel.

"What's he doing now?" he said under his breath, concealing his mouth as he spoke.

"He's still at his desk," Tatyana said. "He's looking at his phone mostly but keeps glancing at the screen."

"I'm on his screen?"

"You and eleven other feeds," Tatyana said. "They rotate."

"Can you tell me if I rotate off-screen?"

"Sure."

Lance kept diddling with the server panel until Tatyana said, "All right. You're good."

Immediately, he hurried over to the safe and started placing the listening devices strategically around the three dials on its enormous door. Each mic was able to independently transmit its data back to Laurel, where it would be analyzed to create an image of the lock's inner workings. It was a tall order, computationally speaking, but Laurel insisted the NSA models she had access to were up to the task.

When Lance had set up the sixth mic, he said, "All right. Devices attached."

"Just a minute," Laurel said. "I'm setting up the learning model."

"Uh oh," Tatyana said.

"The guard?"

"Yes. He's pinned your camera to his screen. He's definitely watching you now."

Lance went back to the server and pretended to examine some cables.

"He's getting up from his desk," Tatyana said. "He looks upset."

"Tell me exactly what he's doing?" Lance said.

Tatyana was quiet for a moment, then said, "He's using the security event logger. He just sent an incident report."

"Can you read it?" He kept fiddling with the cables while she checked.

"It says, 'Cyber contractor in restricted area. Incident reported. Backup called'."

"All right," Lance said. "Laurel, let's get moving."

"You should abort."

"No," he said, hurrying back to the safe. "What do you need me to do?"

"I need you to get out of there."

"I'm not leaving," Lance said. "So you either tell me what to do, or I'll—"

"Fine!" Laurel said. "Shut up a second. Let me think. What's the guard doing?"

"Waiting by the front door," Tatyana said. "Probably watching for his backup."

Laurel hesitated a moment, then said, "Lance, start moving the dials slowly and steadily in a clockwise direction, beginning with the topmost and working down."

Lance began turning the dials.

"That's too fast," she said. "It needs to be nice and slow."

He slowed down, rotating the dials one at a time through their full cycle of positions, the mics picking up every minute click and sound in the internal mechanisms. No one could speak while he did it, though he knew Tatyana would interrupt if necessary. The entire process took about twenty seconds per dial. "Okay," he said when he was done. "Did you get what you needed?"

Tatyana immediately broke in. "Lance, you've got company."

"What is it?"

"A car belonging to the building's private security firm just pulled up out front. Two men, armed, are getting out now. They'll likely be with you in a minute or two tops."

35

Tatyana watched the screen as a second security vehicle pulled up outside the building. Two more guards got out, also armed. It looked like they weren't taking any chances.

"Two more guards," she said into the mic. "That's five now in total, including the guy at reception."

"Where are they?" Lance said.

"Still in the lobby. They're looking at the screen at the front desk, watching you."

"Laurel? How's that model?" Lance said.

"Data's processing. The mechanism is more complicated than expected. This could take time."

"How much time?"

"Hours."

"Hours?" Lance said, hurrying back over to the server so he could again pretend to be doing what he was supposed to be doing.

"If we're lucky," Laurel said.

"And if we're not lucky."

"It could take days, Lance. Or even weeks. We might never get in."

"Weeks! I needn't tell you we don't have weeks, Laurel."

"Even if we did, the NSA would revoke my access. I'm tying up the most powerful computers in the entire government right now."

Tatyana got up and went to Laurel's terminal. Her screen was awash with numbers and letters, digital gibberish scrolling endlessly like stock market figures. On her own screen, she could see that Lance was looking at the server controls, pretending to scribble notes with something that may or may not have been a pen.

"The camera and listening devices can be packed up," Laurel said. "They've done their job."

"And the model?"

"Still processing, Lance."

Tatyana was tense. She understood that the computer was reconstructing the inner-workings of a complicated mechanism based solely on the sounds and clicks that the gears and springs made, she just wished it would do it faster. She went back to her own desk and said, "The guards are moving toward the elevator now."

"Have they called for further backup?"

"No," she said. "They're still in a precautionary stance. They're suspicious, but they don't know for sure you're doing anything wrong. You could be doing exactly what a technician is supposed to be doing."

"They know he's unarmed," Laurel said.

"They figure they have enough guys to take me," Lance said.

"Four just entered the elevator. The first guy remained upstairs."

"How's that model doing, Laurel?"

"If anything happens, I'll let you know."

"The elevator's descending."

"They likely have no idea how important that safe is," Laurel said.

Lance went to the carryall and took out what looked to Tatyana to be a small toolkit. He'd packed for the job without them, picking up the equipment Laurel had requested, though what else he might have had in the carryall, she didn't know. "What's that Lance?" she said. The guards in the elevator could no longer see what he was doing, though they would be connected by radio to the guy upstairs.

"It's a screwdriver."

"Screwdriver?" Laurel said. "We said no fatalities. We're on home soil."

"I know where we are," Lance said, deftly slipping the screwdriver into the sock at his ankle.

"It's very small," Tatyana said to Laurel, but as she did, she saw Lance put something else into a pocket. She hadn't seen what it was and had no idea what he was planning.

"Oh my God," Laurel gasped. "It did it. We're in."

Lance glanced toward the door, then toward the safe. "How much time do I have?"

"Not enough," Tatyana said. "They're getting out of the elevator now. You have fifteen seconds."

Lance ran over to the safe and and said, "Okay, Laurel. Ready when you are."

"Start at the top dial. Left fourteen, right twelve," she said.

Lance began rotating the dial.

"Left forty-one, right sixteen," Laurel said.

"Same dial?"

"Same dial."

"They're at the door," Tatyana said.

"All right, boss," Lance said loudly as the door opened. "Almost done with the servers but I'll need to speak to the guard upstairs."

Spurred by the sound of Lance's voice, the guards hurried into the room, ready for trouble.

"Next dial," Laurel said. "Left seven, right nine, left six, right thirty-two."

"Hey you!" the lead guard shouted, his hand on the firearm at his waist. Lance could see that it was a Glock 22.

Lance finished what he was doing, then turned around and said, "Whoa, fellas, what's going on?"

Tatyana watched the screen closely. The four men neared Lance, seemingly hesitant. They still didn't seem to know if he was doing anything wrong or not.

"Is there a fire or something?" Lance said.

"What are you doing over there?" the lead guard said.

"I'm from Rhino," Lance said, reaching for the lanyard hanging around his neck.

"Don't move!" the man said, drawing his gun.

"Whoa, whoa, whoa!" Lance said, raising his hands. "What's going on? Is there some sort of problem?"

"Building security," one of the other guards said.

"Don't speak to him," the lead man said. Then, to Lance, he said, "Come away from there."

"What's the problem?" Lance said, keeping his hands up and stepping forward slowly. "I checked in with security. I've got a lanyard."

"Well, apparently you're not working where you're supposed to be working."

"That right there," Lance said, indicating the safe, "contains the security protocols for accessing the mainframe controls. I'm the only person authorized to access it, and I can't do my job until I do."

"I don't know about all that," the guard said, "but if you come back upstairs with us, we can sort it all out. All I know is that the area you're in right now is off limits."

"Fine by me," Lance said, keeping his hands on his head. "We bill by the hour. Just tell your guys to put their guns away." The other guards hadn't drawn their guns, but the lead man holstered his. He took Lance by the arm as he approached.

"Great," Tatyana said to Laurel. "Now what?"

Laurel shrugged and leaned over to see Tatyana's screen. The four men were escorting Lance back toward the door. Lance was going with them peacefully. Not resisting. They walked out of the safe area, back past the servers, and then, just as they were approaching the door, there was a loud bang, as if a flashbang had just exploded, and the screen went completely white.

"What was that?" Laurel said.

"I guess he packed a few surprises in that carryall," Tatyana said.

The visuals came back. The room was full of smoke, and what followed was a jumbled hotch-potch of chaotic movement, barely decipherable on the screen. They saw one of the guards emerge from the smoke, rubbing his eyes. Lance followed him, struck him in the neck, and planted a knee in his groin. The man doubled over and dropped his gun, which Lance immediately picked up. He smacked the man on the back of the head with it, then struck another man. The two fought, but Lance got the upper hand, knocking him to the ground as the two other guards approached, guns drawn. Lance reached down to his ankle, pulled out the screwdriver he'd hidden there, and jammed it into the arm of the lead man. The man cried out in pain and grabbed his arm. The last man fired a bullet, but too late. Lance's arm had already swung out and knocked his aim off. The bullet ricocheted into the room, and Lance punched the man in the face, then caught him on the chin with an elbow.

"Lance!" Laurel hissed, looking at the four guards lying on the floor. "Home soil!"

"They'll live," Lance said, then to the men, all of whom were still conscious, he said, "Nobody move."

"The guy upstairs has raised the alarm," Tatyana said. "Police will be all over the place in minutes."

Lance went to each man hurriedly and took his gun and radio, then cuffed them to a pipe using their own cuffs. "Just sit tight, and I'll be on my way," he said. "No one needs to get hurt."

The lead man's arm was bleeding badly, the screwdriver still in it, and Lance pulled it out and tied a makeshift tourniquet at his elbow using the man's own belt.

Then he said to Laurel, "What's the final set of digits?"

Laurel gave him the instructions for the last dial, which he followed, then waited. There was an excruciating second of silence, then the heavy door of the safe swung open smoothly on its well-oiled hinges. They were in!

"What's inside?" Laurel said. "What is it?"

"Police incoming in four minutes," Tatyana said, staring at the satellite view.

And then something strange happened. The screen showing the room went completely blank, like their connection had suddenly been cut. Tatyana tabbed through the other camera feeds in the building. They were all blank. “What the hell just happened?” she said.

“Lance?” Laurel said, then more urgently, “Lance? Are you there? We lost visual.”

There was no answer.

36

"What the hell just happened?" Laurel said, desperately hitting keys on her computer, trying to get back into the building's security system. "All the feeds went down at once. We've been completely locked out. I can't see anything?"

"Look here," Tatyana said, staring at her own screen. She had the satellite feed up of the building's exterior and the surrounding area. "The police are just three minutes out."

"He'll get out," Laurel said, eyeing the screen. "He was in control of the situation. All he has to do is get past that one guard in the lobby."

Tatyana zoomed in closer on the building, though from the angle, it was impossible to see what was going on inside the lobby's enormous glass façade.

Laurel went back to her own computer and

pulled up the comms log. She said into her mic, “Lance? Lance? Can you hear me?”

There was no answer.

“What I don’t understand,” Laurel said, “is why we lost comms when we got kicked out of the building’s system. They were running on separate networks. There’s no overlap.”

“You don’t think....” Tatyana said quietly, her words trailing off.

“Think what?” Laurel said.

“I mean, the comms network is still running. It’s only Lance that went silent.”

“Maybe he lost his earpiece,” Laurel said. “Maybe it fell during the tussle and got stamped on.”

“Maybe,” Tatyana said, but Laurel could hear the trace of skepticism in her voice.

Laurel pulled up the comms log and confirmed that the network was still running. It was just Lance’s node that was down. She pulled up the event log for the building’s security system. And there it was. A number in red, forty-six kilobytes, amidst a sea of green. “Uh oh,” she said.

“What?” Tatyana said.

“It looks like we received a data packet from the building right before the blackout.”

“A data packet? What does that mean?”

“Something protecting the building. It’s what kicked us out.”

“How’s that possible?”

"I don't know. I don't know any—" she stopped speaking mid-sentence.

"What is it?" Tatyana said.

"It came from the camera. There must have been an SD card or something...."

"Please tell me what you're talking about?" Tatyana said.

"It wasn't the building's security that kicked us out," Laurel said. "It was Lance."

"What?"

"He got us kicked out, Tatyana. The script used the camera's transmitter. He must have planned on doing it right from the beginning."

"But why?"

"Whatever was in that safe," Laurel said, "Lance wanted to keep it for himself."

"He did this on purpose?" Tatyana said, turning to Laurel. "I can't believe it."

"Why?" Laurel said, then, looking at Tatyana, suddenly added, "Am I missing something here?"

"Missing something?"

"I mean," Laurel said, "Was there... is there..."

"You don't think—" Tatyana gasped, with a look of absolute shock on her face.

"Was there something going on here that I wasn't aware of?"

"Something between me and Lance? Are you kidding me?"

Tatyana looked mortified, and Laurel felt the same. This was a topic they'd both managed to steer clear of for a long time. The fact was, both of them had harbored feelings for Lance since day one, and they both knew it. It didn't matter that those feelings went unrequited. In fact, that only served to make the topic more sensitive.

"I'm not kidding," Laurel said. She could already feel the error of her judgment, she knew she was way off base, but she couldn't stop herself.

"I was right here with you," Tatyana protested. "The entire time."

"That doesn't mean—"

"Whatever this was," she said, pointing at her screen, "it's got nothing to do with me."

"You two arrived at my hotel room—"

"I came into this with the same information you have, Laurel. And whatever Lance is doing now, I'm as in the dark about it as you are. Believe me."

The two women stared at each other for a moment, and it was Laurel who broke eye contact first. "Sorry," she said quietly.

"We're on the same side," Tatyana said.

Laurel nodded. She knew that was true. "I know, I know," she said. "For a moment there, my nerves just got the better of me. I was out of line."

"It's all right," Tatyana said. "I might have thought the same thing if you hadn't gone there first."

Tatyana still had the satellite view up, and Laurel noticed movement on the screen. "Uh oh," she said. "Here we go."

Tatyana zoomed in closer, and there was no doubting what they were looking at. A man in gray overalls had just walked out the front door of the Skadden Arps building like it was the most ordinary thing in the world. He looked left and right—no sign of the police, they were still a minute and a half out—then began walking briskly in the direction of the nearest subway station. He'd left his carryall behind, but tucked under one arm was a small, brown document folder.

"There he goes," Laurel said.

"And he's got the safe's contents with him."

"Well," Laurel said, "as long as he got what he wanted from us."

They watched him go as far as the subway station and disappear underground. They could have hacked the city's CCTV network and kept following, but neither of them had the heart to do it. It was pointless, in any case. If Lance wanted to disappear, he had all the tools at his disposal to do so. They'd lose him now, and they wouldn't find him again unless he wanted to be found.

"That's it," Tatyana said. "That might be the last time we ever see him."

"Don't say that," Laurel said, feeling a knot of emotion in her throat.

"It's true," Tatyana said, shutting down the satellite connection. "No use pretending otherwise."

Laurel looked at her friend. She knew Tatyana was feeling the same emotion that she was. Neither of them said a word for a full minute, and then

Tatyana threw up her hands. "All right," she said. "We got fucked, lady. Time to move on."

Laurel nodded, but she hardly heard the words.

"Are you ready for me to wipe the drives?" Tatyana said.

Laurel didn't answer her for a second, lost in her own thoughts, then nodded. "Sure," she said. "Wipe everything."

Tatyana began wiping all traces of the operation from her system— there was no need for Agency auditors to see it all and ask questions later. Laurel did the same with her system, then got to her feet.

"Laurel, are you all right?" Tatyana said, looking at her strangely.

"Am I all right?" Laurel said, shaking her head. "I'm going to be honest, Tatyana. I don't know what I am." She gathered her things and walked across the room toward the elevator.

"Wait up," Tatyana said, hurrying after her.

Laurel pushed the button for the elevator but nothing happened. She scanned her keycard and pushed it again. Still nothing.

"Well, there you go," she said, suddenly feeling as if she was about to break down into tears. "That's it. Our passes have been revoked. We're officially out in the cold."

37

When Tatyana's card also didn't scan, she wasn't sure what to feel. "An inglorious end to our time here," she said, looking out across the empty office space.

"How do we get out?" Laurel said.

They both looked toward the stairs at the same time. "It's only six floors," Tatyana said.

Laurel still looked ready to burst into tears. She marched toward the door, pushed through, and Tatyana hurried down the six flights of stairs after her.

When they burst into the lobby on the ground floor, the guard looked up, surprised to see them coming that way. "Everything all right, ladies?"

"No, it's not all right," Laurel said. "Our cards don't work. We couldn't even call the elevator."

"That's odd," he said. "Let me look into that for you."

"It's all right," Tatyana said, already knowing

the problem went way above his pay grade. She recognized him vaguely, though it was only from his name tag that she remembered his name. In any case, the dissolution of the Group was not something he was going to be able to fix. "Don't worry about it."

"Here," he said, reaching out to Laurel for her pass. "Let me take a look." He scanned her card in his reader, and his brow furrowed. "Hm," he said. "I'm sorry. It looks like your clearances have been revoked."

"Ridiculous!" Laurel snapped, spoiling for a fight.

"Come on, Laurel," Tatyana said, taking her by the arm. "Let's go."

"No," she said. "This is unacceptable. I want this fixed."

"There's nothing he'll be able to do."

The guard picked up his phone and said, "I can call my supervisor. If there's some sort of error—"

"Don't bother." Tatyana said. "We're leaving."

"But if this is some sort of mistake—"

"It's not a mistake," she said.

"It *is* a mistake," Laurel said.

"Laurel, come on, let's go."

Laurel pulled her arm free and then looked at them both. Tatyana didn't know if she was going to laugh or cry or run. Instead, she took a deep breath and composed herself. "I need to get out of here," she said. There was an agency car outside, and Laurel crossed the lobby and went out to it. Then she got inside and was gone. Tatyana stood there next to the security guard, watching the car's taillights disappear into the night.

"I suppose I should ask you to call me a cab," Tatyana said at last, absently handing him her card.

"Sorry," he said, looking at it.

"Oh," she said, rolling her eyes. Stupid. She wouldn't be charging anything to the Group's billing code while the card wasn't working. "It's fine," she said with a sigh. "I'll pay cash."

She waited on a bench in the lobby, watching for the cab, and the guard kept catching her eye and nodding sympathetically. She nodded back, utterly humiliated, and when she finally saw the lights of her cab approaching, she gave him a thin smile and said, "So long, Bukowski."

He looked up and gave her a final smile, and that was it. She was out the door. Her final moments at the Agency were over, and they'd been as unceremonious as sitting at a bus stop, waiting for a ride. As she descended the steps to her car, she wondered if she would ever set foot inside the building again.

She'd intended to go straight home, but once she was in the backseat of the cab, she found herself telling the driver to take her to the Old Ebbitt.

"You think it'll be open?" the driver said, glancing at his watch.

"It's open," Tatyana said.

She sat in silence while he drove, watching the

lights of the other cars pass by, her mind running over what had just happened. What was Lance up to? What had he found in the safe? Why cut her and Laurel out of the picture?

When she got to 15th Street, she paid the driver and got out of the cab. It had started raining again, and she hurried into the bar, brushing past the host who attempted to stop her as she passed. “Oh, we’re just closing up, ma’am.”

“I know,” she said over her shoulder, still walking. “I’m just here to see... what’s his name?” She nodded over at her *friend*, the bartender, though when he saw her, he seemed to visibly flinch.

He made a gesture to the host that was definitely intended to stop Tatyana from coming over, but it was too late. She was already inside. She walked up to the bar purposefully, daring the host to try to stop her, and took a seat on one of the bar stools. The bartender was cleaning up from what had apparently been a busy night, and he didn’t stop what he was doing on her account. In fact, it seemed he was doing his best to ignore her, polishing the counter at the far end of the bar, or clearing glassware from tables and disappearing into the back for minutes at a time.

Tatyana knew she wasn’t wanted, and ordinarily, that would have been enough to make her run a million miles, but tonight, for some reason, she couldn’t leave. She couldn’t face going home alone. She’d lost all of her usual poise. She didn’t care if the bartender wanted to see her or not. Even a fight with him would be better than nothing. Even being kicked out, if it came to it, would be preferable.

Back at the entrance, she could see that the host was speaking animatedly to the manager, pointing her way. The manager, dressed in a crisp navy suit, began walking in Tatyana's direction, but even then, she didn't care. Even if they brought security over, she didn't care. The only thing she cared about was getting through the night, getting through the next hour, getting through the next ten minutes. As long as she wasn't alone with her thoughts, as long as she didn't have to think about what was going to happen next, she would take anything.

And then it came, a tap on the shoulder from the manager. He was a surly-looking fellow in his mid-forties, wiry, with a badge on his lapel that said his name was Maxwell. "Excuse me, ma'am," he said.

"If one more person calls me *ma'am*—"

"I'm going to have to ask you to leave, ma'am. We're shutting down for the night."

"Don't worry, I'm not going to order anything."

"That's not the point."

"All I'm doing is waiting for that guy to acknowledge that I exist," she said, nodding at the bartender who'd just re-emerged from the back.

"That *guy*," the manager said, "doesn't seem interested in anything you have to say."

"Hey?" Tatyana called out at him. "Brian. Brandon."

"Bryant," the bartender said, reluctantly coming

over. "It's all right, Max," he said with a sigh. "I'll take it from here."

"See that you do," the manager said, giving Tatyana a final stern look.

"Is that any way to treat a friend?" Tatyana said when the manager was gone.

Bryant was tired, she could see that, but she didn't care. She needed him. Or, rather, she needed *someone*, and he was the closest person to hand.

He looked at her for a minute, then said, "You're not drunk, are you?"

"No," she said, "though that sounds like a good idea." She smiled at her little joke, but Bryant's face remained motionless.

"I didn't think I'd see you back here," he said.

"Oh? Why not?"

"Why not? Because of the way things ended the other night. That's why not."

She knew what he was talking about, she'd been as cold as ice after they'd made love and then snuck out as soon as he fell asleep. She was often that way with the guys she went home with. Men were usually pretty forgiving of it if she ever saw them again. As long as a woman was willing to go to bed, they could be forgiving of almost anything, she'd found. "Oh," she said. "Sorry. I was called in to work."

"You asked me to go another round, and when I said I couldn't, you just walked out."

"That's not what happened."

"Yes it is."

"You fell asleep."

"I did not fall asleep."

She shook her head. "You're crazy," she said. "You fell asleep."

From the look on his face, she didn't think she was going to get what she'd come for, and she suddenly felt very small, very rejected, very humiliated. She looked around the bar—the host was staring at her, so was the manager. Even two drunk businessmen who were as guilty as she was of staying late were staring. She made to say something else to Bryant, but no words came to her, so she just got down from her stool and stormed toward the exit, stumbling on her heel as she passed the manager and host, who watched as if afraid she'd steal something.

What was wrong with her, she thought, pulling her coat tight as she was enveloped by the cold night air. Was she losing her marbles? She tried to hail a cab, but it was late and she didn't see any, so she walked to the corner of New York Avenue and tried again.

"Hey!" someone said from behind her.

It was Bryant, standing there in the cold without his coat.

"What is it?" she said.

"All I was saying is that you could have said goodbye."

"I could have said goodbye?"

"Before you ran out the other night. I didn't know where you'd gone."

"I'm Russian," she said before even fully realizing what it was she intended to say.

"What's that supposed to mean?"

She shrugged. "I guess it means that you get what you get. I'm not going to promise you any more than that."

"I see."

"My people.... We're not good at...."

"At what?"

She thought for a moment, then said, "Explaining ourselves."

He looked at her then as if he didn't understand, as if she was speaking a language from a different planet, which she probably was.

A cab approached, and she put two fingers in her mouth and whistled. It stopped right next to her, and she reached for the door. "Are you coming?" she said to Bryant.

"I don't...."

"You don't what?"

"I don't have my coat."

"Your loss," she said, getting into the car.

"Wait!" he said, hurrying in after her. "I'll come."

38

Tatyana woke with a start. For an instant, she had no idea where she was and glanced around the room frantically, putting together the pieces before realizing she was at the bartender's place, in his bed, bunched up in a ball as far away from him as possible.

He'd performed admirably the night before, and she looked at the chiseled form of his chest as he rose, rubbing his eyes.

She got out of the bed and realized her phone was vibrating on the nightstand. She picked it up. It was Laurel.

"What is it?" Tatyana said.

"I found Lance."

"You're kidding," she said, searching for the clothes she'd so hastily discarded the night before. She looked at the bartender and then said to Laurel, "Can I call you back in five?"

"Sure," Laurel said, and from her tone, she'd guessed the reason.

Tatyana sat down on the side of the bed and rubbed her temples. There'd been a bottle of whiskey, she remembered. She looked around for it. There it was, on the dresser across the room, almost empty. That had been a mistake.

She began pulling on her clothes, and the bartender watched her from his side of the bed. "You're doing it again," he said.

"No I'm not," she said. "This time, I'm saying goodbye."

"Work?"

"Yes."

"What is it you do anyway?"

She looked at him very seriously. "I could tell you," she said, "but then I'd have to kill you."

He rolled his eyes.

She pulled on her coat, gave him a final glance, and a moment later was outside, looking up and down the deserted predawn street and realizing she wasn't going to be hailing a cab anytime soon. It was a residential neighborhood, and she tried to remember the cab ride from the night before. It had taken a while to get wherever it was that they were. She looked at her watch. It was before five in the morning. She'd probably had an hour's sleep max.

She began walking in the direction that looked most promising and pulled out her phone. "Laurel?"

"Lance boarded a flight."

"To where?"

"Istanbul."

Neither of them said anything for a moment. Then Tatyana said, "He's going to Moscow."

"I think so," Laurel said.

"He wants to cut a deal."

"We don't know what he wants."

"Do you think…."

"Do I think what?" Laurel said.

"Do you think Lance would ever…."

"Defect?"

"Sorry," Tatyana said.

"Don't be sorry," Laurel said. "He left us high and dry. Why do that if he wasn't up to something?"

"He did say he wanted to help Roth," Tatyana said. "Cutting a deal with the Kremlin would be one way of doing that."

Laurel sighed. "Let's hope that's it. And let's hope that whatever he found in the safe gives him enough leverage to do it."

"Except, why disappear?" Tatyana said. "Why not keep us in the loop?"

"I don't know. To protect us?"

"Protect us from what?"

"I don't know," Laurel said. "What I do know is that those cameras cut out before he ever opened the safe. That means either he knew what it contained or planned on cutting us out of the picture regardless."

"Something's definitely up," Tatyana said. "He

had another agenda before he ever came to us for help."

"He used us," Laurel said.

"Sure feels that way."

"There's something else," Laurel said. "That whole business in Washington State."

"With his sister?"

"Yeah, except it wasn't his sister. Someone only made it look that way. Someone who wanted to pull Lance into that whole mess. My guess is that it was the Kremlin."

They were both quiet then. Tatyana tried to picture Lance getting off a commercial flight in Moscow and seeking to cut a deal. "If he ends up defecting," she said, "I'll fly back to Moscow myself to kill him."

"Don't joke about that," Laurel said.

"I'm not joking," Tatyana said. She was still walking briskly, getting wet in a light rain, and she was trying to make out what street she was on. There was still no sign of a cab anywhere.

"There's something else," Laurel added.

"That sounds ominous."

"It's not… well, I don't know. Just check your email."

"Oh," Tatyana said, looking at her phone. "I see. The nail in the coffin."

"Things aren't going to be the same, Tatyana."

"You sound maudlin."

"Well, it's been, I don't know how to do these."

"Do what?"

"It's been an honor, Tatyana. Things weren't always frictionless between us, but, well, working with you, it's been an honor."

"Likewise," Tatyana said and was going to say more, but Laurel had already hung up.

Tatyana reached an intersection and was finally able to orient herself. She was at Monroe and 13th. She looked up and down the forlorn street, not a car in sight, and sat down on a bench by a bus stop. Then she opened the email.

The message Laurel mentioned was from the new acting Director of the CIA, Jared Cutler.

> Tatyana Aleksandrova, citizen of Russia, operator of the Special Operations Group, hired by Levi Roth, reporting to Laurel Everlane. This message is formal confirmation that your services will no longer be required by the Central Intelligence Agency and that, as of the transmission of this message, your security clearance and access to CIA resources and systems have been revoked.
>
> As you are aware, the work you performed for the United States was of critical national security importance and, as such, puts you at an ongoing risk of reprisal from foreign powers. Therefore, you are entitled to a full relocation and protection package, including a new name and identity, US citizenship, a place to reside, and a

sizable one-time financial payout. If deemed feasible by our medical team, you will also be entitled to some degree of cosmetic alteration to render you unrecognizable to digital detection systems.

In accordance with Directive 41 of the CIA's Memorandum of Understanding with the US Congress, all record of your service has been permanently deleted. No government agency or employee will ever be able to verify any detail of your service to the country or, indeed, whether it occurred at all. You are also prohibited from speaking of it or doing anything that would compromise the integrity of the arrangements made for your protection. Please report to the personnel office at 1000 Colonial Farm Road, Maclean, Virginia, between the hours of nine am and five pm, Monday to Friday, to make further arrangements for your relocation.

In accordance with the conditions of your service to the Special Operations Group, the United States Government will now begin a deep clean of all records relating to Tatyana Aleksandrova, whether such records exist on US Government databases, the databases of private corporations, or the records of foreign governments.

You no longer exist and, indeed, never did.

Thank you for your service,

Jared Cutler

Acting Director, Central Intelligence Agency

Tatyana let out a long sigh as she read to the end, then deleted the message, got to her feet, and began walking along Monroe toward Michigan Avenue, where she thought she'd have a better chance of at least catching a bus.

39

Lance was seated in the economy cabin of a Turkish Airlines Airbus A321 from Istanbul to Vnukovo International Airport, Moscow. It was a flight of just under four hours and he was making it on his own passport, under his own name. He had little doubt that there would be a welcoming committee waiting for him on his arrival.

The file he'd found in Skadden Arps's safe was stowed safely in a safe deposit box at Istanbul Airport, at the airport branch of İşbank, Turkey's largest bank. He'd rented the box earlier that morning, with the instruction that if he did not come back to claim the contents within seven days, they were to be sent to the Café Americano on Kaplicalar Street in Istanbul, directly across the street from the US Consulate General, with the name Laurel Everlane on the front of the envelope. It wasn't the most direct method of getting it to its intended recipient, but it also wasn't a method anyone would be on the lookout for. The Kremlin would know he'd traveled via Istanbul and could potentially be watching the mail to intercept it.

Additionally, Skadden Arps' rolodex was in a locker at Dulles International Airport in Washington, with instructions that it be sent to the *New York Times* if not collected.

Lance thought about the *kompromat*. It was amazing how much value could be squeezed into one little folder, especially if you knew what you were looking at. That folder could do things that the combined military might of the US and all her NATO allies could not.

That folder was the reason Arps had been killed.

And what it contained was not military secrets, or the blueprints for some new superweapon, or even political documents. No, all it contained was a single, simple medical file. Lab results, original prescriptions in Russian doctors' handwriting, photographs and treatment regimens, x-rays, all for one very important patient, Vladimir Molotov. The contents confirmed beyond a shadow of a doubt that the many rumors regarding the president's health were true, and that he was currently undergoing extensive treatment for pancreatic cancer. If the contents were ever to get into the open, they would utterly undermine the image Molotov sought to project to the world. Molotov was a strongman, an iron-willed dictator, a man who'd already secured the legal basis for his power for another fifteen years. When he completed that term, he would have been in power for longer even than Stalin.

The folder was kryptonite to all of that. How could a strongman maintain his grip on power when the public knew he was dying of cancer? Challengers would proliferate. They'd come out of every nook and cranny, both from within Russia and without. That folder was an existential threat to Molotov's regime.

And that gave Lance leverage.

Lance knew what he was sitting on. He knew the value of it, and the steps Molotov would take to see that it remained secret. And he had little doubt that it could be traded for two things at once.

"Anything to drink, sir?"

He was seated by the window, and the other two seats in the row were empty. In fact, most of the plane was empty. Molotov's aggression against Ukraine was taking a toll, even on the busy route between Moscow and the Turkish capital, which had long been a lifeline for Russians seeking to live and work abroad.

"Coffee," Lance said to the hostess. "Black."

She brought him his coffee and he took a sip. Outside, was nothing but clouds and blue skies. By the time he'd finished the coffee, the pilot was announcing that he was beginning the final descent to Vnukovo. Lance took his phone from his pocket and removed the battery and SIM. He left the handset and battery in the pocket of the seat in front of him, and put the SIM card in the empty paper coffee cup, which he threw in the trash.

He knew that the *Politsiya*, or national police, and probably representatives from the Russian Ministry of Internal Affairs, as well as the GRU and FSB, would be waiting for him when he landed. Indeed, he was counting on it.

40

Lance got to the end of the air bridge and immediately put his hands in the air. In front of him were eight armed police, as well as a man dressed in an ill-fitting business suit who looked more like an insurance salesman than a member of the security services. He was holding a shabby leather briefcase and had on large, thick glasses that slightly magnified his eyes. Behind one ear, he had a plastic pen.

"Gentlemen," Lance said, approaching them with his hands still in the air. "I take it you're my welcoming committee."

"You'll come with us, Mr Spector," the man in the suit said in Russian. Lance wondered if he would introduce himself. He wanted to know which agency he was from. It mattered because whichever section of the Russian intelligence community had taken the lead would tell him a lot. It would affect how things panned out.

The police were regular *politsiya*, which told him nothing other than what he could read from their demeanor. They seemed relaxed. None put their hands on him. There was no unsightly arrest, no handcuffs, no one even patted him down to check if he was armed. Everything was decidedly dignified, almost welcoming.

The airport wasn't busy, and the escort led him through the passenger lounge to a set of large double doors. A sign on the doors read, in bold Cyrillic script, 'Security Personnel Only'. An electronic card was required to gain access, and two cameras monitored the entry. They took him through the doors into a long, anonymous corridor with brick walls painted a glossy white and strong fluorescent lighting overhead. It was now that they patted him down, conducting a thorough search to make sure he wasn't armed. Once satisfied, they brought him to some stairs and down two floors to another corridor, this one wider than the first, with a water cooler and some vending machines lining one of the walls. There were offices on the other side, visible through windows that looked back out at the corridor. Lance saw computers in the offices, shelves laden with folders, and desks covered in papers. The Russian security bureaucracy, he thought, hard at work.

Toward the end of the corridor was a little seating area, like a doctor's waiting room, and four doors leading to four interrogation rooms. Each door bore the seal of the Russian Ministry of Internal Affairs.

Lance was taken into the first of the interrogation rooms and told to sit. The room contained a plain metal table and two chairs facing each other, as well as two cameras mounted to the wall. The same high-powered fluorescent lighting illuminated the room, but it seemed brighter now, given the smaller space available to absorb it. Lance squinted slightly as he took the chair facing the door. There was an old phone on the table, as well as an iron ring for handcuffing suspects to, though it didn't seem they were going to use that on him. There was also another camera, this one on a tripod just inside the door, as well as some sound recording equipment on a steel stand. To his right was a large observation window of reflective one-way glass.

Only the man in the suit entered the room, the police all waited in the corridor, and Lance was not restrained in any way. He took that as another good sign.

The man in the suit remained standing, seemingly searching for the words with which to begin. At last, he spoke. "Mr Spector, my name is Smidovich," he said in heavily accented English. "I am here on behalf of the President of the Russian Federation."

"I see," Lance said.

"You look disappointed," Smidovich said.

"No, no," Lance said. "I wouldn't say disappointed."

"You were expecting a grander welcome, perhaps."

"I wasn't expecting anything," Lance said.

"Yes," Smidovich said, "well, life is full of disappointments, as I'm sure you already know."

"I'm not disappointed," Lance said, still wondering if there was a security agency this man was affiliated with. He had no doubt the Kremlin had more or less summoned him there. They were the ones who'd planted his sister's name in Black Swan. They were the ones who'd wanted him to kill Arps. They must have known that would lead him to the contents of Arps's safe. Now, they'd want to do a trade.

"Can I offer you anything?" Smidovich said. "Something to drink. Water?"

"No, thank you," Lance said.

"I hear you like coffee."

"You hear correctly," Lance said, "but I really don't want to put you to any trouble."

"It's no trouble," Smidovich said, picking up the receiver of the old phone and pushing a button. "Coffee," he said. "Two."

"Thank you," Lance said.

"You see, we're very civilized here in Moscow. I don't know why we get such a bad rap with you Westerners."

Lance shrugged. "Who knows? Maybe it's all the footage we see of cities being shelled. Twenty years ago, it was Grozny. Now it's Mariupol and Kharkiv. Maybe we're wondering who's next."

Smidovich raised his hands as if to say there was nothing he could do about that. "Politics," he said. "It's a dirty business."

"It's not politics that's the problem," Lance said. "It's war."

Smidovich sighed. "Well, I'll have to ask the good people of Iraq and Afghanistan what they think of war."

It was Lance's turn to say nothing, and the two men stared at each other for a moment. Smidovich shrugged then and reached down to his briefcase. He had a folder in it, and he brought it to the table, perhaps to change the subject. Looking at a printout from it, he said, "I see you've packed light. No checked luggage on your flight from Istanbul. No hand luggage."

"I was afraid anything I brought might get lost," Lance said.

Smidovich smiled. "But on your flight from Dulles to Istanbul, it says here that you did have a carry-on for that flight."

"Funny," Lance said.

"Not so much funny," Smidovich said, "as curious. You had a bag on the first flight but not on the second. Now, I'm no logician, but common sense tells me the bag must have gone somewhere. It can't have disappeared."

"That's very true," Lance said.

"Perhaps you left it in Istanbul?"

"Perhaps," Lance said. He knew he wasn't telling the man anything he couldn't deduce. What the man didn't know was where exactly he'd stashed it in Istanbul.

"Yes," Smidovich said. "It must be in Istanbul or on one of the planes. There's nowhere else it could be."

"The planes are a possibility, too," Lance conceded.

"I think Istanbul," the man said, taking the pen from behind his ear and making a note on the printout.

There was a knock on the door, and a policeman came in with two styrofoam cups of coffee and some packets of milk and sugar. "Thank you," Smidovich said, passing one of the cups to Lance.

The officer left and Smidovich put milk and sugar in his coffee. He stirred it with the pen, then offered the same pen to Lance.

Lance looked at him. The last thing he was going to do was put a pen that had been behind this man's ear in his drink. "You're not afraid I'd use that as a weapon?" he said.

"A weapon? Heaven forbid! Why would you say such a thing? You came here of your own free will. We're not enemies. Like I said before, we're very civilized here in Moscow."

"Okay," Lance said.

"I simply thought you'd like to stir your coffee," Smidovich said.

Lance smiled. "I'm fine," he said.

"You take it black, in any case."

"Yes, I do."

Smidovich took a sip of his own and said, "That's in your file."

"That must be a very detailed file."

"We're very thorough here in the—" Smidovich stopped himself before giving away his agency. "Here in the Russian Federation."

"I see," Lance said. "What else is in that file?"

"Oh, lots of things. Personal details. Known contacts. Aliases. Psychology."

"How interesting," Lance said. He got the impression the man was stalling. Killing time. Perhaps even waiting for someone more important to arrive.

As if reading Lance's mind, Smidovich said, "I suppose you'd like me to get to some sort of point. I mean, you didn't come halfway around the world for some bad coffee and the pleasure of my company."

"Don't sell yourself short," Lance said.

Smidovich smiled and looked at his watch. Definitely waiting for someone, Lance thought, and right then, the door opened again. This time it was two members of Molotov's Presidential Regiment who entered the room, dressed in full ceremonial uniform. Speaking Russian, they told Lance to stand and then conducted a thorough search of his person even though he'd already been searched. They scanned him with some handheld devices. When they were done, they left as suddenly as they'd appeared.

"We're not waiting for someone else to join us, are we?" Lance said when they were gone.

Smidovich shrugged. He was about to say something when another man entered the room, this one dressed in black pants and a turtleneck. He spoke quietly in Smidovich's ear, then also left.

"We're waiting for the big man," Lance said. It was a statement more than a question.

Smidovich ignored it. "You know," he said, "I'm really rather surprised that our paths never crossed before today."

"Why would they have?" Lance said.

"I think you can guess that I'm not just a common bureaucrat."

Lance shrugged.

"I'm from the Prime Directorate," Smidovich said.

"Good for you."

"And if our paths had crossed, as much as it pains me to say it, I imagine that one of us would be dead right now."

"Why?" Lance said. "I thought we were all civilized here in Moscow."

"When I said civilized," Smidovich said, "what I should have said is that we know how to play by the rules."

"Rules of your own making."

"No," Smidovich said, "real rules. Universal rules. The rules such games have always been played by."

"What games?"

"Come, Mr Spector. You're an assassin for the CIA. You kill on a regular basis."

Lance said nothing.

"But you don't do it mindlessly," Smidovich continued. "You do it according to an invisible set of rules. Unwritten rules. No one ever told you these rules. You just know them."

Lance shrugged. "If you're from the top floor, then I killed a great many of your friends."

"*Friends*?" Smidovich said with a shake of the head. "Let's call them colleagues."

"All right," Lance said.

"The thing we've noticed about you on the top floor, Mr Spector, is that you play by the book."

"There is no book."

"Oh no?" Smidovich said. "Come now. There's a book."

"I don't know what you're talking about."

"You don't go after your targets in their homes. You don't kill them while they're asleep in their beds, lying next to their wives. You don't do it in front of their children. There's never any unnecessary overhead."

"I've killed people in their homes."

"You only kill people when they're in play. We appreciate that."

"I'm a real gentleman," Lance said dryly.

"The people you kill," Smidovich said, "they're killing your people. You have no choice. It must be done. We understand that."

Lance looked at the man closely, wondering what the point of all this was. "I hope you're not going to ask me out on a date," he said.

Smidovich smiled. "Always the joker."

"It's not a joke," Lance said.

Smidovich breathed in deeply, choosing his next words carefully, then said, "Mr Spector, if I thought there was any chance of persuading you to switch allegiances—"

"There isn't."

Smidovich spread his hands. "Right. As you say. I'm just, what do you call it?"

"Fishing?" Lance said.

"*Shooting the shit*," he said. "Isn't that what you Americans like to say?" He glanced at his watch again and took another sip of his coffee.

"Who are we waiting for?" Lance said.

Smidovich smiled. "I wouldn't like to spoil the surprise."

"Why not?"

Smidovich shrugged. "Perhaps I don't know who's coming."

"You know."

"Perhaps I don't know anything."

"If you didn't, you'd certainly be curious," Lance said, wondering what it was this pasty bureaucrat wanted. What was his position? What had he been told? He definitely wanted something, and Lance was beginning to suspect he needed to get it before whoever was coming arrived. But what was it? And what could he trade in exchange for it?

"Curious?" Smidovich said coyly. "Whatever about?"

"Do you even know why I'm here?" Lance said.

Smidovich shrugged. "I know some things. I don't know others."

"You don't know why I'm here, do you?"

Smidovich shook his head again. "Perhaps my mind is, how you say, immune to curiosity."

"I know that's not true."

Smidovich smiled. "In Russia, we have a saying. I don't know how to say it in English, something like, some things are better left unknown."

"You know the names of my contacts. You know who my targets were. You know I had a handbag on my flight to Istanbul, but not on the flight to Moscow. Hell, you even know how I take my coffee."

Smidovich shrugged.

"Perhaps you know about my past, too," Lance said. "Someone changed the name of a murder victim in Black Swan, Washington, to Raven Spector. Was that you?"

Smidovich didn't answer.

"Do you know something about my sister and mother's disappearance?" Lance said.

Smidovich was quiet for a long moment. Lance

thought he'd lost him, lost the chance to find out what he knew, but then Smidovich picked up the phone. "Are the cameras off?" he said in Russian. He hung up, stood, and confirmed that the sound recording equipment was off too, then came back to the table and said under his breath, "The documents you left in Istanbul, they refer to our president personally, do they not?"

Lance smiled. "You go first, Smidovich. What do you know of my mother and sister?"

Smidovich shook his head solemnly. "We know they both died a very long time ago."

The words hit Lance with more force than he would have expected. On some level, of course, he'd known that all along. Three decades didn't pass without certain conclusions being drawn. But it was still difficult to have it confirmed so bluntly. "How could you know that?" he said.

"Our top floor. It has its methods."

"I scoured every record. I read every police file."

"You could never read as much as an entire division of the Prime Directorate, especially with our access to the Mexican criminal underworld. We have inroads there that even your own government could never match. We work with the cartels. We trade information for weapons. They tell us everything."

"What happened to them?" Lance said.

"Personally, I don't know the details."

"Then what good is this conversation?"

"They're in a file," Smidovich said. "A paper file

in a cardboard folder, very much like the one you left in Istanbul."

"How do I get that file?"

"Easy, now," Smidovich said. "You'll have your chance, though not with me."

"With who, then?"

"He'll be here shortly," Smidovich said. "You'll have to deal directly for that."

"All right," Lance said. "I'll do that."

"But before he gets here," Smidovich said, "perhaps there's something you could tell me about the file you left in Istanbul?"

"I thought you didn't want to know. I thought some things were *better left unknown*." He said the last words mimicking Smidovich's accent.

Smidovich ignored the taunt. "You know something about our president that I don't. Something that even our own security services don't know. Something that could be important to the future of the Russian people."

"It sounds to me like you already know what I have."

"It would be nice to get some confirmation."

"I see," Lance said.

"Like I said," Smidovich repeated, "it could be important to our country. To our people."

"Your president," Lance said, speaking carefully, "is a very powerful man."

"Our president is the most powerful man in the world—"

"By some measures."

"By all measures," Smidovich said.

"Everyone's got their vulnerabilities," Lance said.

"Not Molotov. He'll still be where he is long after your American president is eating jello out of a cup in an old folks home."

"That's not what the documents I saw suggested."

And there it was. The information Smidovich sought. "I see," he said.

Lance knew he was taking a risk in giving it to him, but he also knew that President Molotov had been in power for too long. In Washington, the big fear with replacing Molotov was that no one knew who would come next. *Better the devil you knew*, they said. *The next one could be worse*. For Lance, Molotov had proven himself to be about as bad a devil as you could meet. He'd brought his country and the world back into war. Thousands lay dead on battlefields in the Ukraine. Now, he was reorganizing the Russian economy for a war that could last a decade. For permanent war, some even thought. If there were elements inside the Russian security apparatus that could move against him, Lance didn't mind giving them some encouragement.

"The old man's sick," Lance said. "Is that what you wanted to hear?"

Smidovich said nothing. They both eyed each other for a long moment in silence.

Eventually, Lance broke the silence. "The question is whether there's someone in Russia who'll do something about it."

There was another long silence, and then Smidovich said, "There's always someone ready to do something, I suppose."

41

Smidovich was about to say more, but the door suddenly swung open, and two more guards from the Presidential Regiment entered the room. They were followed by none other than the man himself, the President of the Russian Federation, Vladimir Molotov.

He was dressed in a garish suit that looked like it had come from the costume department of one of Martin Scorsese's more flamboyant gangster movies. Smidovich rose to his feet and bowed slightly. Lance remained seated, eyeing the Russian President intently. He knew the man had spent time modeling his persona on Robert De Niro's character in *Casino*, and even now, his bearing, his facial gestures, the details of his clothing, the slicked-back hair and gold jewelry, all channeled De Niro as conspicuously as if he was getting ready to try out for the part.

He'd also heard that Molotov had Tom Ford

and Gucci send tailors to custom make his suits, and if it was true, he certainly looked the part. He was dressed in a deep blue velvet blazer with matching pants, and apart from a receding hairline and slightly puffy face, Lance never would have guessed he was looking at anyone other than the vigorous strongman Molotov worked so hard to portray. Lance had seen recent footage of him driving a forty-six-ton T-90 tank across a frozen lake in Nizhny Tagil. He'd watched him aim its 125mm smoothbore cannon and hit a target five kilometers away. He'd seen pictures of him topless riding a horse.

Who would have guessed he was dying of pancreatic cancer?

"Lance Spector, we meet again," Molotov said in Russian.

Lance rose then, though he didn't extend a hand.

Smidovich, still bowing, shuffled past the two bodyguards and out of the room. The guards, standing by the door, shut it behind him.

"Mr President," Lance said.

Molotov took his time examining Lance, taking in every inch of him, every detail, like a fighter sizing up a foe. The two had met before, if the circumstances could be called a meeting—and the one thing Molotov seemed to have taken from the encounter was the fact that Lance could have killed him but didn't. That wasn't strange. It wasn't a sign of any special admiration or sympathy. Lance had been simply obeying the standing order of the US President to all members of the Armed Forces, the CIA, the NSA, and especially the Special Operations Group, that none of them, under any circumstances, were to threaten the life of President Molotov.

"The man has more nukes than Santa Claus has elves," the president had said when delivering the order. "We do not target a man like that. We achieve our goals in other ways."

And that had been fine by Lance. He was a soldier, not a general, and despite what the White House might think, he had no trouble obeying orders. It was Levi Roth who'd broken the rules. He was the one who'd gone after Molotov directly. And that was the reason Lance was there now—to clean up that mess. At least, that was one of the reasons. The other was the business in Black Swan.

"I think you're a man who can be bargained with," Molotov said, sitting on the chair vacated by Smidovich.

Lance sat down also. "I am," he said in his flawless Russian, "and I think you know why I'm here."

"You have something of mine."

"I do," Lance said.

"Though you didn't bring it with you."

"Where would be the fun in that?" Lance said.

Molotov smiled, though Lance knew not to try his patience. Molotov was a man known for his temper, for his tendency toward paranoia, and those aspects of his character had only grown more pronounced since his disastrous invasion of Ukraine. He was not known for his sense of humor, especially when the jokes were at his expense.

"I'll say this much," Lance added. "What I found in the safe, if we can come to an understanding, it could be back in your hands before I leave this room."

"That's very trusting of you," Molotov said.

Lance shrugged. "You have a long reach, Mr Molotov. If I can't trust you, I'm in a lot of trouble."

"Very true," Molotov said. "I have a team in Istanbul. I take it they should be at the airport?"

"They should," Lance said, "though, I wonder, aren't you worried that I made a copy?"

"Copies don't concern me," Molotov said. "It's the original that concerns me. There's always something more convincing about the real thing, don't you think? Something that no amount of forgery can match. I want the original back in Moscow, where it belongs. The rest is, how you say, fake news?"

Lance nodded.

Molotov smiled, satisfied, then moved on to the next topic without missing a beat. "I suppose you want to talk about your sister and mother."

Lance felt his heart thumping in his chest. It was a strange feeling to speak so openly about a wound so deep, a wound he'd thought he'd buried in the past and would never have to look at again. "What do you know of them?" he said.

Whatever Molotov said, Lance would have to be

careful. He'd spent the better part of his life scouring police, CIA, and FBI records relating to the sex trafficking around the Mexico-Texas border in the years his mother and sister disappeared. He had access to more intel than anyone, and he hadn't been able to find out a single thing about them. Whatever Molotov claimed to know now would have to be treated with the greatest skepticism.

But at the same time, if there was even a chance of getting the information he sought, Lance had to take it, no matter the risk.

"I know more than you were able to learn from your own government's records," Molotov said.

"How do I know the information is reliable?"

"You'll have to make up your own mind on that," Molotov said. "What I can say is that we used our extensive network in Mexico to fish out this information. And we went after it hard."

"To get to me?"

Molotov nodded. "Like I said before, you're a man who can be bargained with. I like people like that. People I can do business with. I would have tried to blackmail you with *kompromat*, but a man of your... *predilections* can be difficult to blackmail."

"I don't know about that."

"The normal things wouldn't have worked on you. Threats? Embarrassing information? What would you have cared for such things? No, my challenge was to find something you cared about."

"So you found out about my sister?"

"Oh, I did, Mr Spector. I had her name placed

on the murder report in Black Swan, but that was only a teaser. That was just to get your attention. Once you'd been drawn in, I knew you'd follow the path all the way to the end."

"Which is here?"

"This isn't the end," Molotov said. "You know that."

"Where's the end?"

"That will be for you to decide, but first, let's talk about Skadden Arps's file. I knew you'd get it for me. And I knew you'd kill Arps for me, too."

"I didn't kill Arps for you. I killed him for myself."

Molotov shrugged. "It's the same thing in the end, is it not?"

"I suppose," Lance said.

"You retrieved what I needed."

"I did, but you could have gotten it without my help. Why go to all the trouble of drawing me in?"

Molotov smiled. "First, let me tell you what's on offer. I'm going to give you the thing you crave most."

"Closure?"

Molotov laughed. "Not closure, heavens no. There's no closure for a thing like this. No. What I'm going to give you is something far more valuable."

"Revenge?"

Molotov smiled. "That's the trade. Do you think it's fair?"

"Fair doesn't come into this," Lance said. "My

mother and sister disappeared. That wasn't fair. Something bad happened to them. That wasn't fair. Now, I'm going to give you your medical file so that you can go on doing the evil things you do. That's not fair."

Molotov nodded, then went to the door and knocked on it. The man in the turtleneck from earlier appeared and handed him a file. "This is it. This is the truth you seek."

Lance looked at the file but didn't reach for it. "What happened to them?" he said, his voice catching as he spoke.

"It's not a question of what happened," Molotov said, "though you'll find the details inside. The real question is, who did it?"

"I know who did it."

"Sandor Grey," Molotov said, and as he said the words, Lance felt a sudden rush of emotion. A shiver ran down his back.

"But it's not just the name," Molotov said. "There's an address too."

"An address?" Lance said, almost unable to speak. "You're sure he's alive?"

"He's very much alive," Molotov said. "Living peacefully and quietly in the town of Cheboygan, Michigan, under a new name."

Lance looked at the folder in Molotov's hand. He couldn't believe he was finally getting what he'd been seeking his entire life. Molotov held it aloft. Lance's hand was shaking with anticipation as he reached for it.

"Not so fast," Molotov said.

Lance knew there'd be more. There was only one reason Molotov had brought him all this way, and it wasn't because he knew how to break into safes. "There's something else you want, isn't there?" Lance said. "The real reason you brought me here."

"There is," Molotov said.

"You want me to kill Levi Roth."

Molotov's expression remained motionless. He said nothing for what felt like a very long time. He leaned back in his chair and stretched. When he finally spoke, his voice had an edge to it. "Levi Roth broke the rules," he said. "He did the one thing I cannot allow. He came after me directly."

"The fact that I just attended Roth's funeral doesn't make a difference?"

"My people already examined the grave. The coffin you buried was empty. Roth's still alive."

"I'm not going to kill him for you," Lance said. "That's not the deal I came here to make."

"Oh?" Molotov said curiously. "Surely you knew that was what I was going to ask."

"I figured it was," Lance said, "but I came to make you a different offer."

"What different offer?"

"You let Levi live."

Molotov laughed then, a shallow, mirthless laugh, and said, "You know the rules. You know he broke them. He put himself in play. He's fair game."

"I know," Lance said, "but you're not going to go after him. You're going to let him live."

Molotov was surprised by this. The reason he'd worked so hard to bring Lance there was for the exact opposite reason. "And why would I go and do a thing like that?"

Lance looked at Molotov for another long moment, acutely aware that he was looking at one of the most powerful men who'd ever lived, a man with the means to destroy the planet, a man with more blood on his hands than any living leader anywhere. "Because if you don't," he said, his tone deadly serious, "then the next time we meet will be the last."

42

Lance's plane landed after a long and uneventful series of flights, first from Moscow back to Istanbul, then to Dulles. He'd half expected to be arrested on his arrival at Dulles—he had no doubt Laurel and Tatyana had figured out what he was up to—but there'd been no arrest. No welcoming committee. Nothing but a wait in the terminal and a transfer to his domestic flight to Detroit.

He'd sat for four hours on the flight from Moscow and a further eleven hours on the flight from Istanbul, with the file Molotov had given him resting on his lap. Not once did he open it.

Now, waiting to board his flight to Detroit, he still couldn't bring himself to look inside. He'd slept a little on the planes but didn't feel quite himself. The file was like a weight bearing down on him. He'd stared at the cover for so long he almost thought his eyes would burn holes in it, but he hadn't been able to bring himself to read it.

The flight to Detroit boarded, but, again, he couldn't bring himself to open the file. He tried, but his hands just wouldn't obey. He wondered if he should just throw the thing away. Perhaps that was the best thing to do.

What was the point of revenge?

What was the point of staring into the abyss?

They said that if you stared into it long enough, it stared back into you. They said that he who fights monsters must take care not to become one.

It was Nietzsche who'd said all that. Lance wasn't a fan, but the words swirled in his mind nonetheless. Perhaps he'd be better off not knowing, not reading the file, not finding out what had happened to his family, and not finding out where he could find Sandor Grey.

Don't become the monster you seek to destroy, he mumbled as he dozed off. He came back to himself with a sudden jolt.

"Sir, are you all right?" It was the hostess.

"Sorry," he said. "I fell asleep."

"You were making noise."

"Noise?"

"About monsters."

"Right," Lance said, sitting up in his seat and rubbing his eyes. "It's been a long journey. Maybe it's time for some coffee."

"We're on the final descent."

"I see," Lance said, looking apologetically at the

passengers around him that he'd evidently disturbed.

"If you took something to help you sleep," the lady sitting next to him said, "that might be what caused the nightmares. My pills do the same thing."

"Thank you," Lance said, then realized, to his horror, that the file he'd been clutching for the better part of the past twenty-four hours was gone.

In a frantic moment of panic, he looked around his feet before finding it on the ground between his own leg and his neighbor's. "I'm all over the place this morning," he said.

"It's fine," the woman said. She was a little older than Lance, somewhere in her forties, and seemed interested in striking up a conversation.

Lance did her the courtesy of asking a few questions—she was flying into Detroit to visit a man she'd been speaking to online. They'd met on a dating site that catered specifically to dentists. "You want to see his picture?" she said.

Lance looked at the picture and nodded approvingly at an image of a guy on a golf course. "I hope you have fun," he said.

"Oh, honey, I'm not looking for fun. I'm looking for a husband."

In the airport he rented a car, but before beginning the drive north to Cheboygan, while still sitting in the airport parking lot, the man from the rental company looking at him from his little booth, Lance flipped open the file and began reading. It took only a minute to read the contents, which were as brief as they were gruesome. None of it should have surprised him, everything that had happened could have been predicted, indeed, had formed the substance of Lance's nightmares for decades, but it was still harrowing.

The report had been compiled from Mexican records and augmented using Russian assets in Mexico who'd done work on the ground to get to the bottom of the case. Molotov had been right, it couldn't have been done without certain insider information relating to the Mexican cartel system operating around El Paso at the time, which was why Lance hadn't been able to get to the bottom of it himself.

It started with an interrogation the GRU had conducted of a cartel enforcer known only as César. He'd been tracked down by them and admitted to remembering the case. He'd said that both women, Lance's mother and sister, had died within weeks of being transported across the border. Lance was almost glad to know they hadn't spent long in captivity, though he knew they must have gone through hell in those weeks they'd been alive. César confirmed as much, saying both Raven and the mother had been forced to engage in prostitution, and that the reason they were dead was because they'd refused to accept their fate. They'd fought and fought and fought until their captors had no other option but to kill them.

Their bodies had then been photographed and

buried outside the city of Matamoros in the province of Tamaulipas in Northern Mexico. No report was made to local law enforcement. The bodies were buried at a place called Playa Bagdad, a place Lance knew well, indeed had been to on numerous occasions over the years, almost as if invisibly drawn to it. It was still a place under the grip of cartels and drug dealers, a place few people ventured unless they had business there, but Lance had been there so many times he'd lost count. Now, he wondered if it had been more than chance that had brought him there. Had it been some sort of instinct? A sense that his family was buried under all that sand? There'd been a city there once, over a century ago, during the American Civil War. Smugglers had used it when the southern ports were blockaded by the Union Army. Lance remembered saying to Laurel once that a whole world had once been there, a city, a bustling port, merchants and hawkers and smugglers and whores. It had all been there, and now it was all gone.

What was the meaning, he wondered now, of places like that? What was their purpose? What God allowed them to be built only for them to be lost to the sands of time?

He didn't have answers to such questions, but he fired up the engine of the rental car all the same and began the journey north. It was a four-hour drive from Detroit to Cheboygan and he took the I-275 as far as a place called Farmington Hills. Then it was the slatted and cracked concrete of the I-96 to

Brighton, where he got onto the even more cracked, more potholed US-23. When that road was first built in the nineteen-twenties, they'd called it the Dixie Highway, and it extended fifteen hundred miles from Jacksonville, Florida to Mackinaw City, Michigan. West of Flint, the road became Interstate 75, and that was the road Lance remained on until Indian River. From there, it was a very short drive into downtown Cheboygan.

The address in the file was for a second-floor apartment above an abandoned realtor's office on Cheboygan's main thoroughfare. Apparently, Sandor had only returned to the town of his birth a few months ago, which was why Lance's numerous visits to the town had not revealed him. It had been a mistake, coming back, though, because that seemed to be how Molotov's people had zeroed in on him. They'd assigned a sleeper agent already in the area to the task of watching and waiting.

It was a gray, overcast day, and a mist hung in the air. Lance looked at the building for a long time before getting out of the car. He wasn't waiting for anything in particular, though the reconnaissance proved useful because, after about thirty minutes, he saw a man in his sixties shuffling along the street. In an instant, Lance recognized him. He'd aged, of course—thirty years had passed since he'd seen the man—but there was no doubting this was him. This was the son of a bitch his mother had married.

Lance watched him fuss with a key at the door,

and then he got out of the car and walked over as if to help him.

"What do you want?" Sandor grunted when Lance held open the door.

"I'm here for you, Sandor," Lance said.

The man's face went instantly white. He looked up, and Lance knew he recognized him. "You've got the wrong man," Sandor said. "No one by that name here."

Lance smiled. They both knew that wasn't going to cut it. "Come on," Lance said, still holding the door. "Let's you and me go upstairs and have a little chat."

Sandor ambled into a narrow hallway, and Lance followed, making sure the door was locked behind them. When Sandor reached the rickety staircase, he made his move, reaching into his coat for a weapon.

Lance was more than ready, knocking the gun from Sandor's feeble grip to the floor. Lance bent down and picked it up. "What do you carry this for?" he said.

"You never know who'll come calling," Sandor said, and it was uncanny how little his voice had changed over the years.

The sound of it brought Lance instantly back. "Come on," he said. "Up we go."

There were two doors at the top of the stairs leading to two apartments. The building was damp and smelled of mold. There was a light switch in the corridor, but it didn't work. There was also a small window, the glass cracked. Whichever apartment was Sandor's, Lance didn't think the other was likely to be occupied. "Which door?" he said.

"This one," Sandor said, pointing to the nearer of the two doors.

Lance watched him as he took a key from his pocket and fumbled with the lock. He dropped the key, and Lance let him bend down to pick it up. When the old man crouched down, Lance felt an overwhelming desire to kick him to the floor and get it over with there and then.

He didn't, and Sandor got the door open and led the way into a murky room of old, piss-stained furniture, a worn-out carpet, and an atmosphere thick with the smell of cat litter, old cooking grease, cigarette smoke, and the stench of an old man who lived alone. It was daylight outside, but the apartment had ratty old curtains hanging shut in front of every window, making the room dark enough that they needed to switch on the light. The old man hit the switch, and a lone filament bulb came on, casting a deathly white glow over a worn-out sofa, a coffee table laden with dirty dishes, and an enormous, overflowing ashtray. On the wall were wooden shelves, so overladen with old books and magazines that they looked to be in danger of collapsing.

The room opened to a small kitchen on one side and a corridor on the other that presumably led to a bathroom and bedroom.

"Maid's day off?" Lance said.

Sandor said nothing, and Lance nodded toward the ratty sofa. “Sit there,” he said.

Sandor lumbered over to the sofa and was joined immediately by a scrawny tabby cat that emerged from the kitchen.

“Looks hungry,” Lance said of the cat.

The old man shrugged and Lance walked through to the kitchen, where he almost gagged at the sight of all the old food and dishes piled up in the sink. Keeping one eye on Sandor, who hadn’t moved, he walked to the sink and opened the window behind it, letting in cool, fresh air.

The old man reached for something on the coffee table, and Lance went back to the living room, gun pointed. “What are you doing?”

Sandor said nothing, and Lance followed his gaze to the coffee table, where there was a steak knife.

“I’d leave that where it is,” Lance said.

Sandor retreated reluctantly back into the sofa. The cat jumped down from his lap and went to Lance, rubbing against his leg.

“So,” Lance said, picking up the cat with one arm while holding the gun with the other. “I take it that you remember me?”

Sandor was quiet for a long time, and Lance went and sat across from him on one of the disgusting, hair-covered arm chairs.

“I was smaller when you saw me last,” Lance said. “Smaller than that time you put me in hospital.”

Sandor remained silent.

"Remember what you told me when I woke up?" Lance said. Still no answer, and Lance added, "Hey! I asked you a question."

"I don't remember anything," Sandor said.

"Oh, surely you remember what you told me."

"I don't."

"You said that if I told anyone what happened, you'd take it out on my mother and sister. You don't remember saying that?"

"It never happened," Sandor said.

Lance nodded. "Oh, I wish that were true, Sandor. How I wish none of it ever happened, our years with you, living under your iron fist. Believe me, if there were a universe in which that never happened, I'd happily give up this one for it. You have my word on that."

Sandor was chewing his lip. He looked very angry. Very angry and very impotent.

Lance said, "You ended up taking it out on them anyway, though, didn't you? In the end?" He rose to his feet, and Sandor looked startled. "That's right," Lance said. "You should be afraid after the things you've done. This isn't going to go well for you."

"You have the wrong man," Sandor said again.

Lance shook his head. That face, that voice, the mustache, unless Sandor had a twin, this was his man. "I don't think so," he said. "You're the son of a bitch who liked to force himself on women. And on girls."

Sandor was staring at the coffee table, at the

knife that he'd been tempted to reach for, and Lance said, "That was you, right? You were the guy who held a hot iron against my sister's chest and burned her skin so badly she looked like she'd been caught in napalm. I know it was you."

"You're making a mistake."

"Oh?" Lance said. "And what mistake is that?"

"All those things that happened, they were a long time ago."

"They weren't a long time ago for me, Sandor. I remember them like they were yesterday. I dream about them every night. My mother's muffled screams through the bedroom wall, those weren't a long time ago for me, Sandor. They're still happening."

"You're crazy."

Lance shrugged. "I won't argue with you there. I've spent the better part of my life hunting down monsters like you. I only hope you're the last one."

"There are much bigger monsters in the world than me."

"Not to me, there aren't."

"The things I did, trafficking women, selling them, hundreds were doing the same thing."

"And if I could kill them all, Sandor, I'd do it in a heartbeat."

"Let's face it," Sandor said. "What other use is there for a woman like your mother? Your sister? You get what you can from trash like that, and when you're done with them, you throw them away."

The words filled Lance with rage, but he didn't show it. He was in control of himself. Having Sandor here now, in front of him, knowing he was going to kill him—there was a strange calmness in knowing that. "You know they died after you sold them," he said.

"Of course they died. I wasn't sending them to the Ritz."

"What do you think they went through in those weeks before they died?"

"I don't know. I wasn't there. I didn't make the world the way it is, Lance. That's the thing people like you need to learn. You rage against us—"

"Who's us?"

"You rage against us," Sandor said, raising his voice. "You wail and gnash your teeth and rage against the world for being the way it is. The way it's supposed to be. The way God made it."

"What are you talking about?"

"I'm not the reason there are wolves in the world, Lance Spector. I'm not the reason there are snakes and scorpions and rats and dark creatures. I didn't make them that way. I didn't make the world as it is. The things you consider bad, Lance, are as much a part of the world as you and all the things you love. I'm as much a part of God's creation as anyone. And I have as much right to be here."

Lance was tempted to pull the trigger right then and there, but he didn't. Not yet. He wasn't satisfied. He'd spent his life hunting this man, and now, after three decades, all he'd found was a pathetic old slob with no one and nothing in the world. Killing him didn't feel like it was *enough.*

The cat began to mewl, and Lance put it on the ground. "He's hungry," he said for the second time, rising to his feet. "Where's the food."

"Fridge," Sandor said, nodding toward the kitchen.

Lance went to the kitchen and opened the refrigerator. It was a mistake. No sooner did he see the contents, moldy and black, no sooner did the stench reach his nostrils, than he doubled over and hurled his guts.

Sandor took his chance and moved surprisingly quickly. The shuffling and limping had apparently been an act because he was at the door in a matter of seconds. All Lance could do was watch him go.

But Lance wasn't worried. He'd hunted men across continents. Finishing this job was never in doubt. He wiped his mouth, went to the sink and ran the water. The sink was disgusting, but the water was okay. He filled his hand with it and rinsed his mouth. Then he went back into the living room and across to the window overlooking the street.

Sandor came out of the door and onto the sidewalk below. Lance didn't bother opening the window. He raised the gun, aimed, and pulled the trigger.

The glass shattered, then a mist of blood flew from Sandor's head and the old man stumbled and fell.

Cold air rushed into the room from the window and Lance fired off another two shots just to be sure. The bullets thudded flatly into Sandor's back.

Outside, the street was as empty as it had been earlier.

That was it, Lance thought. That was all the closure he was going to get. The conversation was over. The man who'd taken his mother and sister was dead. Everything was right with the world.

Except it wasn't.

Nothing was different. Nothing had changed. Lance had killed enough people in his life that he should have known that would be the case. Nothing momentous ever happened. Nothing was fixed when you put a bullet in a man's skull. No matter how evil the man was, no matter how much you thought you hated him, nothing changed. The evil was never undone. It couldn't be erased. Not with a bullet, in any case.

For some reason, a part of him had thought this one would be different. It wasn't.

He put the gun down and was about to leave when the cat came up to him again, rubbing against his legs. It hadn't even been scared by the gunshots. Lance looked around the apartment, then picked up the cat and brought it with him as he left.

AUTHOR'S NOTE

First off, I want to thank you for reading my book. As a reader, you might not realize how important a person like you is to a person like me.

I've been a writer for fifty years, and despite the upheavals my industry has faced, the ups and downs, the highs and lows, one thing remains constant.

You.

The reader.

And at the end of each book, I like to take a moment to acknowledge that fact.

To thank you.

Not just on my own behalf, but on behalf of all fiction writers.

Because without you, these books simply would not exist.

You're the reason they're written. Your support is what makes them possible. And your reviews and recommendations are what spreads the word.

So, thanks for that. I really do mean it.

While I have your attention, I'd like to give you a little bit of background into my opinion on the events portrayed in this book.

Writing about politics is not easy, and I hope none of my personal thoughts and opinions managed to find their way into this story. I never intend to raise political points in my writing, and I never intend to take a stand. I'm one of those guys who stays out of politics as much as possible, and I would hate to think that any political ideas raised in my book hampered your ability to enjoy the story or relate to the characters.

Because really, this is your story.

These characters are your characters.

When you read the book, no one knows what the characters look like, what they sound like, or what they truly think and feel, but you. It's your story, written for you, and the experience of it is created by you when you read the words and flip the pages.

I write about people who work for the federal government. The nature of their work brings them up against issues of national security and politics, but apart from that, I truly do try to keep any views I might have to myself. So please, don't let any of my words offend you, and if you spot anything in my writing that you feel is unfair, or biased, or off-color in any way, feel free to let me know.

My email address is below, and if you send a

message, while I might not get back to you immediately, I will receive it, and I will read it.

saulherzog@authorcontact.com

Likewise, if you spot simpler errors, like typos and misspellings, let me know about those too. We writers have a saying:

To err is human. To edit, divine.

And we live by it.

I'm going to talk a little about some of the true facts that this book is based on, but before I do, I'd like to ask for a favor.

I know you're a busy person, I know you just finished this book and you're eager to get on to whatever is in store next, but if you could find it in your heart to leave me a review, I'd be truly humbled.

I'm not a rich man. I'm not a powerful man. There's really nothing I can offer you in return for the kindness.

But what I will say is that it is a kindness.

If you leave me a review, it will help my career. It will help my series to flourish and find new readers. It will make a difference to one guy, one stranger you've never met and likely will never meet, and I'll appreciate that fact.

Now that those formalities are out of the way, let's talk about some of the events in this book.

~

This was the ninth and final book in the spectacular Lance Spector series. I truly hope that you enjoyed it. I have always been a big fan of series that drew to a satisfying conclusion, and book nine seemed like an appropriate place to draw Lance's journey to a close. Nine is a satisfying number, allowing as it does for a trilogy of trilogies. Also, with Lance having finally closed the chapter on the disappearance of his mother and daughter thirty years ago, the overarching series arc has been concluded in a manner that I hope you find satisfactory. Thank you for following the Lance Spector adventure through nine action-packed novels. I hope you join me in the next adventure, The Honeytrap, which I promise, kicks off with a bang.

A brand new series is coming. *The Honeytrap* is available to pre-order.

So grab your copy now. I promise, if you enjoyed the Lance Spector series, this new series is going to be even better!

God bless and happy reading,

Saul Herzog

THE NEXT SERIES

DON'T MISS IT!

A stunning new series from the creator of Lance Spector. Join me on my next unforgettable journey with a brand new espionage thriller series. **The Honeytrap** is an ultra-modern, hyper-realistic espionage thriller with a new heroine you can really sink your teeth into. Don't miss out!

Made in United States
North Haven, CT
07 September 2024

57113334R00224